For an instant she felt the terrible cold panic of falling.

She braced herself for the pain of landing on the hard floor—only to be caught instead in a pair of strong muscled arms.

The shock of it quite knocked the breath from her, and the room went hazy and blurry as the veil of her bonnet blinded her. Willing herself not to faint, Emma blinked away her confusion and pushed back the dratted veil.

"Thank you, sir," she gasped. "You are very quick-thinking."

"I'm just happy I happened to be here," her rescuer answered, and his voice was shockingly familiar. A smooth, deep, rich sound, like a glass of sweet mulled wine on a cold night, comforting and deliciously disturbing all at the same time.

It was a voice she hadn't heard in a long while, and yet she remembered it very well.

* * *

Running from Scandal
Harlequin® Historical #1165—December 2013

Bancrofts of Barton Park

Two sisters, two scandals,
two sizzling love affairs

Country girls at heart, Jane and Emma Bancroft
are a far cry from the perfectly coiffed,
glossy debutantes that grace most of Society.

But soon they come to realize that,
country girl and debutante alike, no lady is immune
to the charms of a dashing rogue!

**Don't miss this enthralling new duet
from Amanda McCabe**

**It started with Jane's story
THE RUNAWAY COUNTESS
Already available**

**And continues with Emma's story
RUNNING FROM SCANDAL**

Running from Scandal

—

Amanda McCabe

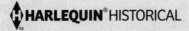

HARLEQUIN® HISTORICAL

Recycling programs
for this product may
not exist in your area.

ISBN-13: 978-0-373-29765-8

RUNNING FROM SCANDAL

Printed in U.S.A.

www.Harlequin.com

Did you know that these novels are also available as ebooks? Visit www.Harlequin.com.

Author Note

When I was about eight, I found a battered paperback copy of *Emma* in a bag of secondhand books at my grandmother's house. I didn't know anything about Jane Austen then (except a vague thought that she'd lived a long time ago and never got married!), but I was drawn in by the two girls in white gowns and feathered bonnets on the cover, and started reading. I was dragged right into the world of Emma Woodhouse and her friends and family in Highbury, and refused to do anything else until I'd finished the book! Then I ran to the library and checked out all the Austen novels. That was the beginning of my Regency love, which goes on to this day.

For a long time I've wanted to try writing a story in the style of an Austen novel. Not in her writing style, of course—no one can copy that—but in what I loved so much about her plots: the life of English villages and country houses, the close bonds that can form between families (especially sisters) and friends in such places, the romances that blossom even when their prospects look bleak.

I finally found the right characters in my Bancroft sisters, Jane and Emma, and the happily-ever-afters they found at Barton Park with their handsome heroes. I started to feel as if I could have lived in that neighborhood, too—it was such a fun world to spend time in, and I was sorry to say goodbye to it all. But I know Jane and Emma go on happily there!

And watch for a little epilogue story coming soon, where we see what happens when Melanie Harding and Philip Carrington find themselves unwillingly married...

Prologue

England—1814

Emma Bancroft was very good at holding up walls. She grew more adept at it every time she went to a party, which was not very often. She was getting a great deal of practice at it tonight.

She pressed her back against the wall of the village assembly room and sipped at a glass of watery punch as she surveyed the gathering. It was a surprisingly large one considering the chilly, damp night outside. Emma would have thought most people would want to stay sensibly at home by their fires, not get dressed in their muslin and silk finery and go traipsing about in search of dance partners. Yet the long and narrow room was crowded with laughing, chattering groups dressed up in their finery.

Emma rather wished *she* were home by the fire. Not that she entirely minded a social evening. People were always so very fascinating. She loved nothing better than to find a superb vantage point by a convenient wall and settle down to listen to conversations. It was such fun to devise her own stories about what those conversations were really about, what secret lives everyone might be living behind their smiles and mundane chatter. It was like a good book.

But tonight she had left behind an actual good book at home in the library of Barton Park, along with her new puppy, Murray. Recently she had discovered the fascinations of botany, which had quite replaced her previous passions for Elizabethan architecture and the cultivation of tea in India. Emma often found new topics of education that fascinated her, and plants were a new one. Her father's dusty old library, mostly unexplored since his death so long ago, was full of wonders waiting to be discovered.

And tonight, with a cold rain blowing against the windows, seemed a perfect one for curling up with a pot of tea and her studies, Murray at her feet. But her sister Jane, usually all too ready for a quiet, solitary evening at home, had insisted they come to the assembly. Jane even brought out some of her fine London gowns for them to wear.

'I am a terrible sister for letting you live here like a hermit, Emma,' Emma remembered Jane saying as she held up a pale-blue silk gown. 'You are only sixteen and so pretty. You need to be dancing, and flirting and—well, doing what young, pretty ladies enjoy doing.'

'I enjoy staying here and reading,' Emma had protested, even as she had to admit the dress was very nice. Definitely prettier than her usual faded muslins, aprons and sturdy boots, though it would never do for digging up botanical specimens. Jane even let her wear their mother's pearl pendant tonight. But she could still be reading at home.

Or hunting for the lost, legendary Barton Park treasure, as their father had spent his life doing. But Jane didn't have to know about that. Her sister had too many other worries.

'I know you enjoy it, and that is the problem,' Jane had said, as she searched for a needle and thread to take the dress in. 'But you are growing up. We can't go on as we have here at Barton Park for ever.'

'Why not?' Emma argued. 'I love it here, just the two of us in our family home. We can do as we please here, and not worry about…'

About horrid schools, where stuck-up girls laughed and gossiped, and the dance master grabbed at Emma in the corridor. Where she had felt so, so alone. She was sent there when their mother died and Jane married the Earl of Ramsay, Hayden. Emma had never wanted her sweet sister to know what happened there. She never wanted anyone to know. Especially not about her foolish feelings for the handsome dance teacher, that vile man who had taken advantage of her girlish feelings to kiss her in the dark—and tried so much more before Emma could get away. He had quite put her off men for ever.

Emma saw the flash of worry in Jane's hazel eyes before she bent her head over the needle and Emma took her other hand with a quick smile.

'Of course we must have a night out, Jane, you are quite right,' she'd said, making herself laugh. 'You must be so bored here with just me and my books after your grand London life. We shall go to the assembly and have fun.'

Jane laughed, too, but Emma heard the sadness in it. The sadness had lingered ever since Jane brought Emma back to Barton Park almost three years before, when Jane's husband, the earl, hadn't appeared in many months. Emma didn't know what had happened between them in London and she didn't want to pry, but nor did she want to add to her sister's worry.

'My London life was not all that grand,' Jane said, 'and I am not sorry it's behind me. But soon it will be your time to go out in the world, Emma. The village doesn't have a wide society, true, but it's a start.'

And that was what Emma feared—that soon it would be her turn to step out into the world and she would make horrid mistakes. She was too impulsive by half, and even though she knew it she had no idea how to stop it.

So she stood by the wall, watching, sipping her punch, trying not to tear Jane's pretty dress. For an instant before they left Barton and Emma glimpsed herself in the mirror, she hadn't believed it was really her. Jane had put her blonde, curling hair up in a twisted bandeau of ribbons and, teamed with her mother's pearl necklace, even Emma had to admit the effect was much prettier than her everyday braid and apron.

The local young men seemed to agree as well. She noticed a group of them over by the windows: bluff, hearty, red-faced country lads dressed in their finest town evening coats and cravats, watching her and whispering. Which was exactly what she did not want. Not after Mr Milne, the passionate school music master. She turned away and pretended to be studiously observing something edifying across the room.

She saw Jane standing next to the refreshment table with a tall gentleman in a sombre dark-blue coat who had his back to Emma. Even though Emma was not having the very best of evenings, the smile on her sister's face made her glad they had ventured out after all.

Jane so seldom mentioned her estranged husband or their life in London, though Emma had always followed Jane's social activities in the newspapers while she was at school and knew it must have been very glamorous. Barton Park was not in the least glamorous, and even though Jane insisted she was most content, Emma wondered and worried.

Tonight, Jane was smiling, even laughing, her dark hair glossy in the candlelight and her lilac muslin-and-lace gown soft and pretty. She shook her head at something the tall gentleman said and gestured toward Emma with a smile. Emma stood up straighter as they both turned to look at her.

'Blast it all,' she whispered, and quickly smiled when an elderly lady nearby gave her a disapproving glance. But she couldn't help cursing just a little. For it was Sir David Marton who was talking to her sister.

Sir David had been visiting at Barton more often of late than Emma could like. He always came with his sister, Miss Louisa Marton, very proper and everything since his estate at Rose Hill was their nearest neighbour. But still. Jane *was* married, even though Lord Ramsay never came to Barton. And Sir David was too handsome by half. Handsome, and far too serious. She doubted he ever laughed at all.

She studied him across the room, trying not to frown. He nodded at whatever Jane was saying, watching Emma solemnly from behind his spectacles. She was glad he wasn't near enough for her to see his eyes. They were a strange, piercing pale-grey colour, and whenever he looked at her so steadily with them he seemed to see far too much.

Emma unconsciously smoothed her skirt, feeling young and fidgety and silly. Which was the very last way she ever wanted to appear in front of Sir David.

He nodded again at Jane and gave her a gentle smile. He always spoke so gently, so respectfully to Jane, with a unique spark of humour in those extraordinary eyes. He never had that gentle humour when he looked at Emma. Then he was solemn and watchful.

Emma had never felt jealous of Jane before. How could she be, when Jane was the best of sisters, and had such unhappiness hidden in her heart? But when Sir David Marton was around, Emma almost—*almost*—did feel jealous.

And she could not fathom why. Sir David was not at all the sort of man she was sure she could admire. He was too quiet, too serious. Too—conventional. Emma couldn't read him at all.

And now—oh, blast it all again! Now they were coming across the room toward her.

Emma nearly wished she had spoken with one of the country squires after all. She never knew what to say to Sir David that wouldn't make her feel young and foolish around him. That might make him smile at her.

'Emma dear, I was just talking to Sir David about your new interest in botany,' Jane said as they reached Emma's side.

Emma glanced up at Sir David, who was watching her with that inscrutable, solemn look. The smile he had given Jane was quite gone. It made her feel so very tongue-tied, as if words flew into her head only to fly right back out again. She hadn't felt so very nervous, so unsure, since she left school, and she did not like that feeling at all.

'Were you indeed?' Emma said softly, looking away from him.

'My sister mentioned that she drove past you on the lane a few days ago,' Sir David said, his tone as calm and serious as he looked. 'She said when she offered you a ride home you declared you had to finish your work. As it was rather a muddy day, Louisa found that a bit—interesting.'

Against her will, Emma's feelings pricked just a bit. She had never wanted to care what anyone thought of her, not after Mr Milne. Miss Louisa Marton was a silly gossip, and there was no knowing what exactly she had told her brother or what he thought of Emma now. Did he think her ridiculous for her studies? For her unladylike interests such as grubbing around in the dirt?

'I am quite the beginner in my studies,' Emma said. 'Finding plant specimens to study is an important part of it all. When the ground is damp can be the best time to collect some of them. But it was very kind of your sister to stop for me.'

'I fear Emma has little scope for her interests since she left school to come live here with me,' Jane said. 'I am no teacher myself.'

'Oh, no, Jane!' Emma cried, her shyness disappearing at her sister's sad, rueful tone. 'I love living at Barton. Mr Lorne at the bookshop here in the village keeps me well supplied. I have learned much more here than I ever did at that silly school. But perhaps Sir David finds my efforts dull.'

'Not at all, Miss Bancroft,' he said, and to her surprise she heard a smile in his voice. She glanced up at him to find that there was indeed a hint of a curve to his lips. There was even a flash of a ridiculously attractive dimple in his cheeks.

And she also realised she should *not* have looked at him. Up close he really was absurdly handsome, with a face as lean and carefully chiselled as a classical statue. His gleaming mahogany hair, which he usually ruthlessly combed down, betrayed a thick, soft wave in the damp air, tempting a touch. She wondered whimsically if he wore those spectacles in a vain attempt to keep ladies from fainting at his feet.

'You do not find them dull, Sir David?' Emma said, feeling foolish that she could find nothing even slightly cleverer to say.

'Not at all. Everyone, male or female, needs interests in life to keep their minds sharp,' he said. 'I was fortunate enough to grow up living near an uncle who boasts a library of over five thousand volumes. Perhaps you have heard of him? Mr Charles Sansom at Sansom House.'

'Five thousand books!' Emma cried, much louder than she intended. 'That must be a truly amazing sight. Has he any special interests?'

'Greek and Roman antiquities are a favourite of his, but he has a selection on nearly every topic. Including, I would imagine, botany,' he said, his smile growing. Emma had never seen him look so young and open before and she unconsciously swayed closer to him. 'He always let us read whatever we liked when we visited him, though I fear my sister seldom took him up on the offer.'

Emma glanced across the room toward Miss Louisa Marton, who was easy to spot in her elaborately feathered turban. She was talking with her bosom bow, Miss Maude Cole, the beauty of the neighbourhood with her red-gold curls, sky-blue eyes and fine gowns. They in turn were looking back at Emma and whispering behind their fans.

Just like all those silly girls at school had done.

'I would imagine not,' Emma murmured. She had never heard Miss Marton or Miss Cole talk of anything but hats or the weather. 'Does your uncle still live nearby, Sir David? I should so love to meet him one day.'

'He does, Miss Bancroft, though I fear he has become quite reclusive in his advancing age. He still sometimes purchases volumes at Mr Lorne's shop, though, so perhaps you will encounter him there one day. He would find you most interesting.'

Before Emma could answer, the orchestra, a local group of musicians more noted for their enthusiasm than their talent, launched into the opening strains of a mazurka.

'Oh, I do love such a lively dance,' Jane said. Emma saw that her sister looked towards the forming set with a wistful look on her face. 'A mazurka was the first dance I—'

Suddenly Jane broke off with a strange little laugh and Emma wondered if she had often danced a mazurka with her husband in London. Surely even though she never mentioned her husband she had to think of him often.

'Jane…' Emma began.

Sir David turned to Jane with one of his gentle smiles. 'Perhaps you would care to dance, Lady Ramsay? My skills at the mazurka are quite rusty, but I would be honoured if you would be my partner.'

For a second, Jane seemed to hesitate, a flash of what looked like temptation in her eyes, and Emma felt an unwelcome pang of jealousy. Jealousy—of Jane! Loathing herself for that feeling, she pushed it away and made herself smile.

'Oh, no, I fear my dancing days are quite behind me,' Jane said. 'But books are not the only thing Emma studied at school. They also had a fine dancing master.'

A horrid dancing master. Emma didn't like him intruding on every moment of her life like this. Would she ever forget him?

'Then perhaps Miss Bancroft would do me the honour,' Sir David said politely. He turned to Emma and half-held out his hand.

And she suddenly longed so much to know what it felt like to have his hand on hers. To be close to him as he led her in the turns and whirls of the dance. Surely he would be strong and steady, never letting her fall, so warm and safe. Maybe he would even smile at her again and those beautiful grey eyes would gleam with admiration as he looked at her. She wanted all those things so very much.

She hadn't felt such romantic yearnings since—since Mr Milne first arrived at her school. And look at what disasters that led to. No, she couldn't trust her feelings, her impulsive emotions, ever again.

Emma fell back a step, shaking her head, and Sir David's hand dropped back to his side. His smile faded and he looked solemn and inscrutable again.

'I—I don't care to dance tonight,' Emma stammered, confused by old memories and new emotions she didn't understand. She had made a mistake with Mr Milne, a mistake in trusting him and her feelings. She needed to learn how to be cautious and calm, like Jane. Like Sir David.

'Of course not, Miss Bancroft,' Sir David said quietly. 'I quite understand.'

'David, dear,' Miss Louisa Marton said. Emma spun around to find that Miss Marton and Miss Cole had suddenly appeared beside them from the midst of the crowd. She'd been so distracted she hadn't even noticed them approach. Miss Cole watched them with a coolly amused smile on her beautiful face, making Emma feel even more flustered.

'David, dear,' Louisa said again. 'Do you not remember that Miss Cole promised you the mazurka? You were quite adamant that she save it for you and I know how much both of you have looked forward to it.'

Sir David gave Emma one more quizzical glance before he turned away to offer his hand to Miss Cole instead. 'Of course. Most delighted, Miss Cole.'

Emma watched him walk away, Miss Cole laughing and sparkling up at him with an easy flirtatiousness Emma knew she herself could never match. She felt suddenly cold in the crowded, overheated room and rubbed at her bare arms.

'I know you think Sir David is rather dull, Emma,' Jane said quietly, 'but truly he is quite nice. You should have danced with him.'

'I am a terrible dancer,' Emma said, trying to sound light and uncaring. 'No doubt I would have trod on his toes and he would have felt the need to lecture me on decorum.'

Jane shook her head, but Emma knew she couldn't really put into words her true feelings, her fears of what might happen if she got too close to the handsome, intriguing Sir David Marton. She didn't even know herself what those true feelings were. She only knew David Marton wasn't the sort of man for her.

Emma Bancroft was a most unusual young lady.

David tried to catch a glimpse of her over the heads of the other dancers gathered around him, but the bright glow of her golden hair had vanished. He almost laughed at himself for the sharp pang of disappointment at her disappearance. He was too old, too responsible, to think about a flighty, pretty girl like Miss Bancroft. A girl who obviously didn't much like him.

Yet the disappointment was there, unmistakably. When she was near, she always intrigued him. What was she thinking when she studied the world around her so closely? Her sister said she studied botany, among other interests, and David found himself most curious to know what those interests were. He wanted to know far too much about her and that couldn't be.

He had no place for someone like Emma Bancroft in his life now and she had no room for him. She seemed to be in search of far more excitement than he could ever give her. After watching his seemingly quiet father's secret temper tantrums when he was a boy, he had vowed to keep control over his life at all times. It had almost been a disaster for David's family and their home when he did briefly lose control. Once, he had spent too much time in London, running with a wild crowd, gambling and drinking too much, being attracted to the wrong sort of female, thinking he could forget his life in such pursuits. Until he saw how his actions hurt other people and he knew he had to change.

As David listened to the opening bars of the dance music and waited for his turn to lead his partner down the line, he caught a glimpse of his sister watching him with an avid gleam in her eyes. Ever since their parents died and he became fully responsible for their family estate at Rose Hill and for Louisa herself, she had been determined to find him a wife. 'A proper wife,' she often declared, by which she meant one of her own friends. A young lady from a family they knew well, one Louisa liked spending time with and who would make few changes to their household.

Not a girl like Miss Bancroft, who Louisa had expressed disapproval of more than once. 'I cannot fathom her,' Louisa had mused after encountering Miss Bancroft on the road. 'She is always running about the countryside, her hems all muddy, with that horrid dog. No propriety at all. And her sister! Where is Lady Ramsay's husband, I should like to know? How can the earl just let the two of them ramble about at Barton Park like that? The house is hardly fit to be lived in. Though we must be nice to them, I suppose. They *are* our neighbours.'

David suddenly glimpsed Lady Ramsay as she moved around the edge of the dance floor, seeming to look for someone. Her sister, perhaps? Miss Bancroft was nowhere to be seen. David had to agree that the Bancroft sisters' situation was an odd one and not one his own highly respectable parents would have understood. The two women lived alone in that ramshackle old house, seldom going out into neighbourhood society, and Lord Ramsay was never seen. Lady Ramsay often seemed sad and distant and Miss Bancroft very protective of her, which was most admirable.

David thought they also seemed brave and obviously devoted to each other. Another thing about Miss Bancroft that was unusual—and intriguing.

Suddenly he felt a nudging touch to his hand and glanced down in surprise to find he still stood on the crowded dance floor. And what was more, it was his turn in the figures as the music ran on around him.

Miss Cole smiled up at him, a quick, dazzling smile of flirtatious encouragement, and he led her down the line of dancers in the quick, leaping steps of the dance. She spun under his arm, light and quick, the jewels in her twists of red-gold hair flashing.

'Very well done, Sir David,' she whispered.

Miss Cole, unlike Miss Bancroft, was exactly the sort of young lady his sister wanted to see him marry. The daughter of a local, eminently respectable squire, and friends with Louisa for a long time: pretty and accomplished, sparkling in local society, well dowered. The kind of wife who would surely run her house well and fit seamlessly into his carefully built life. And she seemed to like him.

Miss Bancroft was assuredly not for him. She was too young, too eccentric, for them to ever suit. His whole life had been so carefully planned by his family and by himself. He almost threw it all away once. He couldn't let that happen again now. Not for some strange fascination.

Miss Cole, or a lady like her, would make him a fine wife. Why could he not stop searching the room for a glimpse of Emma Bancroft?

From the diary of Arabella Bancroft—1663

I have at last arrived at Barton Park. It was not a long journey, but it feels as if I have ventured to a different world. Aunt Mary's house in London, the endless hours of sewing while she bemoaned all that was lost to her in the wars between the king and Parliament, the filth in the streets—here where everything is green and fresh and new, all that is almost forgotten.

I know I must be grateful to be brought here to my cousin's beautiful new manor, this gift to him from the new king. I am a poor orphan of seventeen and must live as I can. Yet I cannot understand why I am here. My cousin's wife has enough maids. I have nothing yet to do but settle into my new chamber—my very own, not shared! Heaven!—and explore the lovely gardens.

But my chambermaid has told me the most intriguing tale—it seems that during the wars one of King Charles's men hid a great treasure near here. And it has never been found.

I do love a puzzle.

Chapter One

Six years later

*B*arton Park. Emma could hardly believe she was there
again, after so much time. It felt as if she had been swept
up in a whirlwind from one world and dropped into another, it was all so strange.

She stood at the rise of a hill, staring down along the
grey ribbon of road to the gates of Barton. They stood
slightly open, as if waiting to welcome her home, but
Barton no longer felt like home. There was no longer
anywhere that felt like home now. She was just a little
piece of gossamer flotsam, blown back to these gates.

She gathered her black skirts in one hand to keep
them from tossing around her in the wind. The carriage
waited for her patiently on the road below, halted on
its uneventful journey from London to here when she
insisted on getting out to look around. Her brother-in-
law's driver and footmen waited quietly, no doubt fully
informed by downstairs gossip about the unpredictable
ways of Lady Ramsay's prodigal sister.

Emma knew she should hurry inside. The wind was brisk and the pale-grey clouds overhead threatened rain. Her old dog, Murray, whined a bit and nudged with his cold nose at her gloved hand, but he wouldn't leave her side. Murray, at least, had never changed.

Yet she couldn't quite bring herself to go to the house just yet.

She'd left Barton five years ago as Miss Emma Bancroft, full of hopes and fears for her first London Season. She came back now as Mrs Carrington, young widow, penniless, shadowed by gossip and scandal. The fears still lingered, but the hope was quite, quite gone.

She held up her hand to shield her eyes from the glare of the light and studied the red-brick chimneys of Barton rising through the swaying banks of trees. Spring was on the way, she could see it in the fresh, pale green buds on the branches, could smell the damp-flower scent of it on the wind. Once she had loved spring at Barton. A time of new beginnings, new dreams.

Emma wanted to feel that way again, she wanted it so desperately. Once she had been so eager to run out and discover everything life had to offer. But that led only to disaster, over and over. It ended in a life with Henry Carrington.

Emma closed her eyes against a sudden spasm of pain that rippled through her. Henry. So handsome, so charming, so dazzling to her entire senses. He was like a whirlwind, too, and he swept her along with him, giddy and full of raw, romantic joy.

Until that giddiness turned to madness and led them on a downward spiral through Continental spa towns where there was plenty of gambling to be had. Henry was always so sure their fortunes would turn around soon, on the turn of the next card, at the bottom of the next bottle. It only led them to shabbier and shabbier lodgings on shadier streets with uncertain friends.

It led Henry to death at the wrong end of a duelling pistol, wielded by the husband of a woman he claimed to have fallen in love with at Vichy. And it took Emma back here to Barton, when she found the scandal had blocked her escape anywhere else.

'Let me help you,' Henry's cousin Philip had said, grasping her hand tightly in his when he gave her the news of the fatal duel. 'Henry would have wanted it that way. And you know how very much I have always admired you. Dearest Emma.'

Philip had indeed always been Henry's friend, a friend who caroused with him, but also loaned him money, made sure he made it home, visited Emma when she was alone and frightened in strange rooms with no knowledge of when Henry might return. She appreciated Philip's kindness, even in moments when his attentions seemed to ease over a line of propriety.

In that moment, with Henry so newly dead and the shock so cold around her, she was almost tempted to let Philip 'take care of her'. To give in to the loneliness and fear. But then she looked into his eyes and saw something there that frightened her even more. A gleam of possessive passion she saw once in Mr Milne, the dancing master, and in that villain who had once kidnapped her in the rainstorm at Barton.

The same look they had just before they violently attacked her.

So she sent Philip away, swallowed her pride, and wrote to her sister. Jane had warned her against Henry when Emma wanted to marry him, had even threatened to make Emma wait a year before she would even agree to an engagement, which led to Emma eloping and causing the first of many great scandals. And then Henry had found out that Jane and her husband had tied Emma's dowry and small inheritance from her mother up so tightly he could never touch them and some of his passion died.

While Emma wandered the Continent in Henry's wake, Jane wrote sometimes, and they even saw each other once when the Ramsays were touring Italy. They were not completely estranged, but Jane would never give in when it came to the money. 'It is yours, Emma, when you need it,' she insisted and so Henry cut Emma off from the Ramsays.

But when Emma wrote after Henry's death, Jane immediately sent money and servants to fetch her home, since Jane herself was too pregnant to travel. Jane would never abandon her, Emma knew that. Only her own embarrassment and shame had kept her away from Barton until now, had kept her from leaving Henry and seeking the shelter of her childhood home. She wondered what she would find beyond those gates.

Murray whined louder and leaned against her. Emma laughed and patted his head with her black-gloved hand.

'I'm sorry, old friend,' she said. 'I know it's cold out here. We'll go inside now.'

He trotted behind her down the hill and climbed back into the carriage at her side. For some months, Murray had seemed to be getting older, with rheumatic joints and a greying muzzle, but he wagged his plumy tail eagerly as they bounced past the gates. He seemed to realise they were almost home.

The drive to Barton was a long, picturesquely winding one, meandering gently between groves of trees, old statues and teasing glimpses of chimneys and walls. In the distance, Emma could see the old maze, the white, peaked rooftops of the rebuilt summerhouse at its centre peeking up above the hedges. In the other direction were the fields and meadows of Rose Hill, the Marton estate, and its picturesque ruins of the old medieval castle, which she had long wanted to explore.

Then the carriage came to a V in the drive. One way led to a cluster of old cottages, once used for retired estate retainers, and old orchards. The other way led to the house itself.

Emma leaned out of the window next to Murray and watched as Barton itself came into view. Built soon after the return of Charles II for one of his Royalist supporters, Emma's ancestor, its red-brick walls, trimmed with white stonework and softened by skeins of climbing ivy, were warm and welcoming.

When Emma and Jane had lived there before Jane reconciled with Hayden, the walls had been slowly crumbling and the gardens overgrown. Now everything was fresh and pretty, the flowerbeds just turning green, the low hedge borders neatly trimmed, new statues brought from Italy gleaming white. Emma glimpsed gardeners on the pathways at the side of the house, busy with their trowels and shears.

So much had changed. So much was the same.

As the carriage rolled to a halt, the front door to the house flew open just as a footman hurried to help Emma alight. Jane came hurrying out, as quickly as she could with her pregnant belly impeding her usual graceful speed. Her hazel eyes sparkled and she was laughing as she clapped her hands.

'Emma, my darling! Here you are at last,' Jane cried. As soon as Emma's half-boots touched the gravelled drive, Jane swept her into her arms and kissed her cheek. 'Welcome home.'

Home. As Emma hugged her sister back, felt her warmth and breathed in the soft, flowery scent of her lilac perfume, she could almost feel at home again. In sanctuary. Safe.

But wandering anchorless around Europe, seeing the dark depths all sorts of people were capable of, had taught her there was really no place safe. And even as she wanted to hold tight to Jane now, the guilty memory of how she had hurt her sister by eloping, of Jane's disappointment, still stung.

Emma stepped back and forced a bright smile as Jane examined her closely. Emma had learned the art of hiding her true feelings with Henry, but still it was difficult to do. 'Barton is looking splendid. And so are you, Jane. Positively blooming.'

Jane laughed ruefully as she gently smoothed her hand over her belly. 'I'm as big as a barouche now, I fear, and twice as lumbering. But I've felt much better this time than I did with the twins, hardly any morning sickness at all. I'll feel all the better now with you here, Emma. I've missed you so much.'

'And I've missed you.' More even than Emma had realised all those lonely months. 'And Barton.'

Jane took her arm and led her into the hall. Emma saw the changes to Barton were not just on the outside. The old, scarred parquet floor was replaced with fashionable black-and-white marble tiles. A newly regilded balustrade curved up along the staircase, which was laid with a thick blue-and-gold carpet runner. A marble-topped table held a large arrangement of hothouse roses and blue satin chairs lined up along the silk-striped walls.

But Emma didn't have much time to examine the refurbishments.

'Is that our Aunt Emma?' a tiny, fluting voice called out, echoing down the stairs. Emma glanced up to find two little faces, with two matching sets of hazel eyes and mops of blond curls, peering down at her from the landing.

'I am your Aunt Emma,' she said, her heart feeling as if it would burst at this sight of the twins, who she hadn't seen in so very long. 'You must be William and Eleanor. You are much bigger than when I last saw you. Back then you were about as large as a loaf of bread.'

The two of them giggled and quickly came dashing and tumbling down the stairs to land at her feet. They peered up at her with curiosity shining from their eyes, eyes that were so much like their mother's.

'You're much younger than we imagined,' William said.

'And thinner,' Eleanor added. 'You should eat some cream cakes.'

'Children!' Jane admonished. 'Manners, please.'

They curtsied and bowed with murmured 'How do you do's' before Jane sent them off to find tea in the drawing room.

'I am so sorry, Emma,' Jane said as they turned to follow the children. 'Hayden and I, and their nannies, work so hard to teach them how to be a viscount and a lady, but they are at such an outspoken age.'

Emma laughed. 'Rather like we were back then? Though I fear I have not quite outgrown it, whereas *you* are the perfect countess.' Suddenly she glimpsed a pile of travel trunks near the drawing-room doors. 'Are you going somewhere?'

'We were planning to go to London for my confinement,' Jane said. 'Hayden thinks I should be near the doctors there. But now that you are here...'

'You must still go,' Emma said firmly, a bit relieved she might have a few days to find her feet without Jane worrying over her as well as the new baby. 'Your health comes first. You can't worry about me now.'

'But you can't rattle around Barton all alone! You could come with us to London.'

London was the last place Emma wanted to be. All those watching eyes and gossiping tongues, all too ready to stir up the old scandal-broth of her elopement and disastrous marriage. 'Actually, I was thinking I could use one of the old cottages. They are so small and cosy, a perfect place for me to decide what I should do next.'

'Live in one of the cottages,' Jane exclaimed. 'Oh, Emma dear, no. This is your house.'

'But you said yourself, it is too big for one person. And I can't go to London now. Not yet. You wrote that Hayden was seeing about releasing my small inheritance from Mama to me soon—I can make do on that in the cottage.'

'But...' Jane looked all set for an argument, but she was, luckily, distracted by the twins calling for her. 'We will talk about this later, Emma,' she said as they hurried into the drawing room.

Emma was sure there would be a long talk later, yet she was set. A small cottage, where she could be alone and think, would be perfect for her now. She would be out of Jane's way, and she could decipher how not to make such foolish mistakes again.

The twins were already settling in next to a lavishly appointed tea table near the windows that looked out on the gardens. Light gleamed on their grandmother's silver tea service and platters of sandwiches and cakes, all cut into pretty shapes and arranged in artistic pyramids.

The children eyed the display avidly, but sat quietly with hands innocently folded in their laps.

'All this for me?' Emma said with a laugh.

'Hannah missed you, too,' Jane said, mentioning the woman who had been their maid for many years. In poorer times she was their *only* maid, but now she was housekeeper of Barton.

'Here, Aunt Emma, you must have *this* cake,' Eleanor said, passing her a pink-frosted confection.

'Thank you very much, Eleanor dear,' Emma said, sure her niece was most serious now about fattening her up. As they sipped at their tea, she studied the gardens outside. The terraces of flowerbeds sloped gently down to the maze and she was sure when summer came it would be a glorious riot of colour. 'What has been happening in the village of late? Anything interesting?'

'Oh, yes, a great deal,' Jane said enthusiastically. 'There is a new vicar, an excellent gentleman by the name of Mr Crawford. He is Lady Wheelington's son from her first marriage. I am sure you must remember my friend Lady Wheelington? She is newly home from abroad herself. Mr Crawford is sadly yet unmarried, but I am sure that will soon be remedied. His mother has hinted of a young lady from Brighton. And old Lady Firth finally won the flower show last year! It was long past time. And Sir David Marton has come back to Rose Hill at last.'

'Sir David Marton?' Emma said, startled by the name. She feared the words came out much sharper than she intended and quickly turned away to nibble at her cake. 'I hadn't realised he ever left. He didn't seem the adventurous sort.'

'So you do remember Sir David?' Jane said.

Of course Emma remembered him. How very handsome he was. The way he seemed to admire Jane's sweet ways so much. The way he would look at Emma, so carefully, so close and calm, until she feared he could see her every secret.

How would he look at her now, after everything that had happened? Would he even speak to her at all?

Somehow the thought of Sir David's disapproval made her heart sink just a bit.

'I do remember him,' she said.

'Yes. He was quite kind to us when things looked rather bleak, wasn't he? And he was such a help that night of the fire.'

He had been kind to Jane, always. 'Yet you say he left the village?'

'Yes. He married Miss Maude Cole. Do you remember her as well?'

Miss Cole, who Sir David had danced with at that long-ago assembly. Pretty, vivacious Miss Cole. The perfect wife for a man like him. 'Of course. She was quite lovely and good friends with his sister, as I recall, so such a match makes sense.'

Jane arched her brow. 'So everyone thought.'

'Was it not a good match after all?'

'No one knows for sure. Lady Marton preferred town life, so soon after the wedding they went off to London and rarely came back here. Hayden and I have mostly been at Ramsay House or here at Barton, but we heard she was quite the toast.'

'Was?'

'Sadly, Lady Marton died last year, and Sir David has come back to Rose Hill with his little daughter. We haven't seen them very much, but the poor child does seem very quiet.'

'She must miss her mother,' Emma said quietly. Surely Sir David also missed his pretty wife. She was sure he would never have allowed his marital life to grow messy and discordant as hers had. The poor little girl, how she must feel the terrible loss.

'Miss Louisa Marton, who is now Mrs Smythe, is said to be most earnestly searching for a new sister-in-law,' Jane said.

'She must surely be disappointed at the lack of scope for matchmaking around here,' Emma said, making her tone light. She didn't want to talk or think about Sir David any longer. It only reminded her of how very different things were now from when she last met with him. 'Tell me, William and Eleanor, do you like to play blindman's buff? It was your mama's favourite game when we were children, though you may not believe me now. Perhaps we could play a round later…'

From the diary of Arabella Bancroft

I think I have discovered one of the reasons I was summoned to Barton. In return for the gift of the estate, the king expects my cousin to host many parties for his court. My cousin's wife's health does not allow her to play hostess to such a raucous crowd, thus my place here. I know little of planning grand balls, but I confess I do love the new clothes—so much silk and lace, so many feathered hats and furred capes!

And the people who come here are most intriguing. I have seldom had the chance for such

*conversation before, and once I am an improved
card player I shall surely fit in better.*

*I have been asking about the lost treasure, but
beyond ever more fantastical tales I can find out
nothing...*

Chapter Two

The silence in the carriage was absolutely deafening.

David looked down at his daughter, Beatrice, who perched beside him on the seat of the curricle. Most of her face was hidden by the brim of her straw bonnet, but he could see the tip of her upturned nose and the corner of her mouth, unsmiling as she watched the lane go by. Her red-gold curls, tied neatly at the nape of her neck with a pink bow, laid in a glossy stream down the back of her blue-velvet spencer.

Bea always looked like the perfect little lady, a pretty porcelain doll in her fashionable clothes, with a real doll usually tucked under her arm as her constant companion. All the ladies they ever met exclaimed and cooed over her. 'A perfect angel, David,' his sister always crowed. 'Why, she never cries or fusses at all! And after all she's been through…'

Louisa was right. Bea *was* an angel, always playing quietly with her dolls or attending to lessons with her nanny. But was she *too* quiet? Too self-contained for a five-year-old?

Even now, on a lovely, warm, early spring day, when children were dashing along the lane with their hoops and skipping ropes, shouting and laughing, she just watched them with no expression on her little face.

'After I conclude my business in the village, perhaps we could go to the toy shop and get you one of those hoops,' David said as he guided the horses around a corner. 'What do you think, Bea?'

She turned to look up at him for the first time since they left Rose Hill. Her grey eyes were unblinking. 'No, thank you, Papa.'

'It shouldn't be hard to learn how to use it. I could teach you in the garden.'

Bea shook her head. 'Aunt Louisa says you have a lot of business to attend to since we came back to Rose Hill and I shouldn't get in your way.'

Of course Louisa would say that. It was his way of avoiding her gatherings, which seemed designed to introduce him to as many eligible young ladies as possible. But his heart ached that Bea took that to mean he had no time for *her.* Bea had been the light of his life ever since she first appeared and everything he did was for her. 'No matter how much business I have, I'll always have time for you, Bea. I hope you know that.'

'I don't need a hoop, Papa.' She turned her attention to the scenery, to the scattered cottages that marked the edge of the village and the square, stone bell tower of the church.

It hadn't always been like that, David thought with a feeling surging through him that felt near desperation. Once Bea had run through the house as lively and laughing as any of the village children. She had thrown herself into his arms, giggling as he twirled her around. She'd served him tea at her tiny table in her tiny porcelain cups, chattering all the time.

Until her mother died. No—he had to say it honestly, at least to himself. Until her mother left them, ran off with her lover, only to be killed with him when their carriage overturned on a rocky Scottish road. Bea knew nothing of that sordid tale. David had only told her Maude had become very ill and gone to take the waters, where she passed away. But ever since then Bea had withdrawn deep into herself, quiet as one of her precious dolls.

David hoped that leaving London permanently and coming home to Rose Hill, near his sister and her family, would bring her out of her shell again. Surely children thrived in fresh air and clear skies? Yet it only seemed to make Bea even quieter.

David liked to be in control of his world; he needed that. He was good at business, at running his estate, improving crop yields, taking care of his tenants and his family. When their parents died, he took care of his sister until she married. He had been a good son, a good brother, and he prided himself on that. He had even been a good husband, had given up his brief wild period of gambling and other women, and devoted himself to his wife. He had seen where such a rakish life led and he hadn't wanted it for himself in the end.

Why, then, had he failed so badly as a husband, and now as a father?

As he looked at his daughter now, her little back

so straight as she perched next to him on the seat, his heart ached with how much he loved her. How much he wanted to help her and could not.

The anger he had long felt towards Maude, which he had tried to shove away and forget, still came out when he saw how Bea had become. Maude—so pretty, so charming. So frivolous. In the beginning, she looked suitable to be his wife, until he found her charm masked desperate emotionalism, a heedless romanticism that made her utterly abandon her family and duties. Just as he had once come so close to doing.

'You should marry again,' his sister told him over and over. 'If Beatrice had a new mother, and Rose Hill had a proper mistress, all would be well. What about Lady Penelope Hader? Or Miss King?'

He had taken Louisa's advice the first time and married her good friend Miss Cole. He should not look twice at any of her candidates again. But she was right about one thing—some day he would have to marry again. But this time he would find a lady of good, solid sense and impeccable reputation and family. A lady who would join him in his duties and be content with a quiet, solid country life.

He was absolutely determined on that. He, and more importantly Beatrice, needed no more romantic adventurers in their lives.

The village was busy on such a fine day. The narrow walkways were crowded with people hurrying on their errands, and the doors and windows to the shops were flung open to let in the fresh breeze. There seemed to be a new energy in the air that always came with the first signs of green, growing things—an invigorated purpose.

David wished he could feel it too. That new, fresh, clean hope. Yet still there was only a strange numbness at his core.

Work was the answer. The forgetfulness of purposeful work. He left the curricle at the livery stables and took Bea's lace-gloved hand in his to lead her out into the lane. She went with him without a murmur, her doll tucked under her other arm.

'I won't be long at the lawyer's office, Bea,' he said. 'If you don't want to visit the toy shop, perhaps we could get a sweet afterwards? You haven't had one of those lemon drops you like in a while.'

'Thank you, Papa,' she murmured.

Their progress down the street was slow, as several people stopped David to offer him greetings or ask questions about his plans for Rose Hill. He hadn't been home long enough for curiosity to fade about his London scandal, and he could almost feel the burn of curiosity in people's eyes as they talked to him. He could hear the careful tones of their voices, from people he had known since he was a child.

Even here the upheaval of his life couldn't quite be forgotten.

As they walked past the assembly rooms, he heard his sister's voice call out to him.

'David, dearest! I didn't know you were coming to the village today. You should have sent me word and I would have made you dine with us before you go back to Rose Hill,' Louisa cried.

David turned to see his sister hurrying toward him, her two little sons tumbling after her and her pregnant belly before her. The boys were shoving and tripping each other, as they so often did, and David felt Bea stiffen next to him.

'I didn't want you to go to any trouble, Louisa,' he said as he kissed her offered cheek under the flowered edge of her bonnet.

'No trouble at all. We see you too seldom,' Louisa answered. She carefully bent down and embraced Bea, who still held her little body very still. 'And how lovely you look today, Beatrice! My, but I do hope *this* one will be a girl. Boys, stop that fighting right now! Bow to your uncle.'

As the boys quickly bowed and muttered before shoving each other again, Louisa whispered in David's ear, 'Beatrice is looking awfully pale, isn't she? You should leave her with me while you conclude your business, she can play with her cousins. I'm sure she is too much alone at Rose Hill.'

Beatrice seemed to hear her and gave David an alarmed glance. 'Thank you for the kind offer, Louisa, but we must return home very soon today. Another time, I promise.'

Louisa sniffed. 'As you like, of course. But you know what Rose Hill and Beatrice need is more children running about the halls there! New little siblings, as you and I were. Have you met Miss Harding yet? She has come to stay with her uncle, Admiral Harding, and I quite admire her already. So pretty, so steady. Just what you need.'

Bea didn't say anything, or even move, but David felt her hand tighten on his. 'No, I have not yet met Miss Harding.'

'Then you must come to the assembly next week. She is sure to be there and I have sung your praises to her already.'

'I still have so much work to do at Rose Hill…'

'Don't say you must work all night as well as all day! You must get out in the world again, David. It would do you so much good. And you will never find a wife if you stay alone at Rose Hill all the time. Will he, Beatrice darling?'

'No, Aunt Louisa,' Bea said dutifully.

'Of course not. Now, David, let me tell you about Miss Harding…'

Louisa went on talking, but David's attention was suddenly captured by a figure hurrying along the walkway on the other side of the street.

She wasn't very tall, but was very straight and slender, with an elegant bearing and purpose to her step that seemed somehow familiar. Yet he was sure she couldn't be someone he knew, for she wore a black gown and pelisse and a plain black bonnet, and there were no recent widows in the village. Still, something about her compelled him to keep watching. Something vital and almost magnetic, something—alive.

David suddenly realised he hadn't felt *alive* in a very long time. Hadn't felt captured by something as he was by the glimpses of the lady in black.

Others, too, watched her as she passed them, turned

to stare at her, stopped in their tracks. But only a few actually offered her a greeting.

She stopped at the window of Mr Lorne's bookshop and, as she turned to examine the haphazard display of dusty volumes behind the cloudy glass, David caught a glimpse of her pale profile against the black ruching of her bonnet, as pure and perfect as a Grecian coin.

'Emma Bancroft,' he whispered, shocked by the sight of her. Now that he saw her again, he was surprised at how completely he recalled a girl he hadn't glimpsed in years. But where he felt a hundred years older than the man he had been at that long-ago assembly, Emma Bancroft looked exactly the same. Golden, sunny curls, a straight little nose dusted with pale amber freckles, rosebud lips curved in a smile as she studied the books. She looked just as young, just as eager to run out and grab life.

Yet she, too, must have faced a great deal since they last met, swathed in black as she was. She pushed open the door to the shop and vanished inside, and David's strangely silent, suspended moment crashed around him. The noisy bustle of the crowd. Bea's hand in his. The ceasing of his sister's stream of chatter.

'Oh, yes,' Louisa said with another sniff. 'Emma Bancroft. I did hear she had returned to Barton Park, though I'm surprised her sister would have her back after everything that happened. Hardly befitting the sister-in-law of an earl.'

David gave her a curious glance and Louisa smiled smugly. She always liked having gossip other people did not and David had lived buried in his own business since he came home. 'You will remember, I am sure, David. Or perhaps you won't, you are always so very busy. Do you not recall her infamous elopement with Mr Henry Carrington?'

David did remember vague whispers about it all. Emma Bancroft eloped with a known rake in her first Season, against her sister's advice. Word of it had floated all the way from London back to Rose Hill, everyone saying how sad it was, but really not very surprising. Miss Bancroft, after all, had always been such an odd girl with strange fancies. Other scandals soon eclipsed it, and by the time David went to London with Maude and their new baby there were only a few titters about Lady Ramsay's wayward sister. He assumed the rake and Miss Bancroft had settled into a reasonable marriage, away from England.

And Maude's own scandal soon quite overtook everything else. But David felt strangely disappointed when he remembered Miss Bancroft's—Mrs Carrington's—true nature. For an instant there, he was actually happy to glimpse her coming down the street, felt a rush of hope. Now the sunny, lively vibrancy he had imagined seemed more hoydenish and dangerously unpredictable.

He couldn't afford any more scandal in his life. Either his own or that of others.

'They say Mr Carrington died in a duel somewhere in France,' Louisa said. 'Now I suppose Lady Ramsay has no choice but to shelter her sister.'

As David had always had no choice in his own family? Faintly irritated, he said, 'Perhaps you think she should have left her sister in a Parisian workhouse.'

'David! You are quite shocking today. Of course Lady Ramsay had to take Mrs Carrington in, though it would have been more politic of Mrs Carrington to stay away after the stir she caused. But family is family, I suppose. I just hope she will stay quietly at Barton Park and not embarrass anyone.'

'I must attend to my business, Louisa,' he said, feeling the urge to defend Emma Bancroft, even from something indefensible. 'The lawyer is expecting me so we can go over my purchase of the lands adjacent to Rose Hill.'

'Oh, yes, of course. I know you are so terribly busy, David dear. Just don't forget about Miss Harding! We shall all be expecting you at the assembly next week.'

Murmuring some non-committal reply, David led Bea off down the street. She went with him quietly, leaving him to brood on that glimpse of Emma Bancroft's face. And wanting even more of what he knew he couldn't have.

Her papa did *not* need another wife. At least not one her Aunt Louisa chose for him.

Bea swung her feet from the tall chair she sat perched on as she waited for her papa to conclude his business. He and the grey-haired, saggy-faced lawyer, Mr Wall, talked on and on with words she didn't understand and the warm close air of the office smelled of old cigars and dust, but Bea didn't care. The more they talked, and the more they ignored her as she sat quietly in the corner, the more she could watch and think.

It was a strategy that had worked very well for her since her mother went away. Things had been so very confusing for a while, the doors of the London house slamming and people coming and going at all hours. Her Grandfather Cole shouting and red-faced. Her papa, who usually played with her and laughed with her, so quiet and serious all the time.

And every time he looked at her he seemed very sad. There were no more tea parties or quiet hours for reading books together. He would send her to the park with her nanny and lock himself in the library.

And no one ever told her anything at all. Tears and shouted questions got her nothing but pitying looks and new dolls. While the dolls *were* nice, she still wanted to know where her mother had really gone and when her real papa was coming back to her.

That was when she learned to be quiet and watch. When she tucked herself away in corners, people forgot she was there and talked about things in quiet, calm ways with no baby-speak. Bea *hated* baby-speak. Her father had never spoken to her that way and most grown-ups had long ago given it up with her, until her mother left. Then no one talked to her any other way.

Especially Aunt Louisa. Bea sighed as she smoothed her doll's silk skirt and thought of Aunt Louisa. She was a very good sort of aunt, always kind and generous with the lemon drops, but her insistence that Bea play with her horrid sons was a nuisance. Those boys had no interesting conversation at all, and they always tried to steal her dolls. Once they even cut the curls off one, making Bea cry and Aunt Louisa scream.

Days at Aunt Louisa's house were not much fun. Even waiting here in this dull office was better.

But what made time with Aunt Louisa even worse was that she always told Papa he should marry again as fast as possible. She even insisted Bea needed a new mother.

Bea did not want a new mother. She'd hardly ever seen the one she once had, except for glimpses out the window when her mother was climbing into a carriage to go off to a party. She'd been as beautiful as an angel, all sparkling and laughing in her lovely gowns, but not much use. Nor would a mother like Aunt Louisa be much fun, always calling for her vinaigrette when she wasn't telling everyone what to do.

Not that Bea *completely* objected to the idea of a mother. Mothers in books always looked like lovely things, always tying their daughters' hair ribbons and reading them stories. And Papa did need someone to help him smile more.

Aunt Louisa's Miss Harding, niece of Admiral Harding, didn't quite sound like what Bea had in mind. Anyone Aunt Louisa chose would surely be entirely wrong for Rose Hill. Bea knew she was only a little girl, but she also knew what she wanted, and what Papa needed.

She just didn't know where to find it.

'...in short, Sir David, the sale of the lands should go through at that price with no problems whatsoever,' the old lawyer said. 'Your estate at Rose Hill will be considerably enlarged, if you are sure more responsibility is what you truly desire right now.'

'Have you heard complaints about my lack of responsibility, Mr Wall?' Papa said, with what Bea suspected was amusement in his voice, though she didn't understand the joke. She hoped he might even smile, but he didn't.

'Not at all, of course. You have a great reputation in the area as a good, and most progressive, landlord with a great interest in agriculture. Once you get those lands organised, you'll have no trouble whatsoever leasing the farms. But there can be such a things as working *too* hard, or so Mrs Wall sometimes informs me.'

'Is there?' Papa said quietly. 'I have not found it so.'

'A wife, Sir David, can be a great help. The right sort of wife, of course, an excellent housekeeper, a hostess, a companion. But I fear we are boring pretty Miss Marton here! Would you care for a sweet, my dear? Sugared almonds—my grandsons love them, so I always keep them about.'

'Thank you, Mr Wall,' Bea answered politely. As she popped the almond into her mouth, she thought over what Mr Wall said. A hostess for Rose Hill—another thing to put on her list of requirements for a new mother.

As they took their leave of Mr Wall and stepped back out into the lane, Bea shivered at the cool breeze after the stuffy offices.

'We should get you home, Bea, before you catch a chill,' Papa said as he took her hand.

But Bea didn't quite want to go back to the quiet nursery at Rose Hill just yet. Neither did she want to go visit Aunt Louisa. 'Could we go to the bookshop first?' she asked. 'Maybe Mr Lorne has some new picture books from London. I've read everything in the nursery at least twice now.' And Aunt Louisa and her sons never went in the bookshop. It was always quite safe.

Her papa seemed to hesitate, which was most odd, for he was usually most agreeable to visiting Mr Lorne's shop. He glanced towards the building across the street, his eyes narrowed behind his spectacles as if he tried to peer past the dusty windows. But finally he nodded and led her across the street to the waiting shop.

Chapter Three

Emma smiled at the familiar sound of rusted bells clanking as she pushed open the door to Mr Lorne's bookshop. It had been so long since she heard them, but once they had been one of the sweetest sounds in the world to her. They had meant escape.

Could she ever find the same sanctuary in books again? The same forgetfulness in learning? Or did she know too much about what lay outside the pages now?

As she closed the door behind her, she thought about the way people watched her as she walked down the street, silent and wide-eyed. She hadn't left the grounds of Barton much since her arrival, wanting only the healing quiet of home. Days wandering around the rooms and gardens, reminiscing with Jane and playing games with the children, had been wonderful indeed. She'd almost begun to remember herself again and forget what she had seen in her life with Henry.

But now Jane and Hayden had gone off to London, and without them and the boisterous twins the estate was much too silent. Emma needed to purchase some things for her refurbishment of her cottage and she needed reading materials for the quiet evenings at her small fireside. That meant a trip into the village.

She hadn't been expecting a parade to greet her, of course. She had been gone for such a long time and in such an irregular way. Yet neither had she expected such complete silence. They had looked at her as if she were a ghost.

Emma was tired of being a ghost. She wanted to be alive again, feel alive in a way she hadn't since her marriage to Henry fell apart so spectacularly in its very infancy. She just wasn't sure how to do that.

Mr Lorne's shop seemed like a good place to start. Emma smiled as she looked around at the familiar space. It appeared not to have changed at all in the years she had been gone. The rows of shelves were still jammed full of haphazardly organised volumes, wedged in wherever there was an inch. More books were stacked on the floors and on the ladders.

The windows, which had never been spotless, were even more streaked with dust than ever, and only a few faint rays of daylight slanted through them. Colza lamps lit the dark corners and gave off a faint flowery smell that cut through the dryness of paper, glue and old leather. Once Emma's eyes adjusted to the gloom, she saw Mr Lorne's bushy grey head peeking over a tottering tower of books on his desk.

'Good heavens,' he said. 'Is it really you, Miss Bancroft?'

Emma laughed, relieved that she really wasn't a ghost after all. *Someone* could acknowledge her. She hurried over to shake Mr Lorne's hand, now worryingly thin and wrinkled.

'Indeed it is me, Mr Lorne,' she said. 'Though I am Mrs Carrington now.'

'Ah, yes,' he said vaguely. 'I do remember you had gone away. No one pestered me for new volumes on plants any more.'

'You were always ready to indulge my passion for whatever topic I fancied,' Emma said, remembering her passion for botany and nature back then. Maybe she should try to find that again?

'You were one of my best customers. So what do you fancy now?'

'I'm not quite sure.' Emma hesitated, studying the old shop as she peeled off her gloves. The black kid was already streaked with dust. 'I'm refurbishing one of the old cottages on the Barton estate, but I'm not sure what I'll do after that. I don't suppose you ever did come across any old writings about the early days of Barton?' Before she left home, Emma had been passionately involved in researching her family's home, especially searching for the legendary Barton treasure. But nothing had ever come of it.

'I don't think so.'

'Then maybe some novels? Something amusing for a long evening?'

'There I *can* help you, Mrs Carrington.' Mr Lorne carefully climbed down from his stool and picked up a walking stick before leading her to a shelf against the far wall. Just like always, she saw he had an organisational system understood only by himself. 'These are some of the latest from London. But I fear I can't help you decide what to do next any more than I can help myself.'

Emma glanced at the old man, surprised by the sad, defeated tone on his voice. The Mr Lorne she remembered had always been most vigorous and cheerful, in love with his work and eager to share the books on his shelf. 'Whatever do you mean, Mr Lorne?'

'I fear I must close this place before too long.'

'Close it?' Emma cried, appalled. 'But you are the only bookshop in the area.'

'Aye, it's a great pity. I've loved this shop like my own child. But my daughter insists I go and live with her in Brighton. I can hardly see now and it's hard for me to get around.'

Emma nodded sympathetically. She could assuredly see that a shop where stock required unpacking and shelving, and accounts required keeping, might be too much for Mr Lorne now. But she couldn't bear to lose her sanctuary again so soon after refinding it.

'That is a very great pity indeed, Mr Lorne,' she said. 'I'm very sorry to hear it.'

'Ah, well, there should be plenty of books for me in Brighton, even if I have to get my grandchildren to read them to me,' Mr Lorne said. 'And maybe someone will want to buy this place from me and restock it with all the latest volumes.'

'I do hope so. Though it would never be quite the same without you.'

Mr Lorne chuckled. 'Now you're just flirting with an old man, Mrs Carrington.'

Emma laughed in reply. 'And what if I am? I have never met another man who could talk about books with me as you do.'

'Then you must find a few of those novels and we'll talk about them when you've read them. I'm not tottering away just yet.'

As Mr Lorne made his way back to his desk, Emma scanned the rows of titles. *Mysterious Warnings. Orphan of the Rhine.* They sounded deliciously improbable. Just what she needed right now. Something a bit silly and romantic, preferably with a few haunted castles and stormy seas thrown in.

She climbed up one of the rickety ladders to look for more on the top shelves, soon losing herself in the prospect of new stories. She opened the most intriguing one, *The Privateer,* and propped it on the top rung to read a few pages. She was soon deep into the story, until the bells jangled on the opening door, startling her out of her daydream world. She spun around on one foot on the ladder and her skirts wrapped around her legs, making her lose her balance.

For an instant, she felt the terrible, cold panic of falling. She braced herself for the pain of landing on the hard floor—only to be caught instead in a pair of strong, muscled arms.

The shock of it quite knocked the breath from her and the room went hazy and blurry as the veil of her bonnet blinded her. Willing herself not to faint, Emma blinked away her confusion and pushed back the dratted veil.

'Thank you, sir,' she gasped. 'You are very quick-thinking.'

'I'm just happy I happened to be here,' her rescuer answered and his voice was shockingly familiar. A smooth, deep, rich sound, like a glass of sweet mulled wine on a cold night, comforting and deliciously disturbing at the same time.

It was a voice she hadn't heard in a long time and yet she remembered it very well.

Startled, Emma tilted her head back and looked up into the face of Sir David Marton. Her rescuer.

He looked back at her, unsmiling, his face as expressionless as if it was carved from marble. He appeared no older than when they last met, his features as sharply chiselled and handsome as ever, his eyes the same pale, piercing grey behind his spectacles. His skin seemed a bit bronzed, as if he spent a great deal of time outdoors, which gave him the appearance of vigorous good health quite different from the night-dwelling pallor of Henry and his friends.

David Marton looked—good. No, better than good. Dangerously handsome.

Yet there *was* something different about him now. Something harder, colder, even more distant, in a man who had always seemed cautious and watchful.

But Jane had said he too had had his trials these last few years. A lost wife. Surely they were all older and harder than they once were?

His face was expressionless as he looked down at her, as if he caught falling damsels every day and barely recognised her. How could this man make her feel so unsure, yet still want to be near him? Made her want to know more about what went on behind his infuriatingly inscrutable expression?

Suddenly Emma realised he still held her in his arms, as easily and lightly as if she was no more than a feather. And her arms were wrapped around his shoulders as they stared at each other in heavy, tight silence.

He seemed to realise it at the same moment, for he slowly lowered her to her feet. She swayed dizzily and his hand on her arm kept her steady.

'I'm so sorry,' Emma said, trying to laugh as if the whole thing was just a joke. That was the only way she had ever found to deal with Henry and his friends, by never letting them see her real feelings. 'That was terribly clumsy of me.'

'Not at all,' he answered. He still watched her and Emma wished with all her might she could read his thoughts even as she hid hers. With Henry's friends, who had tried to flirt with her or drunkenly lure her to their beds, she had always known what they were thinking and could easily brush them off. They were like primers for children once she learned their ways.

David Marton, on the other hand, was a sonnet in Latin, complicated and inscrutable and maddening.

'I fear I startled you,' he said, 'and these ladders are much too precarious for you to be scurrying along.'

Emma laughed, for real this time. So Sir David hadn't entirely changed; she remembered this protective quality within his watchfulness before. Like a medieval knight. 'Oh, I've been in much more precarious spots before.'

A smile finally touched his lips, just a hint at the

very corners, but Emma was ridiculously glad to see it. She wondered whimsically what it would take to get a *real* smile from him.

'I'm sure you have,' he said.

'But I haven't been lucky enough to have anyone there to catch me until today.'

And finally there it was, a smile. It was quickly gone, but was assuredly real. To Emma's fascinated astonishment, she glimpsed a dimple set low in his sculpted cheek.

No man should really be allowed to be so good looking. Especially one as cool and distant as Sir David Marton.

'It's good to see you at home again, Miss Bancroft,' he said.

'Ah, but she is Mrs Carrington now, Sir David,' Mr Lorne said, sharply reminding Emma that she wasn't actually alone with David Marton.

She quickly stepped back from his steadying hand. The warmth of his touch lingered on her arm through her sleeve and she rubbed her hand over it.

'Indeed she is,' Sir David said, his smile vanishing behind his usual polite mask. 'Forgive me, Mrs Carrington. And please accept my condolences on your loss.'

Emma nodded. She was so disappointed to lose that rare glimpse of another David and be right back to distant, commonplace words. Or maybe she had only imagined that glimpse in the first place. Maybe *this* really was the true David Marton.

'And I am sorry for your loss as well, Sir David,' she

said. 'My sister told me about your wife. I remember Lady Marton, she was very beautiful.'

'You knew my mother?' a little voice suddenly said.

Startled, Emma turned to see a tiny girl standing beside Mr Lorne's desk. She was possibly the prettiest child Emma had ever seen, with a porcelain-pale face and red-gold waves of hair peeking from beneath a very stylish straw bonnet. She was very still, very proper, and if her demeanour hadn't convinced Emma this was Sir David's daughter her grey eyes would have.

Emma walked toward her slowly. She was never entirely sure how to behave toward small children. The only ones she really knew were William and Eleanor, and the rambunctious twins seemed as different from this girl as it was possible to be. Once, when she first married Henry, she'd longed for a child of her own. But later, when she saw his true nature, she knew it was a blessing she had never had a baby.

Yet this girl drew Emma to her by her very stillness. 'Yes, I knew her, though not very well, I'm afraid. I saw her at dances and parties, and she was always the prettiest lady there. Just as I suspect you will be one day.'

The little girl bit her lip. 'I'm not sure I would want to be.'

Sir David hurried over to lay his hand protectively on the girl's shoulder. 'Mrs Carrington, may I present my daughter, Miss Beatrice Marton? Bea, this is Mrs Carrington. She's Lady Ramsay's sister from Barton Park.'

Miss Beatrice dropped a perfect little curtsy. 'How do you do, Mrs Carrington? I'm very sorry we haven't seen you at Barton Park before. I like it when we visit there.'

Emma gave her a smile. There was something about the child, something so sad and still, that made her want to give her a hug. But she was sure the preternaturally polite Miss Beatrice Marton would be appalled by such a move.

Much like her father.

'I've been living abroad and have only just returned to Barton,' Emma said. 'I fear my sister and her family have gone to London for a while, but you may call on me any time you like, Miss Marton. I am quite lonely there by myself.'

'So what brings you to my shop today, Sir David?' Mr Lorne interrupted. 'Has your uncle, Mr Sansom, finally decided to sell me his library?'

'I've just come to find Beatrice a new book. She's already read the last ones you sent to Rose Hill,' David said. 'As for my uncle, you would have to ask him yourself. I fear he never leaves his estate now, though you are certainly quite right—his library is exceedingly fine.'

'Such a pity.' Mr Lorne sighed. 'I am quite sure I would find buyers for his volumes right away. Books should have loving homes.'

As Mr Lorne and Sir David talked about the library, Emma watched Beatrice sort through stacks of volumes on the floor. She came back not with children's picture books, but with titles like *The Environs of Venice* and *A Voyage Through the Lands of India*.

'Do you wish to travel yourself, Miss Marton?' Emma asked, quite sure such volumes should be too weighty for such a little girl.

Beatrice shook her head, hiding shyly behind the

brim of her bonnet. 'I like to stay at home the best. But I like looking at the pictures of other places and when Papa reads me the stories. It's like getting to be somewhere else without actually having to leave.'

'Yes, that's exactly what books are,' Emma said. 'Like trying on a different life.'

'Have you been to these places, Mrs Carrington?'

'A few of them.'

Beatrice hesitated for a moment, then said quickly, 'Perhaps you would tell me about them one day?'

Emma's heart ached at the girl's shy words. She heard so much in them that she tried to hide in herself: that uncertainty, that need for life, but the fear of it at the same time. 'I would enjoy that very much, Miss Marton.'

'Beatrice, we should be going soon,' Sir David said. 'Have you found something you like?'

Once everyone's purchases were paid for, Emma left the shop with Sir David and his daughter. As it was nearing teatime, the street was not as crowded and there was no one to stare at her. But she did notice Mrs Browning, the old widow who lived in the cottage across the street, peering at her through the lace curtains at her windows. Mrs Browning had always known everything that happened in the village.

'Did you bring your carriage from Barton, Mrs Carrington?' Sir David asked.

'No, I walked. The exercise was quite nice after the last few rainy days.'

'But it looks as if it might rain again,' he said. 'Let us drive you back.'

Against her will, Emma was very tempted. Her old intrigue with Sir David Marton, formed when she was no more than a naïve young girl, was still there, stronger than ever. When she looked into his beautiful, inscrutable grey eyes, there was so much she wanted to know. If she did sit beside him on a narrow carriage seat, all the way back to Barton, surely he could not always maintain his maddening mystery?

Yet she was no longer that girl. She had seen far more of the world than her old, curious self could ever have wanted. And she knew that men like Sir David—respectable, attractive—could not be for her. No matter how tempted she might be.

She saw the curtains twitch at the house across the street again and could almost feel the burn of avid eyes. In the cosmopolitan, sophisticated environs of Continental spa towns, where everyone was escaping from something and no one was what they appeared, she had forgotten what it was like to live in a place where everyone knew everyone else's business. Where they knew one's family—and one's past.

Emma had vowed to atone, both for the sake of herself and especially for Jane and her family. She couldn't let her sister come home to Barton to find fresh gossip, which was surely what would happen if she drove off now with the eligible David Marton. Nor did she want Sir David and his lovely little daughter to face that, only because he was being polite.

And she knew politeness could surely be all it was for him.

The curtain twitched again.

'You are so kind, Sir David,' she said. 'But I do enjoy the walk.'

'Just as you like, Mrs Carrington,' he said, still so polite. He put on his hat and the shadow of its brim hid him from her even more than he had been before. 'I hope we shall see you more often, since you have returned home.'

'Perhaps so,' Emma answered carefully. 'It was good to see you again, Sir David, and know that you are well. And very good to meet you, Miss Marton. I always love meeting other great readers.'

Little Miss Beatrice gave another of her perfect curtsies before she took her father's hand and the two of them made their way down the lane. Once they were gone from sight, the curtain fell back into place and Emma was alone on the path.

She looked up and down the street, suddenly feeling lost and rather lonely. She'd grown rather used to such a feeling with Henry. After all, he usually left her in their lodgings while he went off to find a card game. But even there she could usually find a few people to talk to, or a task to set herself. Here, she wasn't sure what she should do.

And being with David Marton made her feel all the more alone, now that he was gone.

She glanced back at the window of the bookshop behind her, at its dusty glass and empty display shelves. Like her, it seemed to be waiting for something to fill it. Suddenly a thought struck her, as improbable as it was exciting.

Maybe, just maybe, there was a way she could find

her path back into the life of this place once more. A way she could redeem herself.

She spun around and pushed open the door, moving resolutely inside. Mr Lorne, who was bent over an open volume, looked up with wide, startled eyes under his bushy grey brows.

'Mr Lorne,' Emma blurted before she could change her mind. 'How much might you ask as the purchase price for your shop?'

'Mrs Carrington is very pretty.'

David glanced down at Bea, startled by the sudden sound of her little voice. She'd said nothing at all since they left the village, the empty road and thick hedgerows rolling past peacefully on the way back to Rose Hill.

In truth, he himself had not been in a talking mood. Not since his last glimpse of Emma Bancroft—no, Emma Carrington—standing alone outside the bookshop. David had always lived his life in a rational way— he had to, if his estate and his family, especially his daughter, were to be safely looked after. But when he held Emma Carrington in his arms, felt her body against his, he hadn't felt in the least bit rational.

He felt like a sizzling, burning bolt of white-hot lightning had shot through him, sudden and shocking and just as unwelcome.

He remembered what a pretty young lady she had been before she left Barton Park and he married Maude. Her green eyes had been as bright and full of life as a spring day and she had always seemed just on the cusp of dashing off and leaping into whatever caught her attention. Her life since then more than fulfilled that promise of reckless trouble.

And now she was back, startlingly beautiful. Her pretty girl's face had matured into its high cheekbones and large eyes, and her black clothes only set off her golden hair and glowing skin. The high collar and dull silk couldn't even begin to hide the slender grace of her body.

The body he had held so close—and hadn't wanted to let go.

David's gloved hands tightened on the reins, causing the horses to go faster. He shook his head to clear it of thoughts he shouldn't even be having and brought himself back to where he should be. In the present moment, in the full knowledge of who he was and the responsibility he had.

'Don't you think so, Papa?' Bea said.

David smiled down at her. She looked up at him from beneath the beribboned edge of her bonnet, and for the first time in a long while there was a spark of real interest in her eyes.

But it was an interest she should not have. David would never let a woman hurt his daughter as his wife had when she eloped. If he did marry again, which he knew one day he would have to, it would be to a lady as fully aware of her duty as he was, someone steady and quiet. *That* was the sort of woman Bea should like and want to emulate.

Unfortunately, it seemed to be the spirited Emma

Carrington who sparked Bea's interest. And his own, blast it all.

'Isn't Mrs Carrington pretty?' Bea said again. She held up her doll and added, 'Her hair is just the same colour as my doll's.'

'Yes.' David had to agree, for really there was no denying it. Mrs Carrington *was* pretty. Too pretty. 'But there are things more important than looks, you know, Bea.'

Beatrice frowned doubtfully. 'That's what Nanny says too. She says the goodness of my soul and the kindness of my manners are what I should mind.'

'Nanny is very right.'

'Then are you saying Mrs Carrington doesn't have a good soul?'

David laughed. 'You are too clever by half, my dear. And, no, that's not what I'm saying. I have no idea what Mrs Carrington's soul is like.'

'But she is Lady Ramsay's sister and Lady Ramsay is kind.'

'Indeed she is.'

'And Aunt Louisa says you should marry again.'

This was more than Bea had spoken at one time in many weeks, and for a moment David couldn't decipher the quick, apparent changes in topic.

Then he realised, much to his alarm, that maybe they were all of *one* topic.

'Perhaps one day I will marry again,' he said carefully. 'You should have a new mother and Rose Hill a mistress. But I am sure we have not met her yet.'

'Aunt Louisa said Mrs Carrington's husband died, just like Mama did.'

'Yes. But Mrs Carrington isn't ready to marry again. And neither am I. We're happy on our own for now, aren't we, Bea?' David felt a bolt of worry over his daughter's sudden worry over his marital status. He had thought she was happy at Rose Hill, that once her mother's death had receded into the past she wouldn't be so quiet. He had thought his love and attention would see her through it all. What if he had been wrong?

'Yes, Papa,' Bea said quietly. She settled back on the seat and was silent for the rest of the drive home.

David could only hope she accepted his words and was truly content. Emma Carrington wasn't the sort of lady who could ever fit into his vision of their future and he surely wasn't the sort of person who could attract her. Not if her first marriage was her standard. He knew himself and he knew all of that very well.

Why, then, couldn't he get the memory of her sparkling eyes out of his mind?

From the diary of Arabella Bancroft

I have met the most fascinating gentleman at the dinner tonight. His name is Sir William and he appears to have no estate yet, but the king favours him. I can see why. He is so very charming, and knows much about music and theatre and books. And most astonishing, he spent much time talking to me, despite my insignificance in such company. Indeed, he did not leave my side all evening and I did not wish him to.

He has asked to walk with me in the garden tomorrow...

Chapter Four

Miss Melanie Harding was quite, quite bored.

She sighed and propped her elbows on the window-sill as she stared down at the street below. It had surely been an hour since she sat down there and not more than ten people had gone by! None of them were at all interesting either. Why had her mother sent her off to this forsaken place? It was most unfair.

She glanced back over her shoulder at her uncle, who as usual sat snoring by the fire. That was all he ever seemed to do. And she had so hoped that the home of a retired admiral would at least be full of handsome officers. That was her only consolation when her mother declared she was sending Melanie off to stay with her uncle in a backwater village no one had ever heard of.

'But why?' she had wailed in despair as she watched her mother toss gowns and slippers into a trunk at their small house in Bath. 'Why must I go *there?*'

'You know very well why,' her mother had said, never pausing an instant in her odious task. 'Because no one there will ever have heard of Captain Whitney and your unfortunate behaviour. Your uncle will keep a close eye on you.'

The Captain Whitney thing *had* been unfortunate, but surely that was his fault, not hers. She had only believed him when he said his pretty words of love and devotion and sent her such darling poems. How could she have known they were copied from a dusty old book by someone named Marlowe—or that Captain Whitney's promises were just as false?

Captain Whitney, as well as looking splendid in his red coat, had a good income and respectable connections to a viscount's family. If all had gone as Melanie hoped, as he promised, her mother would have been in ecstasy. She would have congratulated Melanie on her fine catch. But she had been deceived and now she was being punished for it.

'Why can I not go to Aunt Mary in London, then, if I must be sent away?' she had sobbed to her hard-hearted mother.

'Because London is certainly no place for you,' her mother said, still packing away all of Melanie's worldly possessions. 'There is too much scope for trouble there. No, you will stay with your uncle until you learn to behave. This family has never had a scandal on its name and we won't start now.'

So here she was. In hell. Bath was a dull enough place, full of old invalids and retired parsons, but at least once in a while someone interesting came along. But here—here there was nothing at all.

Her uncle snored even louder, shifting in his chair. Melanie knew this was the way it would be until teatime, then he would expect her to read to him from some book of sermons or naval reports or a history of the Armada.

The only people besides her uncle and his servants she had even met in the village were shopkeepers, old Mrs Browning and Mrs Louisa Smythe, who at least had some interesting conversation on the few times they had met. Mrs Smythe knew lots of gossip, even from London as well as of local worthies Melanie hadn't met yet. Mrs Smythe had invited her to an assembly, which seemed like the only bright spot on Melanie's horizon.

As she stared out the window, kicking her feet under her hem, she saw a carriage rolling past. It was the first she'd seen in over an hour and she leaned forwards eagerly to see who it was.

She glimpsed a man she hadn't met before, and from what she could see beneath his hat he was rather handsome. And not old. Plus the curricle seemed to be an expensive one, if painted a rather dull dark-green colour rather than a fashionable yellow. She stood and watched until the equipage was out of sight, her spirits considerably raised.

At least there was one handsome gentleman somewhere in the vicinity! Now she just had to find out who he was. And she knew just who could tell her more about him—her new friend, Mrs Louisa Smythe.

Chapter Five

Emma turned her face up to the sky and closed her eyes as the warmth of the sun touched her skin. After the grey, rainy days, it felt like heaven.

She pulled the door of her cottage closed behind her and hurried up the narrow path of her little garden. She wasn't sure where she was going, she just knew she had to move. She tied her shawl around her shoulders and pushed up the sleeves of her old yellow muslin gown, the first thing not in black she'd worn for weeks. The warm breeze brushed against her skin, drawing her out into the world again.

She ran up the gentle slope of a small hill and spun around to look at Barton spread out all before her. Jane had just sent her a letter that morning saying the baby hadn't arrived yet, so they would be in London for a while longer. So the house was still shut up, but Emma could see the gardeners scurrying around the grounds getting them ready for summer and the new life that would soon fill them. New flowers, new trees—new babies.

Emma felt the stirrings of something new inside herself, too. Some hint of her old restlessness that stirred up what she had thought were cold, dead embers of life.

She turned in a slow circle, taking in the old maze, the outline of her own cottage, where she had left Murray snoring by the fire in his dog dreams. It was her own home, the first she had ever had, and though it was small and quiet it felt like a place where she could be herself. Where she could hide. But maybe, just maybe, she didn't want to hide any more.

Emma took out a letter she had tucked into the folds of her shawl. It had arrived most unexpectedly with that morning's post, from a man named Mr Charles Sansom at Sansom House. When she got the direction from Mr Lorne, she hadn't really expected to hear back. After all, Mr Sansom had already said he wouldn't yet sell any of his extensive library to Mr Lorne, so why should he sell it to her?

But here it was. Emma unfolded it and read it again.

To Mrs Carrington—such a delightful surprise to hear from you, and to know that such a valuable business as Mr Lorne's will go on as before. I have placed many an order with him and he found me some rare volumes in our younger days. Also, though you will not remember it, I knew your late father, who was an excellent authority on local architecture and history. I do not go out into society a great deal now, but you must come and inspect my library at any time that is convenient.

*I have a few volumes on Barton Park itself you
might find of interest.
Yours very sincerely,
Charles Sansom.*

Volumes on Barton Park. Emma found herself most
curious to see what those could be. Once, before she
married, she had found a diary belonging to a lady who
lived at Barton in the seventeenth century. It sent her
off on an ill-fated treasure hunt, yet another reminder
that she had to learn caution.

But surely whatever books Mr Sansom had could
do no harm? He had said he knew her father, who had
also been fascinated by the legend of the Barton treasure. She really did want to get a glimpse of that library.

And she had certainly not forgotten that Mr Sansom
was David Marton's uncle. Not that she thought she
could catch a glimpse of Sir David at Sansom House.
She hadn't seen him since that first day she ventured
into the village and that was all for the best.

She tucked the letter away again and twirled around
to study the long, snaking grey line of stone wall that
divided Barton from Rose Hill. All she could see of that
estate from her perch atop the hill was rolling green
fields and a few white dots of sheep, but she knew it was
there. In the distance she could see the tumbling stone
ruins of the old medieval castle. Who knew what went
on behind Rose Hill's serene pale-grey walls? It was
like a book in a language she didn't yet know.

The wind suddenly swirled around her, catching at
her skirts and hair. It tugged strands from their pins

and tossed them around. Emma laughed and twirled with it. She took off running down the hill, letting the bright day carry her.

She hadn't run in so very long. Life had been small and confined for so many months. Now, just for a moment, she felt free. Faster and faster she went down the hill, the momentum of her movement carrying her until she almost flew over the ground.

She knew there was no one to see her there, no one to judge, and she had almost forgotten how that felt. She ran all the way to the stone wall and twirled around in a little dance step. Maybe life would be well after all. Maybe she could redeem herself, find her place. Maybe…

'I fear I've quite misplaced my dancing pumps,' someone suddenly said.

Emma gave a startled shriek and spun to a sudden halt. But her skirts didn't quite stop with her. They wrapped tightly around her legs and made her stumble against the rough stone of the wall.

For an instant she thought she must have been imagining things, because she couldn't see anyone nearby but two indifferent sheep. Then she glanced up and saw David Marton perched up in a tree beyond the border of the wall, watching her as she ran and twirled and generally behaved like a hoyden.

He *did* have a great talent for catching her unawares.

She held on to the wall and wished that the ground would just swallow her up. The sense of delicious freedom she had felt just a moment before drifted away like a curl of smoke and the coldness of shame she remembered too well from her time with Henry took over.

But then she pushed the coldness away and realised something amazing. David Marton was in a *tree*.

Mystified by the strangeness of the moment, she watched as he climbed down, branch to branch, and leaped to the ground. His lean body moved with a fluid, powerful grace, much like a troupe of Russian acrobats Emma had once seen perform. They had amazed her with the deceptive power of their elegant movements and Sir David could easily have been one of them, tumbling and twirling along thin wires. Rescuing fair damsels from thorny towers.

You have been reading too many novels, Emma told herself sternly. Imagining David Marton as a rescuer of fair ladies, slayer of dragons...

Oh, dear heavens, but he wore no coat. Emma stared at him, hoping she wouldn't go slack-jawed like some country milkmaid, as he reached for a blue coat slung across a low branch. His shirt was very white in the sunshine and the breeze moulded the thin linen to his back and shoulders as he stretched for the coat.

Obviously, he did not spend all his time poring over estate ledgers in the library, or carousing and gambling as Henry and his friends had. The strong muscles she had felt as he caught her in his arms were no illusion. His broad shoulders and powerful arms tapered to narrow hips and long legs encased in tight doeskin breeches.

Emma turned sharply away before she could gawk at his tight backside.

'Out enjoying the fine day, Mrs Carrington?' he asked.

She heard the rustle of fabric as he slid into his coat and only then did she look at him again. The coat concealed his torso, but he wore no cravat and the throat of his shirt was open to reveal the tanned skin of his neck. The wind caught at his glossy dark hair, tousling it over his brow.

In such dishabille, with his hair dishevelled, he almost looked like a different person. Just as handsome as ever, but younger, freer, wilder. More at home here, under the sun and sky, on his own land, than he was in an assembly room.

Perhaps, just perhaps, she had judged Sir David too hastily? Perhaps there was more to him than the serious and responsible estate owner?

Then he slid his spectacles from the pocket of his coat and covered his beautiful grey eyes with them again. A faint frown flickered over his lips as he looked at her and her instant of wild hope was gone.

'Yes,' she said brightly, suddenly remembering that he had spoken to her. 'I was just out for a walk. I hadn't realised I was so near to the edge of your estate.'

'Shall I have you arrested for trespassing, Mrs Carrington?'

For an instant, Emma was shocked, sure he was serious. Then she saw his frown whisper into a smile and her shock grew. Had he made a *joke?*

'Only if I cross the wall,' she said. 'And I shall be very careful not to.'

He laughed and it sounded startled and a bit rusty,

as if he didn't do that very often. 'Fair enough. Then I will stay here and we can talk at a safe distance.'

Yes, that would surely be best if she stayed at a safe distance. Especially since she had seen what he looked like without his coat. 'Were you climbing trees?' she asked, unable to contain her curiosity any longer. 'I wouldn't have thought it of you, Sir David.'

He shook his head ruefully. 'It's not my usual pastime, I confess. Not since I was about Bea's age, anyway.'

'I find it hard to imagine you as a child,' Emma blurted out. Somehow Sir David seemed the sort of person who would spring into the world, Athena-like, fully grown and ready to take care of business.

'We all must come from somewhere, Mrs Carrington. I gave up the tree-climbing after I was caught as a boy by an exceptionally stern tutor, though.'

'Then what drove you back to it today?'

'All of this…' He gestured toward a wide swathe of flat-grounded meadow, from the cluster of trees near the wall to a small, open-sided shelter in the distance. 'This used to be an orchard and quite a productive one. Until my grandfather took the trees out to try and make a more picturesque vista. These few trees are all that is left and they've given us a good apple crop every year until now. My gardener suggested I take a look, but I know little of such things. I'd like to see them restored, though; I was hoping to expand the orchard again.'

Emma peered up at the tree. 'I can see little sign of disease from here. You should read James Lee's volume, it is very helpful in such matters.'

'Ah, yes. I had forgotten your interest in botany.'

'I haven't studied it in a long time, but I do remember Mr Lee. I wanted to use some of the information to make some improvements on the gardens here at Barton.' She glanced back at the house, all peaceful and shimmering in the sun. 'There wasn't much use for such things after I left and my interests turned to other matters.'

'Your sister said you have been living on the Continent,' he said, in that maddeningly neutral tone of his.

'Yes.' Emma started strolling slowly along the wall and Sir David fell in step with her on his side of the divide.

'Barton Park must seem dull to you now.'

'It's not dull at all,' Emma protested. 'I get to be close to my sister again, to be at home. I've missed it.'

'And you don't miss things like balls and routs? Meeting new people and seeing new sights? The village bears little resemblance to Paris or Rome, I fear.'

Emma laughed, remembering the crowded, smelly streets of Paris, the hordes of people jostling together between the tall, close-packed buildings and the glittering shop windows. 'No, it's not like Paris. I confess I do miss the great scope for people-watching there. But the village does have its own pleasures.'

'You enjoy people-watching?' he asked, sounding doubtful, as if such a pastime was not quite…correct.

'Of course. Doesn't everyone? People do such endlessly fascinating and strange things. I suppose that's the only thing I miss in being by myself at Barton, though I do have the characters in the books I read.'

'You should come to the assembly next week, then. The crowds won't be as fashionable as Paris, but they ought to supply you with conversation enough.'

Emma had moved a few steps ahead of Sir David, but now she stopped and turned to look at him. Had he really said she should come to the village assembly? 'I haven't been to a gathering there in a long time.' Not since the party where she watched him dance with Maude Cole, the two of them so beautiful, so perfect-looking together. As if they belonged there, in that very place with those very people, with each other.

Suddenly she felt terribly selfish for ever thinking Sir David only cold and aloof. He had lost his wife, the mother of his adorable daughter. She, too, had lost her husband, and even though Henry had proved to not be what she had hoped for in the end, she had mourned him. Mourned the possibility of what he might have been. How much worse it must be for Sir David.

She didn't know quite what to say to him and for once she held herself back from blurting out commiserations he surely did not want, not from her. Instead she just smiled at him and said, 'I remember how enjoyable events at the assembly rooms were. But I'm not sure I should go.'

His head tilted a bit to one side and he gave her a narrow-eyed, quizzical look, as if he was confused by her sudden smile. Emma resolved to be friendlier in the future, to not always leap to conclusions about people.

'Because you are still in mourning?' he said.

'Actually I should be in half-mourning now,' Emma answered. She just didn't have the money to replace her black with greys and lilacs, not until her inheritance from her mother came through. And then most of that would go to buying Mr Lorne's shop and replenishing its stock. But Sir David didn't have to know that. 'Appearing at an assembly shouldn't cause much comment, unless I become completely foxed and dance about wildly on the refreshment tables.'

David laughed again. Twice in one day. Emma was sure it had to be a milestone. 'Do you do that often?'

'Only when the mood strikes me,' Emma said breezily. 'But here at home I'm sure I would be a pattern-card of propriety. I'm just not sure many people would be happy to see me there. Not after...'

After the scandal she caused by eloping. The infamy would surely follow her always. Emma felt her cheeks turn warm and she turned away to sit down on the edge of the wall, busying herself with arranging her skirts around her.

'You have more friends here than you realise, Mrs Carrington,' David said gently. 'They would all be glad to see you again, dancing wildly or not. And if you plan to run the bookshop...'

Emma looked up at him in surprise. 'You know about that?'

'I was in the village again yesterday and Mr Lorne mentioned it.'

'You don't think that's terribly shocking—for a female to run a shop?'

David sat down next to her on the wall and was silent for a moment. She had the sense he was weighing his thoughts. He always seemed to do that. She wished she could learn how.

He braced his palms on the wall and said, 'It is not the usual thing, of course. But it's not as if you were proposing to take over the butcher shop. Many young widows find projects to fill their days. Charity, embroidery—why not books?'

Emma was startled. She would never have thought David Marton would espouse such an open-minded attitude. Maybe his years of marriage had changed him. Or maybe the years had changed her. Hadn't she just decided she should not judge people hastily? They were too ever surprising. 'Or an orchard?'

He looked down at her, his brow arched. 'An orchard?'

'Young widowers surely need to distract themselves as well,' she said. 'You are said to be the hardest-working landowner in the area.'

'I take my responsibilities at Rose Hill seriously,' he answered slowly.

'My sister says you lived much in London when Lady Marton was alive. You must be going through many—adjustments now.'

'As you are, Mrs Carrington?'

'Yes. As I am.' Emma had always felt as if she and David Marton were such different personalities they could scarcely talk together, no matter how much she enjoyed looking at his handsome face. But perhaps now they had become more alike, both suddenly adrift in a new, uncharted sea.

His compass, though, seemed more reliable than

hers. He had his purpose at Rose Hill, his secure place in the life of this village. She was still floundering.

'My wife preferred town life,' he said. 'Luckily London is within easy enough distance that I could take care of Rose Hill from there and still see to my family. But when she died I wanted Bea to know her home.'

'Miss Marton is very pretty,' Emma said. 'And she seems quite clever, if the books she chose are anything to go by.'

David smiled, and just as he had when he first jumped out of the tree he looked suddenly younger. Lighter. His grey eyes seemed to glow as he thought about his daughter. 'Bea is too clever by half. And, yes, she is very pretty, though I do say so myself as her papa. I fear it may get her into trouble one day.'

'Not with such a fond papa watching over her,' Emma said. Surely any man who cared about his child so had to be good inside? She thought of her own father, so distracted by his own projects, but so much fun when he was with her.

'She has had a difficult time since she lost her mother. I was hoping that coming back to Rose Hill would help her, yet she still seems rather lonely. There are few children here her own age for her to befriend and my sister's sons—well, Bea has little in common with them.'

Emma thought of Mrs Smythe's boys, romping through the streets of the village. 'I would imagine not.'

'I sometimes wonder if a school might not be good for her.'

'Oh, no!' Emma cried, unable to stop herself. 'Not a school, Sir David, I beg you.'

David's brow arched again. 'You don't think a school would be a good idea?'

'I—I don't mean to interfere in your own family business, of course. But I went to school for a time after my sister married, and it was not where I wanted to be. Girls who love books and dreaming, as it seems Miss Marton does...'

'Could easily get lost there,' David murmured. 'Thank you, Mrs Carrington. You have confirmed that I should indeed be selfish and keep her with me. It is hard at times for a father to know what best to do for his daughter when she has no mother. My own parents died too young and I had to look after my sister. I fear it has all made me too protective.'

Emma nodded. He did seem to understand, in a way few men would. It certainly surprised her. 'Miss Marton can always come visit me at the bookshop and read all she likes, since you say my shopkeeping has not shocked you too much,' she said, trying to tease him, to make him laugh. To put herself on more familiar ground with him, when she was shaken by the sudden surge of tender feelings.

He didn't say anything. Before he looked away, Emma saw a shadow flicker through his eyes. Even though he was obviously too correct, too reserved, to say anything, Emma felt the familiar cold touch of faint disapproval. Of course a man like him would not want his young, impressionable daughter spending much time with a woman like her. Her past mistakes were still there with her.

Emma jumped up from the wall, unable to sit so close to him any longer. She felt like a fool, wanting him to like her, wanting to know him better, but knowing he would not. The old wildness that had always plagued her, always lurked inside of her, swept over. She clambered atop the low wall and danced over it, balancing on her toes, letting the wind brush over her and tug at her hair again.

'Mrs Carrington, be careful,' Sir David called. He jumped up from the wall and held up his hand as if he would catch her.

Somehow the gesture only made her feel sadder. She twirled away and called, 'It's a beautiful day, Sir David! You should dance here with me.'

'This wall is a bit rougher than a dance floor, I fear,' he said, his hand still held out to her.

'All the better, then, because there is no one to see us.' Emma held out her arms and ran lightly over the uneven stones. He stayed close beside her, and when she spun around again she heard him make a choked sound, half between a laugh and a disapproving growl.

She glanced down at him, at his eyes shielded behind his spectacles and his windblown hair, and she wanted to touch him. To feel those locks against her fingers, the warmth of his skin on hers. She turned sharply away. 'Don't worry, Sir David. I can take care of myself— I've been doing so for a long time.'

'Sometimes in life we have to let other people take care of us, Mrs Carrington.'

Surprised by his solemn words, Emma stumbled to a halt and looked down at him again. She thought of what Jane had said, of how he took care of Rose Hill and all its tenants and servants, took care of his giggly sister and his daughter and his wife. 'Oh, Sir David. I'm not sure you are quite the right person to teach that lesson.'

He stared up at her and his handsome face hardened. It seemed like a veil dropped before his eyes and he was even more hidden from her than ever. 'Please get down from there now, Mrs Carrington.'

Feeling chastened, Emma finally reached out for his offered hand. But the toe of her half-boot caught on a crevice of the stone and she stumbled and started to fall towards the ground.

But his arms closed around her waist and swept her up again, saving her from disaster. Disaster of her own making.

Emma held on to him and closed her eyes tightly as she tried to breathe. 'Th-thank you. Again.'

'So you can always take care of yourself?' he asked, a hint of lurking amusement in his voice.

Emma's eyes flew open and she looked up into his face. That handsome face that always dazzled her and that hid so much of his true self behind it. 'Perhaps— not always. Not by choice, anyway. But sometimes we have no choice.'

'No,' he answered quietly. 'Sometimes we don't have a choice.'

'If *you* ever need someone to catch you…'

Sir David laughed and suddenly spun around with her

in his arms. Emma squealed and held on to his shoulders as the world turned blurry and giddy around her.

'Would you stand below my ladder and my wall, waiting for me to tumble down?' he shouted over the wind. 'I fear you would send us *both* crashing down!'

'I'm stronger than I look,' Emma cried, laughing.

'Now that I do believe.' David came to a sudden halt, but Emma was still dizzy. As she struggled to catch her breath, to stop laughing, he went very still.

She looked up at him and was caught, mesmerised by what she saw there. He stared down at her, his grey eyes glowing, unwavering, and she knew she couldn't have turned away from him if the world was crumbling around them. He was all she could see, all she knew. He leaned towards her; his lips parted, and she knew, knew with the most certain certainty of all her life, that he would kiss her. And that she wanted him so desperately. His mouth barely brushed hers...

'Papa!' At the sudden cry, David pulled back abruptly. A look of raw horror crossed his handsome face before it went all mask-like again and he carefully lowered her to her feet.

Emma spun away from him to press her hands to her warm cheeks. She was so bewildered, so excited and sad and confused all at the same time that she didn't know what to do. What to feel. She only knew she had to compose herself before David's daughter saw her. Before she faced him again after what they had almost done, what she had wanted so desperately for him to do.

'What are you doing today, Bea, my dearest?' she

heard David say. His tone was light, affectionate, betraying none of her turmoil.

'I'm out for my walk, of course,' Bea answered. Emma heard the sound of footsteps rustling over grass, the whisper of muslin and silk stirred by the wind. 'Is that Mrs Carrington?'

'Indeed it is,' David said. 'I met her on her own walk.'

Emma pasted a bright smile on her face. At least she had learned *that* in her life with Henry, how to put on a social face to hide her true feelings. She turned to see Miss Beatrice beside the wall, a stout older lady in a starched grey nanny's uniform hovering nearby. Watching everything, as if she planned to talk about this encounter in the servants' hall later.

Beatrice was beautifully dressed again, in a pink pelisse and ribbon-trimmed bonnet, her small hands encased in pink kid and a book tucked under her arm. But today she actually had a shy smile on her pretty, pale little face.

'How do you do, Miss Marton?' Emma said. 'I'm very glad to see you again so soon after the bookshop. Have you been enjoying your new volumes?'

'Oh, very much indeed,' Beatrice answered enthusiastically. 'I should like to tell you all about what I read about India, it's ever so interesting. Have you ever seen an elephant, Mrs Carrington?'

'As a matter of fact, I have,' Emma said. 'In a menagerie in Austria. Though I fear he was quite an elderly fellow and not decked in grand jewels as I'm sure they are with the maharajahs.'

Beatrice's eyes widened. 'Really? Oh, Mrs Carrington, you must tell me if—'

'Bea, dearest, I'm afraid Mrs Carrington was on her way home now,' David said, much more abrupt than his usual carefully polite style. 'We must not detain her.'

Beatrice bit her lip. 'No. Of course not, Mrs Carrington.'

'I am sure we will meet again very soon, Miss Marton, at least I hope we will,' Emma said quickly. She meant every word. Her heart was touched by this quiet little girl, who seemed so alone despite the love of her father. Beatrice Marton reminded her too much of her childhood self. 'I can tell you all about the elephants then, as well as the parrots and monkeys I saw.'

'I would like that,' Beatrice said quietly. 'Good day, Mrs Carrington.'

'Good day, Miss Marton—until next time.' Emma watched as Beatrice's nanny bustled forwards to take her hand and lead her away. Beatrice glanced back once and gave a little wave, which Emma returned with a smile.

David bowed politely. 'I'm glad I happened to be here to catch you, Mrs Carrington,' he said quietly.

'Again, you mean?' Emma smiled and curtsied. As she straightened to her feet, the letter from Mr Sansom fell from her shawl.

She bent to pick it up just as David reached for it. He glanced down at it as he held it out to her.

His brow arched in that way she was coming to hate. It always seemed to mean something disapproving. It made her feel so cold, so—in the wrong. 'You are writing to my uncle?' he said.

'Yes, Mr Lorne was kind enough to send me Mr Sansom's direction,' she said. 'I wanted to know more about his library. He says he knew my father.'

Sir David's jaw tightened. 'My uncle is an elderly man who just wants to be left alone with his books. He already told Mr Lorne he doesn't want to sell.'

Emma was confused. 'Yes, but I—'

'You what, Mrs Carrington?' he said, his tone too polite, too quiet.

She tucked the letter away. 'You've made it clear that you don't entirely approve of how I live my life, Sir David, but I assure you I mean no harm to your uncle. I merely wished to enquire about his library. Thank you for rescuing me—again. Good day.'

She spun around and hurried away before she could become careless yet again and say things she would regret. She had determined to make a new chapter in her life, a more respectable one, and she had to do that.

No matter how angry or unsure Sir David Marton made her feel. Or how very much she longed for him to kiss her.

By Jove. Had he actually almost kissed Emma Bancroft?

David, after an hour of trying to go over the Rose Hill accounts, finally gave up and tossed down his pen. Images of Emma's eyes, greener than a summer meadow, brighter than his mother's old emerald ring, kept getting in the way of black-and-white numbers.

Usually nothing could have distracted him from his work, but Emma did it now.

You've made it clear that you don't entirely approve of how I live my life, she had said, those eyes flashing.

And he didn't. He couldn't, not after Maude. He had too much to protect, and he had never known a freedom quite like the kind that shone all around Emma. After his father's hidden flashes of raw anger when he was a child, David had vowed to always keep tight control over himself.

For a time in his youth he had let himself loose, let himself run wild, and it hadn't ended well. Emma just brought out those old feelings.

And yet—yet he also couldn't help but grudgingly admire Emma as well. She had come back here, to a small place she hadn't seen in a long time, and was trying to rebuild something. To make herself useful. That could not be an easy task.

But that didn't mean he would let her bother his elderly uncle, who needed rest and quiet. Nor could he let her beautiful eyes disrupt *his* life. He would never make such a mistake again. When he remarried, it would be for practical, sensible purposes.

Two things Emma Bancroft could never be.

A knock sounded at the library door and he welcomed the distraction. 'Come in,' he said, carefully closing the ledger.

It was Bea's nanny who stepped into the room and made a wobbly curtsy. She was a good woman who in her younger days had been a junior nursemaid to Louisa and David, and later took care of Louisa's brood before coming to look after Bea following Maude's death. But David had begun to notice she was getting older, less sturdy, and even a quiet child like his daughter could get away from her at times.

One more thing he would have to take responsibility for very soon.

'Yes, Nanny, what is it?' he said. 'Is Miss Beatrice unwell?'

'Not at all, Sir David,' she answered. 'But she has been pestering me today for more books. I can't do anything beyond lessons on some Bible verses and such, and I fear she will become bored and troublesome. Perhaps more education is needed soon? More advanced books to keep her occupied?'

David laughed ruefully. *More educated—more books.* It sounded very much like the lady he had just been trying so hard not to think about.

But it seemed she wouldn't let herself be forgotten, even here in his own house.

Chapter Six

'I say, Phil, but you are racing off too early tonight. It's hours 'til dawn. Plenty of trouble to get into before then.'

Philip Carrington laughed as he tied the elaborate loops of his cravat. He studied Betsy's reflection in the mirror as she lolled around on the rumpled bed behind him. Her long, bright-blonde curls were tangled up with the sheets and she pouted at him.

'I never want to leave you, Betsy my beauty,' he said. 'You know that.'

'Then why go? You were gone abroad for ever so long, I just got you back.'

'I'm afraid I left some business undone on the Continent,' he muttered, reaching for his brocade waistcoat. 'So tomorrow I have to go to the countryside and finish it.'

'The country! I wouldn't think you'd like it *there,*' Betsy said. She sat up against the haphazard piles of pillows and wrapped the blue-satin blankets around her luscious nakedness.

'No, I certainly will not. But it must be done.'

His troublesome cousin Henry, rot his soul, had died owing him and Philip was not a man to forget debts owed. If Henry weren't here to do it, then Henry's widow would have to.

At the thought of Emma, Philip's fingers tightened on the carved buttons of his waistcoat. Emma—so beautiful, so sweet. Henry never knew what he had in her, always running off and leaving her alone and vulnerable.

It should have made his task easier. Seduce that idiot Henry's grateful, lovely bride and find what he needed. What Henry stole from Philip's father. But Emma had proved more loyal than Henry deserved and only professed gratitude for Philip's 'friendship'. And then she had left before Henry even knew she was gone.

But Henry was dead now. Surely Emma's time alone had made her want company? And he found himself strangely eager to see her again.

'It has to do with money, doesn't it, Phil?' Betsy said. Usually Betsy was all fun all the time, always up for a dance or a bottle of wine or a romp in the bedchamber. That was why he liked her, why out of all the lightskirts in London he kept coming back to her.

But now she sounded serious. Hard, even. Philip turned to look at her and she peered at him over the garish satin blankets with narrowed green eyes.

Green, like Emma's.

'Why would you say that, my dove?' he asked. 'Have I not taken care of you sufficiently today?'

He glanced pointedly at the bracelet on her wrist, the

one his jeweller threatened to be the last one he would get on credit.

'You've been worried ever since you got here,' she said with a little pout. 'And I know nothing would take you to the blighted country unless it was dire. Must be money.'

Philip dropped the coat he had just picked up and strode across the room to the bed instead. He couldn't bear the look of worry and scepticism in Betsy's eyes any longer. She was the only one who ever thought he could do no wrong. He didn't want her to think differently, as his family always had.

At the thought of his family and their demands, a wave of hot anger washed over him. He pushed it away and kissed Betsy instead, devouring her with his mouth, demanding she help him forget.

But Betsy held him away, staring up at him with her hard eyes. 'You should marry, Phil,' she said.

He choked out a laugh. Betsy was certainly full of surprises tonight. 'Marry?'

'That's how toffs like you get money when they need it, right? From what I hear, the streets of Mayfair are paved with heiresses just ripe for the plucking.'

'Not exactly,' he answered, bemused. Marriage had never been in his thoughts; there was too much fun to pursue in life to worry about such matters. But maybe Betsy had a point, in her own way... 'And heiresses tend to come with strict guardians.'

'I wager you could charm the guardians as well as the heiresses,' Betsy said. She lay back down beneath him and stretched her plump white arms over her head as she grinned up into his eyes. 'You have to marry some day, right? Might as well make it of good use.'

Philip laughed and kissed her again, feeling the sweet, yielding softness of her lips on his. He would fix this any way he could, no matter what he had to do. And Emma Bancroft Carrington had to be the key.

Chapter Seven

Emma drew in a deep breath as she looked up at the assembly rooms before her. During the day, the building was a rather dull, low, squat rectangle of dark brick and green-painted shutters, quiet and still. A place to hurry past on the way to the draper's or the bookshop.

Now, in the gathering blue-black twilight, with its shutters and doors thrown open, and light and music and laughter spilling out, it seemed an entirely different place. A place full of life and movement.

It had been quite some time since Emma went to dance, and even longer since she attended a gathering here at home. She swallowed past a nervous lump in her throat and stared up at the amber glow of the windows as if they were about to swallow her up.

You can go home, a tiny voice whispered in her head. Run back to the shelter she had made of her little cottage. She glanced back over her shoulder to see that Jane's coachman had already driven away. She couldn't flee without chasing him down, or walking home in her satin slippers.

Besides, Sir David was right. She had to meet people if she wanted to be part of the life of the village, if she wanted them to come to her bookshop. She had to find a way to get them to like her again.

And, if she was being honest with herself, she wanted to see David Marton again. That was really why she had taken such care with her appearance tonight.

Straightening her shoulders and holding her head high, she marched up the stone steps and through the open doors into the vestibule. Girls she didn't recognise, girls who had probably been children when she left, were gathered in front of the mirrors there, giggling together and exclaiming over each other's gowns. They made room for her with no judging glances—so far so good.

Emma glanced in the mirror. She had borrowed one of the housemaids at Barton to help her with her coiffure, a girl eager to gain lady's maid's experience, and the results weren't half-bad. Not as elaborate as the stylish young ladies around her, but surely most presentable. Her blonde waves were smoothed into curls and bound with blue-and-black ribbons. She wore one of her black gowns, her only new evening dress of taffeta and a pattern of sheer silk ribbon embroidery. She had added a bunch of blue-silk forget-me-nots at the sash and her mother's pearl pendant.

Surely she looked respectable and presentable. Maybe even a bit—pretty?

Emma sighed. It had been so long since she felt pretty. It seemed like a lot to ask now.

'Mrs Carrington? Is that really you?'

Emma turned to see a lady hurrying towards her through the crowd that had just swept between the front doors. A purple-plumed turban bobbed above grey-streaked dark curls and bright brown eyes. With a flash of delight, Emma recognised Jane's friend Lady Wheelington.

'Lady Wheelington,' she called, trying to fight her way upstream through the swirling crowd to the first familiar face she'd seen that night. 'How lovely to see you again. Jane said you had recently returned home.'

'I had to, my dear.' Lady Wheelington reached Emma at last and reached for her hands. 'My son Mr Crawford is the new vicar. What's your excuse for coming back?'

Emma laughed, suddenly more at ease. This was not entirely a foreign land; it was her home, or it once had been. She was the one who had changed, not it. 'I missed you all too much, I suppose.'

'You mean you missed our thrill-a-moment ways? Why, Mr Price's pig, who won some terribly important agricultural show just last month, escaped from his pen and ran quite amok in Mrs Smythe's flowers…'

Without faltering over a word in her tale, Lady Wheelington took Emma's arm and steered her neatly toward the doors leading into the ballroom. She couldn't escape then if she wanted to.

And she was very glad to have a friendly face beside her as she stood before the gathered crowd. It seemed as if everyone in the village, from the ninety-year-old Mrs Pratt who had once run the draper's shop, in the corner with her ear trumpet, to a little toddler in leading strings lunging for a tray of lemon tarts, was gathered there. And they all turned to look at her with shocked expressions on their faces.

Emma held her head high and made herself keep smiling. She had as much right to be there as anyone else. She was their neighbour; she had bought a ticket. And she intended to make her new life here among them.

Curiosus semper—cautious always. That was the motto of the Bancroft family and Emma meant to live up to it now.

'My dear Mrs Carrington, you remember my son Mr Crawford, do you not?' Lady Wheelington said as they came to a couple standing near the tall windows at the back of the room. 'He is finally living here. And this is his new fiancée, Miss Leigh of Brighton.'

Emma smiled at the two of them, as young and adorable and eager as pretty puppies, and luckily, they smiled back. The approval of the local clergy was always important.

'Best wishes to you both on your engagement. I did enjoy your sermon last week, Mr Crawford,' Emma said. She had slipped into the back pew of the old church, near her own father's memorial plaque, and left when the last notes of the closing hymn died away. But Mr Crawford's sermon had indeed been mercifully short and spiced with hints of humour. She would happily attend his services every week.

'Wasn't he wonderful, Mrs Carrington?' Miss Leigh said, gazing up starry-eyed at her betrothed. 'Mr Craw-

ford writes the most eloquent sermons I have ever
heard.'

As she chatted with their little group, Emma sur-
reptitiously scanned the crowded room. The little rip-
ple of shock caused by her entrance seemed to have
faded, though everyone who passed would slow down
to stare at her. She gave them smiles and nods, which
sent some scurrying away, but also brought some to
greet her. Soon she found herself in the midst of quite
a group, Lady Wheelington leading their conversation
about plans for an upcoming garden fête to benefit the
church's efforts to restore some of the medieval monu-
ments that were crumbling away.

Emma tried to picture Henry here with her, listening to such chit-chat about local affairs as the amateur
musicians noisily tuned their instruments in the corner.
He would have fled in a panic as soon as they stepped
through the doors, running until he found a card room.
Only he would have fled there as well, as Emma remembered that only penny-ante wagers were allowed there.
And old Mrs Pratt always won anyway.

Emma almost laughed to imagine Henry's reaction
if she had asked him to live this life with her. Then she
glimpsed David Marton just coming into the ballroom
and her smile faded.

He was taller than everyone around him, so for a
moment she could see him quite clearly. He looked so
different than when he had leaped out of that tree, in
his fashionably sombre dark-blue coat and impeccably
tied cravat skewered with a small pearl pin. His dark
hair was combed back to reveal the austerely carved

lines of his face, the metallic glint of his spectacles. Emma felt a warm rush of excitement flow over her to see him again.

For an instant he was very still, studying the gathering as if they were a scientific experiment that was not going quite as he hoped. But then he bent his head and smiled, and his face softened.

Emma saw that it was his sister, Louisa Smythe, on his arm. Mrs Smythe went up on tiptoe to whisper something frantically in his ear as she tapped his sleeve with her fan. As Emma watched, Mrs Smythe used that fan to wave someone over. It was a lady in a pretty pink-sprigged muslin gown trimmed with fluttering pink ribbons, with more pink ribbons in her fashionably tumbled pale curls.

The two ladies embraced as if they were long-lost bosom bows and then the pink lady curtsied to Sir David.

The lady half-turned as she smiled up at David and Emma saw she was as pretty and spring-fresh as her dress, with blushing cheeks and a dimpled chin. She swayed close to him as he talked to her, her eyes wide as if she could see only him. Finally he held out his arm to her and she took it with a soft laugh. He led her towards the gathering dancers, while Mrs Smythe looked after them with a cat-in-cream smile on her face.

And Emma felt foolish for feeling that warm rush of excitement on seeing his face again. It seemed as if she had been catapulted back to the last time she was there in those very rooms. Watching Sir David dance with Miss Maude Cole.

This lady, whoever she was, seemed to be the image of his late wife. The perfect pretty bride, where Emma had long ago blotted her copybook beyond any hope of being such a thing.

'That is Miss Harding,' Lady Wheelington said close to Emma's ear, pulling her back to where she was. Who she was.

'I beg your pardon, Lady Wheelington?' Emma said.

'The young lady whose gown you seemed to be admiring. Her name is Miss Harding and she is a new arrival to the village. Her uncle, Admiral Harding, retired here last year and she has come to stay with him for a time. She and Mrs Smythe are always seen together of late.'

'Are they?' Emma murmured. An admiral's niece *and* best friends with his sister. Of course Sir David would want to dance with her.

And smile at her. Emma watched as the music started and the dancers skipped down the line, David hand in hand with Miss Harding. They twirled around, perfectly in step with each other.

'I shouldn't trust it,' Lady Wheelington said. 'Look what happened last time poor Sir David listened to his sister's marital advice.'

Last time? *Poor* Sir David? Emma turned to Lady Wheelington, concerned. 'Whatever do you mean, Lady Wheelington?' she asked, but her question was lost as Lady Wheelington turned to greet Mrs Smythe as she joined their small group.

'Mrs Carrington!' she exclaimed with a little flutter of her silk-gloved hands in front of her obviously en-

ceinte belly. 'Such a surprise to see you here tonight.
I've seen you rushing around the village here and there,
but I didn't think to see you out in society just yet.
But then, you always did have your own way of doing
things. Just a *joie de vivre*.' She gave a trilling laugh.

Emma politely smiled. She could see echoes of Sir
David in Mrs Smythe's pretty face and dark hair, in the
blue-grey eyes she squinted slightly as if she eschewed
her brother's spectacles even though she needed them.
But Mrs Smythe had none of his calm stillness, his careful observation. She was like a bird, fluttering around,
always looking for the next moment.

'It was getting very lonely at Barton with my sister
gone, Mrs Smythe,' Emma said. 'I wanted to see old
friends again.'

'But I see *you* have been making new friends, Mrs
Smythe,' Lady Wheelington said. 'Was that Admiral
Harding's niece you were greeting? Such a pretty girl.'

'Oh, yes!' Mrs Smythe cried with another of her trilling laughs. 'And she is quite as sweet as she is pretty. I
have quite come to admire her in the short time we've
known each other. Such an asset to our little community.'

They all turned to look at where Miss Harding was
dancing with Sir David, graceful and light in her little
hopping steps as she turned under his arm and smiled
up at him.

'I am hoping she can somehow be persuaded to stay
here much longer than the planned visit with her es-
teemed uncle,' Mrs Smythe said. 'It is so hard for my
poor brother to find dance partners who match him so

well in grace. Especially after my poor darling sister-in-law.'

Mrs Smythe sniffled and Lady Wheelington gave her a sideways glance Emma couldn't quite read. She did, however, read Mrs Smythe's intentions quite well. She was set that her brother should marry the pretty Miss Harding.

Emma watched the two of them dancing, so well matched, like the picture of a perfect couple in a novel. She suddenly wished there was a wall nearby in need of being held up so she could hide there.

She didn't know why her spirits should sink at the thought of Sir David standing at the altar with Miss Harding, kissing her, holding her, taking her to Rose Hill to take her rightful place as the second perfect Lady Marton. Emma had so little in common with Sir David. She shouldn't even want to be in his company, let alone feel sad he should marry again. She had made such mistakes with her emotions before, with Henry and long ago with Mr Milne, the dance master. She could not be trusted now.

And yet—and yet there was the way she felt when he held her in his arms. So safe, so right, so full of excitement and peace all at the same time.

'Excuse me for a moment,' Emma murmured to Lady Wheelington and Mrs Smythe. 'I suddenly feel in need of some refreshment.'

'Are you quite all right, my dear?' Lady Wheelington asked with a concerned frown. 'You do look rather pale.'

Emma made herself smile to hide her confusion.

'Nothing a glass of punch can't cure. I will return directly.'

She threaded her way through the thick crowds around the edges of the dance floor. A few people even greeted her and issued tentative invitations to tea, a sign of some progress, she hoped. Yet she was always aware of David dancing with Miss Harding so nearby. It was a distraction she couldn't afford.

At last she reached the refreshment table and gratefully sipped at a glass of cool, sweet punch. She noticed Mrs Smythe's portly, usually absent husband lurking nearby, putting away a silver flask in his coat pocket. She wished he would splash some of it into the punch bowl for the rest of them.

The room suddenly felt too warm, too close-packed. The music and laughter and indistinct voices blended into a blurred roar that made her head spin. She closed her eyes and imagined her little sitting room waiting for her, a fire in the grate, a pot of tea and some toasted cheese, a pile of books and Murray snoring at her feet.

But then the contented image shifted and someone was sitting in the chair next to hers, reaching for her hand. He raised it to his lips for a warm, lingering kiss and whispered, 'Now isn't this so much better than going out on a chilly night?'

In her daydream, Emma shivered at the kiss and looked up—to find David Marton smiling at her in the firelight, his beautiful eyes full of promise.

Emma's own eyes flew open in shock. She was still in the crowded ballroom, still standing by herself. And David was finishing his dance with Miss Harding.

Emma quickly swallowed the last of her punch and scanned the room for some escape route. Tucked in a darkened corner she saw a door that she knew led out to a small garden attached to the assembly rooms. She hurried towards it, hoping no one would notice her hasty exit, and slipped outside.

The garden, a formal expanse of winding gravel paths past orderly flowerbeds and groupings of stone benches, was usually a place for resting between dances, exchanging whispered secrets—or for gentlemen to escape their wives for a few minutes. Even though Emma could tell such escapees had recently been there by the faint smell of cigar smoke in the air, the space was nearly deserted. Except for one young couple sitting close together on one of the benches, staring into each other's eyes, she was alone for a moment.

Emma made her way to a low iron railing that divided the garden from its neighbour. There was a cluster of tall old trees there where she could hide. She could hear the echo of laughter from where the coachmen waited in the narrow lane behind the building, but where she stood was blessedly quiet and dark.

No one could see her ridiculously flushed cheeks there.

Emma drifted to the far end of the garden, where a large, ancient tree offered shade to strollers by day and shelter to shy wallflowers at night. And Emma needed a place to shelter at the moment.

When she first came back to Barton, she'd expected many challenges. But she certainly hadn't expected David Marton to be one of the greatest. When he was near, she couldn't concentrate on anything else. She wanted him to notice her—but then she was scared of what he thought when he did. And he had looked so right dancing with Miss Harding...

Emma leaned back against the rough trunk of the tree, letting its strength hold her up as she examined the darkened windows of the bookshop across the lane. *That* was what she needed to think about. What she needed to do next. Not things she couldn't have.

As she studied the quiet street, she heard the assembly-room door open. There was a blast of music and laughter, quickly cut off, and the soft rustle of footsteps on the pathway.

Emma quickly straightened and pasted a bright smile on her face before she turned to face the newcomer. But her smile faltered when she saw it was David who stood there.

She was now alone with David in the moonlight.

He gave her a small, quick flash of a smile and laid his palm against the tree. 'Diagnosing the diseases using Mr Lee's treatise, Mrs Carrington?'

Emma gave a choked laugh. 'Since this is an oak, Sir David, I am sure it can have nothing to do with your orchard. I just needed a breath of fresh air.'

'Perfectly understandable. I find it hard to breathe at such things myself.'

'But you seemed to be enjoying the dance,' Emma said. She thought of how he smiled down at Miss Harding as she turned prettily under his arm. Emma shivered, wondering why the night felt so cold.

'Are you chilled, Mrs Carrington?' he said. To her

surprise, he quickly shrugged out of his coat and gently draped it over her shoulders.

She was suddenly wrapped in the warmth, the clean scent of him. And yet it made her shiver all the more.

He drew the edges of his coat closer around her, yet he didn't move away. Emma stared at the white glow of his cravat in the darkness and felt him watching her closely. She slowly reached out and rested her hands on his shoulders.

'I do like to dance sometimes, Mrs Carrington,' he said, his voice rough. 'But I like it best with the right partner.'

It had been so long since she was close to a man like this, and even back when she thought herself so in love with Henry it hadn't felt like she did now. So giddy and dizzy, like a glass of sparkling champagne! So warm and safe, like a summer's day. All of her senses whirled and all she could think about was David so close to her. The way his strong shoulders felt under her hands, so hard and warm and alive.

'We—we shouldn't be here like this...' she managed to whisper.

'Definitely not,' he said hoarsely. Yet his head bent toward hers and she instinctively went up on tiptoe to meet the kiss she so longed for.

The touch of David's lips was soft at first: warm, gentle. When Emma whimpered and wrapped her arms around his neck to hold him with her, he deepened the kiss. Their lips parted, tasted, and with that taste they slid down into urgent heat.

Something deep inside Emma, something reckless

and passionate she had tried so hard to banish, surged back to life at the taste of that need. Passionate need— from David Marton! And, oh, but he was such a *good* kisser, his lips moving over hers so skilfully, his tongue sliding over hers to draw her into him. Who could have ever guessed? He knew just how to touch her to make her want to touch him back. *Need* to touch him.

Something in her heart called out to him, a rough, wild excitement that burst inside of her until she knew she would explode from it. She moaned and pressed her body even closer to his as his arms held her tight. She forgot everything: who she was, who he was, the crowd in the building just behind them. Scandal mattered nothing to how he made her feel in that one perfect, frozen moment.

A moment too quickly shattered by a laugh from behind the tree that hid them from view. Emma's sensuous dream shattered like a fragile glass bubble and dropped her back down to the heavy earth. She tore her mouth from David's and drew in a deep breath of air. It felt like surfacing too fast after diving into a warm pool.

It was too dark for her to see his face, but she feared she wouldn't like what was written there if she could.

He stepped back from her, his shoulders heaving with the force of his breath. 'Oh, blast it all,' he said roughly, and she could swear she heard nothing but horror in his hoarse voice. 'Emma. Emma, I am so…'

'No,' she whispered. She pressed her fingertips to her tender lips and willed herself not to cry. She hadn't cried in so very long; tears never solved anything. But she wanted to cry now, from some strange, ineffable, hollow sense of loss.

Was she sad because he had kissed her so unexpectedly, awakening needs she had thought she had banished? Or because he had stopped?

'Don't say you're sorry, I beg you,' she said.

'But I am sorry. I don't know what insanity came over me. Forgive me, Mrs Carrington.'

Insanity. Of course. That was surely what he thought it had to be if he desired her. Emma shook her head, beyond words. She spun around and dashed out of the garden, careful to keep to the shadows where no one could see her. His coat tumbled from her shoulders. Somehow she found her way to the blessedly empty ladies' withdrawing room.

She barely recognised the sight that greeted her in the mirror. Her cheeks were very red, her hair dishevelled. She had lost the silk forget-me-nots at her waist and her sash was half-untied. She quickly set about tidying herself.

She had just smoothed her hair and tugged her gloves into place when the door opened to let in another blast of music and laughter from the party outside. Emma tensed, but then saw it was only Lady Wheelington.

'There you are, Mrs Carrington!' she cried, joining Emma at the mirror to adjust her turban. 'I wondered where you disappeared to.'

'I found myself a bit overwhelmed,' Emma confessed. 'I needed a breath of air.'

Lady Wheelington nodded sagely. 'I completely understand, my dear. All of us feel that way sometimes when faced with Mrs Smythe. She is quite the chatterer, I fear.'

'I often got the feeling when I lived here before that she did not like me very much,' Emma admitted.

'Of course not. You are much too smart for her.' Lady Wheelington turned sideways to study the fall of her dress in the glass. 'Their parents, rest their souls, were kind people and very dutiful, but it's always been quite clear their son inherited whatever brains were in the family tree. Sir David is a treasure to our community indeed. I hope he shan't make the mistake of taking his sister's marital advice again. What a mistake that would be.'

Against her will, Emma felt her curiosity piqued. Hadn't she just vowed to stay away from Sir David? Vowed never to let her emotions rule her again, as they had with Henry and Mr Milne? That David was bad for her peace of mind, for the future she wanted for herself. Yet here she was, eager to hear any gossip about him.

'Was it a mistake the first time?' she asked, hoping she sounded only light and neutral. She looked down to fuss with the button on her glove. 'I left Barton before Sir David's wedding to Miss Cole, but I remember what a handsome couple they were.'

Lady Wheelington gave a sound that sounded suspiciously like a snort. 'Handsome in appearance, mayhap. And certainly Miss Beatrice Marton is the prettiest of children. We must hope she inherits her father's steadiness and not her mother's sad flightiness. What a scandal it was!'

'A scandal attached to Sir David's name?' Emma said, startled. 'I can hardly warrant it.'

Lady Wheelington's eyes widened in the glass. 'My dear, never say you don't know?'

Confusion swept over Emma, a feeling she was becoming all too familiar with. 'Don't know what?'

'Oh, yes. I forgot you have been gone for a long while, and your dear sister is probably not the sort to share local gossip in her letters. Well, Mrs Carrington, what *do* you know?'

'Only that Sir David and Lady Marton lived mostly in London while they were married and that Lady Marton died there.'

Lady Wheelington pursed her lips. 'Yes, but I fear that is not all of it. Lady Marton died in a carriage accident near the Scottish border—where she had eloped with her lover, a cavalry officer. A handsome young rake, so I've heard. We all wondered why she insisted on living in town, when Sir David has always been so devoted to Rose Hill. When she died, it all became clear. She wanted to be close to her lover.'

Emma had never been so deeply shocked in her life. Sir David's wife had run away from him with a lover? Eloped and left her husband with a little daughter and a terrible scandal hanging over their heads? How awful it must have been for such a proud, reserved man to face down such a thing. And poor little Beatrice…

Then Emma sighed as another terrible thought struck her. Lady Marton was a romantic eloper, just as Emma herself was. No wonder David looked at her with such distance sometimes. No wonder she could never quite read his thoughts. Surely he looked at her and saw the shadow of his late wife.

But why, then, would he kiss her, so wonderfully and thoroughly?

Her head was spinning with it all.

'…but Mrs Smythe was delighted when he married Miss Cole, though the rest of us had our reservations that they suited as a couple,' Lady Wheelington was saying. 'I hope he won't listen to his sister's advice now about Miss Harding. She may be a perfectly lovely girl, of course, but who around here knows her?'

Emma shook her head, trying to bring herself back to the present moment and out of her own shock and confusion. 'Isn't Miss Harding an admiral's niece? That sounds most respectable.'

'Yes, but who are her other people? Why was she sent to stay with her uncle so suddenly? Sir David should be doubly cautious now. After Miss Cole, and little bits of gossip we heard about him in his youth…'

Cautious about associating with questionable ladies. Emma understood that very well. And she was sure any 'bits of gossip' about David himself had been only that. Gossip. 'So should we all, I think,' she murmured.

Lady Wheelington gave her a kind smile. 'Oh, my dear, you needn't worry about such things now. You are home again. You must come to tea soon and tell me how you are settling in.'

Emma started to reply, when the door opened and Mrs Smythe and Miss Harding appeared, arm in arm, heads bent together as they giggled over some joke.

'Oh, Lady Wheelington! And Mrs Carrington,'

Mrs Smythe cried. 'How lovely it is to see you out and about.'

'Thank you, Mrs Smythe,' Emma said politely, even though Mrs Smythe already told her that once.

'You must meet my new friend Miss Harding, who has quite brightened our little corner of the world since she arrived,' Mrs Smythe said. 'Miss Harding, you know Lady Wheelington of course, but this is Mrs Carrington, who is sister to Lady Ramsay at Barton Park. She has been gone for quite some time.'

Emma and Miss Harding made their polite curtsies and greetings, and Emma studied the other lady as Mrs Smythe went on chattering. Miss Harding's smile quirked, as if she had got the measure of Emma and found her no threat. And Emma was sure she could *not* be a threat where Sir David was concerned, not after all that had happened in her life.

But then, it was not her business who Sir David Marton married, she reminded herself. She had caused scandal just like his wife had and therefore wouldn't be suitable in his eyes or the eyes of their friends. And he did not even know everything she had seen in her life with Henry. No, Miss Harding was obviously a pretty and suitable young lady. And Emma shouldn't even be thinking about David, or anything else but repairing her life.

Why, then, did she just want to hide in a quiet corner somewhere and cry?

David scooped up his coat from the ground and paced to the end of the garden and back to the tree, a terrible restlessness seizing him. He had guarded against such passions all his life, fearing a hidden temper like his father's lurked inside of him. But with Emma he couldn't guard against anything at all.

When he looked into her wide green eyes, so full of life, he could see nothing else.

He had to be rid of these feelings. They could do nothing good, for either him or her. The more he saw her, the more he *wanted* to see her. The more he admired her boundless spirit.

But it was the kind of spirit that led only to ruin in the end.

David shook his head, trying to rid himself from memories of that kiss. Of the way Emma tasted, the warm, soft sweetness of her body against his.

A ray of moonlight caught on something at his feet and he bent to study it. It was the branch of silk forget-me-nots fallen from Emma's sash. He slowly picked it up and turned it between his fingers. They smelled faintly of Emma's perfume as he inhaled deeply.

And something drove him to slip the flowers into his coat and carry them with him back to the assembly rooms. He would have to return them to her later…

From the diary of Arabella Bancroft

> *My first kiss! I feel foolish indeed admitting to such a thing after my time here in such sophisticated company, but there it is. I have just had my first kiss tonight, in the garden with Sir William. And it was all I could have dreamed of. He told*

me I was beautiful, that he could see my true heart as it is like his. I know better than to believe such poetry, but those words were sweet to my ears.

For a moment I was sure I found a place where I truly belonged.

Chapter Eight

Melanie Harding struggled to climb up the slope of the hill, holding on to her bonnet as the wind tried to snatch it away. Nature really was terribly horrid. But going for a walk seemed like the only way she could escape her uncle's snoring for a while.

She reached the top of the hill and turned to study the village laid out before her as she tried to catch her breath. She could see all the little streets laid out in their short, straight lines, the old church, the people moving in and out of the shops like lines of ants.

Once she had thought Bath a poky little place, boring and narrow. Now she saw what 'narrow' really meant. She longed to escape, to run away, yet she knew there was no place to go. This terrible little village was where she was trapped.

She had to find an escape within her purgatory, clearly. And Melanie had learned to be resourceful if nothing else. Captain Whitney had abandoned her. Even her own mother had sent her here to rot. She could only depend on herself now.

And on the few friends she had been able to make. Melanie studied the stolid stone building where the assembly was held. Assembly—it was hardly worthy of the name, nothing like the assembly rooms in Bath where at least there was real music and a choice of dance partners. But at least she was able to wear her pink muslin again instead of letting it moulder in her trunk.

And she had also met Mrs Smythe's brother there.

Melanie made another impatient grab at her flying hat. Mrs Smythe was indeed a good friend, the only person of any interest she'd met since she arrived at her uncle's house. Mrs Smythe knew about London fashions and *on dit,* and was always ready for a laugh. Everyone else here seemed too serious to laugh, too preoccupied with nonsense like crops and fences and tenants. Mrs Smythe cared for none of that and she seemed glad to have Melanie's company, too.

Mrs Smythe also had a very handsome brother. A handsome brother with a nice estate and a good income.

Melanie turned her back on the horrid little village to look towards where she knew Rose Hill lay. She'd walked by it on one of her escaping rambles before, peeking over walls and past gates for a glimpse of the house. It was quite fine and modern. It could use some extension and renovation, of course, but that was what the mistress of a house was for.

Yes, Rose Hill definitely had potential. And gossip said the estate was prosperous enough to fund a London house as well. That was most important. It wasn't as if he was an earl or marquess, but at that point she would happily settle for being Lady Marton of Rose Hill.

The fact that Sir David was good looking and smelled nice, and was not an old, bald man with gout like her uncle's cronies, made it even better. He wasn't much fun, of course, not like Captain Whitney…

Captain Whitney. Melanie sighed as she remembered him and his flirtatious laughter. Being with him had been like being swept away on a tidal wave, giddy and fast and wonderful, but so quickly gone. How she missed him! Sir David was nothing like that. She had a feeling that days—and nights—with him would be something of a trial, no matter how handsome he was.

But maybe, with the security of money and a proper name behind her, there could be men like Captain Whitney again. With no harm done this time. If she was clever and careful, as she knew she could be. She had learned her lesson.

Yes, she was lucky in Mrs Smythe's friendship, as Mrs Smythe's brother was her best chance in a long time. She wasn't about to let it go.

Suddenly fed up with the wind catching at her skirts and the annoying birds wheeling overhead, Melanie strode back down the hill towards the road. She turned back towards the village, thinking maybe she could take tea at Mrs Smythe's before she had to go back to her uncle and his silent, stuffy house. She trudged slowly beside the hedgerow, caught up in thoughts of Rose Hill and being a wealthy married lady at last.

For several long moments all she could hear was the whine of the wind, which carried the stench of damp grass and woolly sheep to her nose. Yet another horrid country thing.

Then she heard something else, the rumble of hooves pounding on gravel behind her, coming on fast. She peered over her shoulder, holding on to her bonnet, to see a large, gleaming black horse barrelling down on her. It was suddenly so close she could see the sheen of sweat on the beast's flanks and the capes of the rider's greatcoat flapping around him like wings.

Terrified, she shrieked and dived toward the hedgerow, sure she would be trampled by the hooves. She tripped and fell into a puddle, her redingote quickly soaked.

'Blast it all,' she cursed. Tears of rage choked her. What else could go wrong with her life? It was all so terribly unfair!

Melanie pounded her fists on the ground, sending up more muddy splashes. Now she would have to go straight back to her uncle's house to bathe and change, no consoling gossip with Mrs Smythe.

'Are you quite all right, miss?' a man shouted. 'I am so terribly sorry. I thought no one was around.'

Melanie looked up to see the greatcoated man swooping down on her. He swept off his wide-brimmed hat and for an instant she was dazzled by the halo of light around him.

She blinked and saw that he really was quite angelic-looking. Dark coppery-blond hair fell in curls to his collar and his eyes were a deep, dark, chocolate brown set in a handsome face. Surely he was some sort of dashing poet, like Lord Byron!

She felt like she was caught in a beautiful dream.

'Are you injured?' he said.

'N-no,' Melanie gasped. 'I do not think so.'

'But I did at the very least cause you a fright, for which I am profoundly sorry,' he said. 'Please, let me help you to your feet.'

Melanie held out her hand to him. His gloved fingers closed around hers, strong and warm, and he supported her as he raised her up. He held on to her until she could stand on her own, the dazzling dizziness slowly righting the world around her. All the boredom she'd felt only moments before was gone when she looked at her rescuer.

'I have not seen you here before, sir,' she whispered.

'I have just arrived in the area on a business matter,' he said with another dazzling grin. 'I would have come much sooner if I had known there were such beauties to be seen. May I beg to know your name?'

Dizzy with his compliments after so long in the arid loneliness of no society, she laughed. 'I am Miss Melanie Harding, sir.'

'And I am Mr Philip Carrington, very pleased indeed to make your acquaintance,' he said. He lifted her muddied glove to his lips for a gallant kiss. 'Please, let me see you home to begin to make amends for my terrible behaviour.'

'Thank you, Mr Carrington,' she answered. The name was vaguely familiar to her, but she couldn't quite fathom why amid the delightful feelings of Philip Carrington's touch on her arm as he led her to his horse.

Not since Captain Whitney first appeared in her life had she felt that way.

He lifted her up into his saddle, his hands strong and steady on her waist. Then he swung up behind her, holding her close to him as he urged the steed into a gallop. The wind rustling past her seemed exhilarating now where before she had hated it.

Suddenly the world seemed fun again.

Philip watched as his pretty damsel in distress dashed up the narrow steps to a village house. She paused at the door and turned to give him a flirtatious little wave. Even under the dust of her fall to the road, Philip could see how lovely her pert little face and the pale curls peeking from beneath her bonnet were.

An angel lurking in the dismal depths of the countryside. Who could have imagined such a thing?

Miss Melanie Harding. Philip tipped back his head to peer up at the tall, narrow house. He had a feeling he would be hearing that name again soon. He was determined to see that fair face and slender figure once more.

Philip sighed and wheeled his horse around. In the meantime he had to find lodgings and seek out the agent of this dismal journey—Emma Carrington.

At least things looked a little more fun now...

Chapter Nine

Sansom House didn't look very forbidding, Emma thought as she studied its front door. All the novels she had been reading lately led her to think the house of a recluse would look like a medieval fortress. That it would come complete with a moat and a watchtower, at the very least some crenellated walkways where the hidden occupant could lurk about and watch for intruders.

She was a bit disappointed there was nothing like that at all. Sansom House was more a large cottage than a castle, comfortable and modern with a pretty front garden and smoke curling out of the chimney. It wasn't even particularly hidden, merely tucked off the main lane behind a stand of trees.

Mr Sansom hadn't been seen about in a long time, but Emma supposed if one had to be reclusive it could be done just as well in comfort. She wondered what sort of man she would find inside. Would he be something like an older version of Sir David?

Emma rather hoped not. She'd already spent too much time thinking about Sir David since they last met at the assembly. She kept images of him away well enough during the day, as she walked Murray on the Barton grounds, worked on decorating her little house and spent time with Mr Lorne learning how to run a bookshop. When she was busy, there was no time to remember how it felt when he kissed her. How it felt to feel life stirring within her again.

But at night, when her cottage was quiet around her and she had only the company of a book and her dog, the thought of him would not be banished. That was when she dreamed of what it would have been like if his kisses had gone even further…

Emma shook her head and climbed down from the seat of the pony cart she'd borrowed from Jane's stable. She couldn't have Sir David in her life. She knew that very well, especially after hearing the sad tale of his wife's scandalous elopement. She shouldn't even have thoughts of him.

A groom hurried over from the side of the house to take the reins and she made her way along the walkway to knock at the front door. She straightened her bonnet and smoothed her new lilac-coloured spencer jacket that she had bought now she had received her inheritance. Surely Mr Sansom could not be so very fearsome, yet she still felt quite unaccountably nervous as she waited. Her reception in the village had been so varied, she didn't know what to expect here at this house.

A neatly clad maid in a white cap and apron opened the door and took Emma's card. 'Of course, Mrs Carrington,' she said, bobbing a curtsy. 'Mr Sansom is expecting you, if you'll just follow me.'

She was expected—that was surely a good sign. Emma trailed behind the maid as she was led through narrow, winding corridors and past closed doors. She could see why Mr Lorne was so eager to do business with Mr Sansom. Every inch of space was taken up with books, piles and stacks and overflowing shelves full of books. They blotted out most of the light from the windows and she was eager to stop and peruse the titles, to explore the treasures that might be hidden there.

But the maid kept up too brisk a pace for any explanation and Emma had to keep up with her. They came to the end of a dim hallway and the maid pushed open a door.

'Mrs Carrington to see you, sir,' she said.

'Send her in, send her in,' a voice, much heartier than Emma would have expected, called. 'And fetch us some tea, please.'

Emma ducked past the low doorway and into what seemed a cave of wonders. There was a crackling fire in the grate and comfortable dark-velvet chairs and sofas grouped around it, but every other inch was covered in more books. Stacked on every table, around the floor, teetering on shelves. Finally, behind the highest stack of all, Emma saw a man.

He sat in a deep armchair close to the fire, wrapped in a warm shawl with another over his legs, despite the mild day outside. Except for the spectacles perched on his nose, he didn't much resemble Sir David. He was thin and waxy-white, with sparse, untidy waves of grey hair. But his blue eyes were bright as he waved her forwards.

'Mrs Carrington, so good of you to come to my little house,' he said. 'Do forgive me not standing, my rheumatism you see…'

'Oh, not at all, Mr Sansom!' Emma cried as she hurried to greet him. 'I don't want to put you to any trouble at all. It was kind of you to answer my letter.'

Mr Sansom pushed forwards a chair for her and gave her a twinkling smile that made her like him right away. 'Not at all. I'm always happy to meet another book lover. Mr Lorne is a good friend, but we have known each other so long we have little left to say to each other. It seems all my other old friends have left the world without me.'

'Life does have a way of changing when one isn't looking, doesn't it?' Emma said.

'Quite right. But books are always the same. Books can always be relied upon. I know you must agree with me, as you are your father's daughter. Now there was a man who valued learning.'

'So he did, Mr Sansom,' Emma said. 'I was so excited to learn that you knew him.'

'We shared many interests. And I'm sure he would be most intrigued to learn you intend to take over the good Mr Lorne's shop.'

'I hope to. I need something useful to occupy myself and earn my bread, and books seem to be the only thing I know well. That is why I'm hoping you could help me.'

Mr Sansom chuckled. 'By letting you sell my books? I confess I would find it very hard to part with my old friends, though I know some day I must. I suppose seeing them go to new homes where they would be appreciated would be best, even if they must be separated.' He gestured to the portrait hung over the fireplace mantel, an image of two young, dark-haired ladies in the stiff satin gowns of the last century. 'You see them?'

'Yes,' Emma answered. 'They are very pretty.' And she couldn't help but notice the younger one had very familiar-looking bright grey eyes.

'My sisters. Anna, the elder, married a diplomat and went off to ports unknown, where she used to write the most fascinating letters to me. My health never let me travel as much as I would have liked, but through her I did. She died young with no children. Amelia, the younger, married Sir Reginald Marton of Rose Hill and lived close, but sadly she was a girl of little imagination. Her only son is a most intelligent man, but he is so busy he does not have the time to read as he should. So I have no family who would want all these dusty tomes.'

Emma thought Miss Beatrice Marton might one day want the 'dusty tomes', as well as Anna Sansom's letters from ports unknown. She was dying to ask Mr Sansom more about David. What was he like as a child? What other secrets lurked in his family's past? But fortunately the maid appeared with the tea tray before she could appear too eager to learn about his nephew.

'Perhaps you could pour, Mrs Carrington, while I find the books I have here that once belonged to your father,' Mr Sansom said. As Emma sorted out the tea, he dug about in the piles of volumes next to his chair.

'I was most excited to hear you had some of them, Mr Sansom,' Emma said.

'Yes, he sent them to me before he died, my poor

friend. Was afraid your mother might sell them off if he didn't, I dare say.'

Emma had to laugh. 'I fear she might have. Mother wasn't a great reader, nor did she share some of my father's—ideas.' Like the search for the lost Barton treasure. The idea of it consumed her father and sent her mother into fits of temper, and he never even found it in the end.

Nor had Emma.

'I like you, Mrs Carrington. You are not missish at all. I can't bear missish women.' Mr Sansom came up with a bundle of faded green leather-bound volumes. 'Ah, here they are. Handwritten, of course, and not the easiest to read, as I'm sure you will find. But rewarding, if you are interested in local history as your father was.'

'I am indeed,' Emma said. She passed Mr Sansom a plate of cake and took the books in exchange. 'I hope to settle here again and learn all I can about the area.'

'Done with wandering, are you, Mrs Carrington?'

'I hope so.'

'Then I do hope you can make a go of the bookshop. This place would be an utter desert without it. Tell me your plans for it.'

As they finished their tea, Emma told him some of her ideas for expanding Mr Lorne's business and finding new, further-flung clients interested in antiquarian works. She also told him about Jane and Hayden's work at Barton Park and listened to some of Mr Sansom's most recent studies. The time was passing so pleasantly that Emma was startled when the maid reappeared.

'Sir David Marton is here to see you, sir,' she announced.

'Well, well! Two visitors in one day. I am becoming quite popular,' Mr Sansom said cheerfully. 'Send him in. Mrs Carrington, you have met my nephew, have you not?'

'We have met a few times,' Emma murmured. She felt her cheeks turn warm at the memory of what happened the last time they met, the overwhelming kiss that exploded between them. The memory that wouldn't leave her. She turned to stare into the fire, hoping she could excuse her sudden blush on its heat.

'It is very good to see you again, Mrs Carrington,' David said quietly. 'I am sorry, Uncle. I didn't realise you had a guest or I would have called another time.'

Mr Sansom chuckled. 'Because I usually live so hermit-like? That is very true, David, but Mrs Carrington has kindly come along to remedy that. Sit, join us for some tea.'

David stood in the doorway for a long moment and Emma began to wonder if he would make his excuses and leave. If he couldn't stand to be around her and remember his uncharacteristic loss of control. But then she heard the echo of his boots on the old wooden floor and he moved some books from the chair next to hers before he sat down.

He was so close Emma could feel the warmth of his lean body brush against her skin, more enticing than any fire on a cold, lonely day. He smelled of the sun and the wind, and of the faint, clean cologne she remembered from the assembly. It made her want to bury her nose in his cravat and inhale him, to be as close to him as she could.

But she just glanced at him and gave him a tentative smile, half-fearful of his response. He smiled at her in return, a careful, polite smile, but it was a start. At least they could be in the same room together without her melting into a puddle of embarrassment.

Hadn't Mr Sansom said he admired her for not being missish? She felt terribly missish now, as if she would start giggling at any moment! That simply wouldn't do.

'Shall I ring for more tea?' she said briskly as she pushed herself to her feet. She hurried across the room to tug at the bell pull.

'Don't go to any trouble for me,' David said. 'I shouldn't stay long and interrupt your conversation.'

'We were just talking about books, weren't we, Mrs Carrington?' Mr Sansom said. 'An endlessly fascinating topic. Mrs Carrington is going to run the bookshop.'

'So I have heard.' David watched Emma as she went back to her seat next to him. The firelight glinted on his spectacles, hiding his eyes from her. 'Were you trying to beg my uncle's books, Mrs Carrington? After he declared to Mr Lorne he didn't want to sell at the moment?'

Emma felt vaguely discomfited by his question, as if she were caught doing something she shouldn't. She knew that feeling very well. She fidgeted with her skirt, trying to decide what to say.

'Don't be so ungallant, David,' Mr Sansom said with another chuckle. 'It's not at all like you. Mrs Carrington was merely offering assistance in finding good homes for my friends.'

'Forgive me, Mrs Carrington,' David said with a small bow.

'Not at all,' Emma answered, still pleating her skirt between her fingers. 'You are quite right to look after your family. Perhaps Miss Beatrice would care to take some of Mr Sansom's library? She seems to have very advanced reading tastes for her age.'

David picked up the large volume on top of the teetering stack next to him and glanced at the spine. 'Perhaps not quite ready for Tacitus. But you are right that she has advanced beyond lessons with her nanny.'

'A bluestocking in the making, is she?' said Mr Sansom, clapping his hands in delight. 'Most gratifying indeed. You must take her any of these books you think she would like.'

David picked up another book and examined it. He didn't look at Emma, but she glimpsed the quirk of an almost-smile at the corner of his lips. Was he—could he be—softening toward her?

'Perhaps Mrs Carrington should advise us what Beatrice might like to read, Uncle,' he said. 'My daughter has said more to her in the few times they've met than she has to anyone else of late.'

Emma couldn't help a warm flush of pleasure at the knowledge that Miss Beatrice liked her, for she was a most intriguing child. But did this mean that David would let her be around his daughter, after his wife's scandalous elopement? 'I would be happy to help Miss

Marton any way I can,' Emma said. 'She's a lovely child.'

'That all sounds settled, then,' Mr Sansom said. 'You must both help me sort out which books to sell and which to start little Miss Marton's library. In the meantime, David, tell me if you could use anything in those agricultural pamphlets I sent you. I could make little of them, but then I am not a farmer...'

After another half-hour of tea and pleasant chatter about books, Emma took her leave along with David. She found her pony cart waiting at the garden gate, along with David's horse, saddled and ready to go.

'Your uncle is a most interesting man,' Emma said. She concentrated on tugging on her gloves, uncomfortable to be suddenly alone with him.

'He is that indeed,' David said. 'I always enjoyed our visits to him as a boy. I have been trying to help him with his financial straits lately, as he has not been in good health.'

'Yet you don't think he should dispose of his books, Sir David?'

David shrugged. 'They are his books to do with as he sees fit. I just worry that he would find himself too lonely if they were gone, and then his health would decline even further. You heard how he calls them his friends. He shouldn't be pressed to dispose of them before he is quite ready. I'm always here to help him if he requires it.'

Of course he was. If there was one thing Emma had heard about David Marton, it was that he always did his duty. He always looked after his own. And that was a trait Emma had seen so rarely in the men in her life. She couldn't help but admire it.

Even when she longed to see another glimpse of the *other* David Marton, the one who kissed her so passionately, so freely. The one she was sure he kept locked down inside somewhere.

'It was good to see you again, Sir David,' she said as she put her foot on the rail of her cart to climb in. 'Please give my greetings to your daughter and your sister.'

He suddenly reached out and took her hand to help her up. His hand was warm and strong and steady through her glove. Like when he touched her, she felt— safe. Secure. As if he would never let her fall in any way.

But Emma knew that was only a sad illusion. Men like him weren't for women like her.

'May I see you home, Mrs Carrington?' he said. 'There is something I should like to talk to you about, if you can spare a few moments.'

Surprised by his words, Emma stared down at him from her perch on the seat. He looked back at her, the greyish light carving his face into solemn, beautiful lines.

'Of course, Sir David,' she said. 'I have no social occasions this afternoon. Perhaps you would care to follow me? I am staying at the old gatekeeper's cottage at Barton.'

'Not in Barton itself?' he said. She couldn't read his tone. Was it surprised—or disapproving?

'It's much too large for me with Jane in Town. I'm cosier in the cottage, though it can be a bit hard to find.'

'I will follow you, then. Lead on, Mrs Carrington.'

Emma nodded and gathered up her reins as David swung up into his saddle. She tried to look as calm as possible, but inside she was utterly bursting with curiosity. Whatever could he want to talk to her about?

She could hardly wait to find out.

Chapter Ten

'It isn't much,' Emma said cheerfully as she pushed open the door to her cottage. 'But I call it home.'

She led David through the short hall to her sitting room and hurried around opening the curtains to let in the light. She didn't look at him as she tried to hastily tidy things up, but she was avidly aware that he stood there in her doorway, watching her.

That David Marton was in her house. She never could have fathomed it before, despite her strange and fleeting fantasies of him beside her by the fire. She couldn't help but be nervous, wondering what he thought when he looked at her little room.

She quickly swept a tangle of ribbons and thread into her workbox and glanced around to make sure there was nothing embarrassing around.

Everything seemed to be in order. The room was small but tidy, furnished with modern, bright pieces Jane had sent over from Barton, shelves full of books, and a few knickknacks from Emma's travels. The colours were light and fresh, all yellows and pale blues, with a watercolour of Barton hanging over the fireplace and miniature portraits of Jane and the children on the mantel. Surely Sir David couldn't object to any of that?

Then Emma saw the book she had been reading lying open on her favourite chair. *Lady Amelia's Scandalous Secret.* She quickly swiped it into the workbox with the ribbons and gave him a bright smile.

'It's charming,' he said. 'It suits you, Mrs Carrington. But do you not get lonely here? It seems some distance from the main house.'

'Not at all. I would be much more lonely there with Jane gone,' Emma said. She watched as Murray roused himself from his bed by the fireplace and trotted over to greet their guest. David knelt down and rubbed at Murray's greying head, making the dog's plumy tail sweep across the carpet. 'I have Murray here, as you see, and a maid comes over to help me every day. She's probably in the kitchen reading fashion papers now. She has a cherished ambition to be a lady's maid. But I think she can scramble together some tea for us.'

'You mustn't go to any trouble, Mrs Carrington,' he said. 'I don't want to take up too much of your time.'

'Not at all. Please, do sit down, Sir David, and let me ring for tea. Like your uncle, I'm glad of the company,' Emma said. Then she suddenly felt flustered, remembering how he hadn't seemed very happy she had visited his uncle. She hurried over to ring the bell and leave her hat and gloves on the table.

He sat down in the chair next to hers, looking a bit stiff and not entirely at ease. Murray followed him, resting his head on David's knee.

'I'm so sorry,' she said. 'Let me put him back in his bed before he leaves fur all over you.'

'No, please, let him stay,' David said. 'It's been a long time since I had a dog. It's quite nice.' He smiled down at Murray, who wagged his tail even faster.

Emma watched him, astonished. Murray was never an unfriendly dog, but life with Henry had taught him to be wary of men and protective of Emma. That he would be happy to see David, so quickly, amazed her. Against her will, she felt her feelings growing tenderer towards David again. He was baffling.

'Murray does seem to like you,' she said.

'I remember when he was a puppy, when you last lived at Barton,' David said. 'Now he's getting as grey as me, poor fellow.'

Emma laughed. 'I don't see any grey in *your* hair, Sir David.'

He smiled up at her. 'That's because I have a valet who is very clever at cutting hair. He hides my decrepitude from the rest of the world.'

'Decrepit indeed,' Emma murmured. She thought of the easy, powerful way he rode his horse as they made their way to Barton, as casually elegant in the saddle as if he were a centaur. The grace of his dancing. The strength of his arms around her as he kissed her…

Fortunately, Mary the maid hurried in to interrupt such wildly distracting thoughts. Emma ordered tea and sat down in her chair, carefully arranging her skirts.

'Oh, Mrs Carrington, the post just came,' Mary said as she turned toward the door. She took a bundle of papers from her apron pocket and left them on Emma's worktable. 'There was a letter from London, as you've asked me to look out for.'

'Thank you, Mary,' Emma said happily. 'It must be from my sister, Sir David. I have been longing to hear how she's doing.'

'You must read it, then. I shall talk to Murray while you do.'

As Emma reached for the letter on top, with the direction written in Jane's neat hand, she smiled to see how content Murray seemed to be, still leaning against Sir David's leg. 'He does seem to enjoy your company.'

'Perhaps I should get Beatrice a dog. Something a bit smaller than Murray, though, I think.'

'Everyone should have a dog.' Emma broke the seal on her letter and quickly scanned the contents. It wasn't very long, as it seemed Jane was still confined to bed, but the news Emma had been aching to hear was good. 'At last!'

'Good tidings, I hope?' David said.

Emma smiled up at him. 'Very good. My sister is safely delivered of a healthy daughter, named—little Emma! They are both recovering very well. She says they hope to return to Barton by the summer.'

'That is indeed excellent news. You must send my congratulations to Lady Ramsay.'

'Of course I will.' Emma carefully refolded the letter, remembering how, years ago, she had suspected Sir David admired her sister. Nothing could have ever come of it, of course. Jane was married, even though she and Hayden were then estranged. And surely David was too much a gentleman to ever pursue such a thing. Still,

Jane *was* pretty and such a perfect lady at all times. Unlike her younger sister…

'You wanted to talk to me about something, Sir David,' she said quickly, pushing away such memories.

He blinked, as if surprised by the sudden change of topic. But he nodded and followed her lead. 'It was about Beatrice.'

'Would you like me to find a puppy for her?'

David laughed. 'Perhaps one day soon. I would only know how to procure farm dogs, not young lady's pets. But I would like to ask a rather presumptuous favour.'

'I doubt it could be very *presumptuous* if it involves Miss Marton. I quite enjoy her company and would like to help her if I can.'

'That is very kind of you. I do my best for her, but it cannot be easy for a girl of her age without a mother to help her. Her own mother…'

Had not been much of a mother. Emma remembered the tale of Lady Marton's sad elopement and wild ways. Surely something like Emma's own misjudged past. Yet here he was asking her for a favour for his daughter. Surely that was some sort of good sign, a kind of progress?

'I am going to look out for a suitable governess for her,' David said. 'Someone who can teach her a little more than French and etiquette. She is becoming too clever for her nanny and me.'

'A bluestocking in the making?' Emma said, remembering Mr Sansom's jolly words.

'I don't know where she gets it. My mother and sister

were never readers and Beatrice's mother—well, Maude knew a great deal about hats and the theatre, I suppose.'

'But not much about books concerning travels in India.'

'Quite. I know Beatrice has been very quiet since she lost her mother and we came back to Rose Hill, but she does seem to enjoy learning. And she also seems to like you.'

Was that a note of doubt in his voice? Did he marvel that Beatrice could like her at all? 'I enjoy her company as well.'

'Then would you perhaps be willing to give her a few lessons until I can find a suitable governess? She could come to you here, or at the bookshop, and I would provide any volumes you need. I think it might help to distract her.'

'I would be most happy to give Miss Beatrice lessons,' Emma said, surprised but delighted. 'It would give me distraction as well and something useful to do. I am not sure I know enough to actually teach her, but I am willing to find out. Perhaps she and I can discuss new topics together.'

'I would be most grateful to you, Mrs Carrington. In return, perhaps I could help sort through my uncle's books and see what might suit you.'

'I thought you didn't like me "bothering" your uncle, "pestering" him to let me have his books.' Emma couldn't help but tease, just a bit.

David gave her a rueful smile. 'I do tend to be quite protective of my family.'

'And quite right.' Emma felt a bit wistful as she wondered how it would feel for him to protect *her*. But at least, perhaps, they were starting to be friends. It was better than nothing and the best she could expect.

Mary came back with the tea tray and arranged it neatly on Emma's worktable. As the maid left, Emma studied the china cups and bowls of sugar and lemon, and a mischievous thought seized her.

'I think I have quite had my fill of tea for one day,' she said. 'My sister's news deserves a bit of celebration, don't you think, Sir David?'

A doubtful frown flickered over his handsome face. 'A celebration?'

'Yes,' Emma said firmly. She hurried across the room to rummage through a crate she hadn't yet un-packed. It was full of odds and ends of her peripatetic life with Henry that she hadn't yet been able to dispose of—including a bottle of fine French champagne he had won at the card tables one night. She had hidden it before he could drink it, then he had died the next week in that duel.

'I think this is fitting to toast the new baby,' she said. 'I was told it's quite a rare and expensive vintage.'

David laughed. 'What *is* that?'

'Champagne, of course. Don't tell me you have never seen such a thing before, Sir David, for I happen to know there is reported to be quite a fine cellar at Rose Hill.'

'Yes, my father was a collector. But where did you get it?'

'From my husband. Henry won it in a card game. I was utterly furious when he brought it back instead of money for the rent.' Not as furious as she was a week later, though, when Henry fought that fatal duel. And his weeping, married lover landed on her doorstep to tell her about it. Emma pushed away those terrible memories and held the bottle up to the light. 'It's terribly dusty, but it should still be good, I think.'

'You should have sold it. It would have paid your rent for many weeks, I think.'

'Really?'

'Yes.' David came and took the bottle from her hands to study the label. 'It's a '96. A very fine vintage.'

'Truly?' Emma peered closer at the label, which was so faded she could hardly make out the French words. 'Perhaps things were not so hopeless as I feared, then.'

He held it out to her. 'You should put it in a safe place.'

Emma shook her head. 'I still think we should drink it. To toast baby Emma's good health.' And perhaps to celebrate her tentative new hopes for friendship with Sir David.

'Are you quite sure?'

'Yes. Can you open it?'

He nodded and turned away to do something complicated to get the bottle open. 'I confess I am quite curious to taste it. Since the war, bottles have been quite rare.'

'I'm glad to be of help, then.' Emma laughed and clapped her hands as the cork popped free with a fizzy little explosion.

David laughed too, a wonderful sound she had never heard before. He quickly poured out some of the pale gold liquid into the teacups and passed her one. His bare fingers slid along hers, warm, enticing and too quickly gone.

He stepped back and held up his cup in a salute. 'To baby Emma.'

'To baby Emma,' Emma agreed. She clinked the gilded edge of her cup with his and took a long sip. It slid over her tongue in a sweet, effervescent rush, making her shiver. 'Oh, that *is* nice. Like—like liquid sunshine.'

David also took a deep drink and smiled. It was a sweet, deeply satisfied smile and Emma couldn't help but wish he would smile at *her* like that. 'Very fine indeed. Are you sorry now you didn't open it sooner?'

'Not at all. This seems like the perfect moment for just such a thing.' Emma sat back in her chair and happily sipped at her champagne until, all too soon, it was gone. David refilled their cups, and a delightful, warm, comfortable feeling spread over her.

After a few quiet moments, David suddenly said, 'Did your husband gamble quite often?'

Emma frowned, some of the warmth ebbing away. She didn't want to think of Henry, not now when she was having such fun. 'Why do you ask?'

David held up his cup. He seemed to notice then it was empty again and he refilled both his and hers. 'Because you said he brought home wine instead of rent money from the gaming tables.'

'Oh, yes. That.' Emma took another sip and Henry once again seemed very far away. A pleasantly blurry memory, which was just what he should be. 'He was very fond of a card game, as well as many other things he couldn't quite handle. I didn't quite realise that when we married.'

'Things such as what?' David asked. 'What sort of man was your husband?'

The wrong sort for any lady. 'But I don't want to think about Henry any more!' Emma cried. She jumped up out of her chair, suddenly unable to sit still any longer. Her whole body felt like the champagne itself, fizzy and warm and alive. Alive—as she had not felt in so very long!

David laughed and she spun around to look at him. She could hardly warrant this was the same man who first came into her cottage so cautiously. He leaned back in his chair, his long, lean legs stretched in front of him. His cup dangled loosely from his elegant fingers and his hair curled over his brow. He smiled up at her lazily and suddenly she couldn't breathe.

'What do you want to think about, then?' he asked.

'I want to dance,' Emma blurted out. At least she didn't say the very first thing that popped into her head—*I want to kiss you.* 'It's been too long since I danced.'

David set aside his empty cup and slowly rose to his feet, as graceful and deceptively powerful as a panther. He reached for her hand and gave a low, courtly bow as Emma watched in thunderstruck astonishment.

'And there is no finer ballroom for it,' he said. 'Mrs Carrington, may I have the honour of this waltz?'

Emma laughed and curtsied deeply before taking his hand. 'Sir David, I would be honoured.'

He took her into his arms and hummed a waltz tune

as they twirled around the room, faster and faster until they were both laughing, until she had to cling to him to keep from falling.

'I've never waltzed like this before!' she cried.

In answer he whirled her around faster and faster, until they stumbled to a stop. Their laughter faded as they stared at each other in the hazy daylight.

Emma reached up to touch his face, trailing her fingertips over his finely carved features as she marvelled at him. He was so contradictory—she couldn't decipher him at all. One moment so strict, so remote, and the next, closer to her than anyone had ever been. He made her feel so safe with his quiet strength, but at the same time he made the world crumble around her until she didn't know what was happening.

She swept a light caress over his sensual lips and he smiled against her fingers.

'Emma…' he said roughly, and then he did what she so longed for. He kissed her.

She went up on tiptoe to meet him, twining her arms around him so she wouldn't fall. So he couldn't leave her. His hands closed hard around her waist, pulling her even closer to him.

Emma marvelled that they seemed to fit so perfectly together. Their mouths, their hands, their bodies—as if made to be just like they were now. She parted her lips and felt the tip of his tongue sweep over hers. Lightly, enticingly, but it made her feel as if she had tumbled straight down into the sun itself. The kiss turned frantic, full of raw need and burning desire.

She felt him press her back against the wall, his

hands strong and hungry as they slid over her shoulders and traced the soft curve of her breasts through her muslin bodice. Emma was astonished and delighted at his boldness, at the way he seemed to know just how she needed to be touched. She moaned at the delicious sensations that shivered through her, like sunrays and snow showers all at the same time.

Oh, this is terrible, she thought. Terrible and wonderful all at the same time. She knew she shouldn't be doing this, but she couldn't stop.

Through the silvery, sparkly haze of desire, she heard him whisper her name.

'Emma, Emma,' he said, as if he was in pain. 'What do you do to me?'

What did she do to *him?* He cracked apart her whole world and reformed it, just by being near her. She didn't know why or how. All she could do was hold on to him.

She felt his fingertips trace the edge of her bodice, caressing the bare skin of the soft upper curve of her breast. She was shocked—and delighted. She drew him closer to her, desperate for him not to leave her. To have him touch her again. She'd felt so cold, so alone, for so long, and now she finally felt warm again.

Because of David.

Her head fell weakly back against the wall and her eyes drifted shut as she tried to blot out everything but the feel of his touch on her skin. His warm, slightly rough fingertips, the brush of his cool breath—it was all so wondrous. She wanted more of it, and yet more and more.

He bent his head to press a hot, open-mouthed kiss

to her neck, to the soft, sensitive spot just below her ear. She shivered as his kiss trailed over her collarbone, the curve of her shoulder over the thin muslin of her gown, like a silky ribbon of fire.

The tip of his tongue lightly traced a teasing circle on the slope of her breast, just above the ribboned trim of her gown. His touch came teasingly close to her aching nipple, just the merest brush, but it made her cry out.

Emma arched against him. Through the layers of her dress and his doeskin breeches, she felt the heavy length of his manhood, hard with a desire that echoed her own. As her body touched his, he groaned against her skin and his mouth found hers again.

Emma buried her fingers in the silky waves of his hair, almost sobbing at the intense force of connection that flowed between them.

The haze of her passion cleared a bit as she felt him draw back. His kiss slid away from her lips, leaving her chilled. His hands loosened their hold on her waist, his fingers tense on her skin, and he braced his forehead on her shoulder. Their rough breath mingled and Emma was sure he could hear the pounding of her heart in the sudden silence of the room.

She reached up to smooth a gentle caress over his rumpled hair and her hand trembled. She wanted to cry with the terrible yearning that grew inside of her, the longing for what she couldn't have. A new life, a new beginning. Her mistakes had made those impossible. But she still longed for them, here with David.

'Oh, Emma,' he whispered hoarsely. 'What is it that you do to me? What is happening here?'

Emma choked out a laugh. 'I have no idea,' she managed to answer. She pressed a lingering kiss to the top of his head, clinging to him for as long as she dared before she let him go. She feared this precious moment close to him would be the only one she might ever have.

As his touch left her, she turned away from him and adjusted her gown. She drew in a deep breath, then another and another, until she felt her trembling slowly stop. Her thoughts still swirled, but at least she could feel the ground under her feet again.

Behind her, David braced his fists against the wall, his head hanging between his shoulders. His inner struggle almost felt like a physical thing between them, a building of a wall as thick as any stone. How could they be as close as any two people possibly could be one moment, and so far the next? She longed to know what he was thinking, for him to take her in his arms again and tell her what was happening.

She glanced back at him shyly, just in time to see him stand up very straight. He seemed to draw the invisible protection of his infallible dignity around him. He straightened his coat and raked his hands through his hair.

'Emma, I...' he said, his voice rough and sad.

'No, David, please,' she answered, trying to laugh, to be light. Not to cry. 'Don't say you're sorry. I should never have opened that wine. I never had a head for it. It seems to cast such a strange spell...'

'Not just the wine,' he muttered.

No—not just the wine. Emma shook her head. She had more words, no more excuses.

'I hope that my behaviour doesn't mean you won't spend time with Beatrice in the future,' he said.

Emma was shocked. She would have thought he wouldn't *want* her to tutor his daughter, not after her wantonness. 'Of course not.'

'Thank you,' he said, his voice still tight, as if he held all his emotions on the tightest of leashes.

Emma wished she could do the same. She felt as if she was about to crack with it all and just wanted to be alone so she could cry.

'I am sorry, Mrs Carrington,' he said. 'I don't know what madness came over me.'

Madness. Of course. That was what it had to be, if he desired her. Emma swore she could hear her heart cracking apart inside of her…

'Is that someone at your door?' David said.

'Wh-what?' she gasped. The whole world seemed to be spinning madly around her and for an instant she wasn't sure where she was. She tilted back her head and stared up into David's glowing grey eyes.

He seemed almost as bewildered as she felt, a frown forming on his brow as he stared down at her. His hair was tousled, his eyes intent as he looked at her. He had never looked so attractive to her, like a flame she beat against helplessly, like a moth drawn again and again to the very thing that was worst for it.

She opened her mouth, only knowing that she had to say something, *anything,* to snap the taut, sizzling tension between them. Then she heard the loud pounding sound again and she realised it was *not* her heart.

Someone was at the door.

'I suppose I should get that,' she said, feeling very slow-witted indeed.

David nodded and slowly stepped back. Emma swayed, hoping she could walk without tumbling down on her trembling legs. She spun around and hurried toward the door, her feet moving automatically.

In the hallway, she glanced back over her shoulder just in time to see David stoop to pick up his spectacles from the floor. Murray gave a confused little whine and David absently reached out to rub at the dog's head. David stared down at the spectacles in his hand, frowning. She longed to go back to him, to feel him touch her again and beg him to tell her what he was thinking.

But she knew very well that he wouldn't tell her. He'd said it himself; he was sorry for what had just happened. Probably sorry he had lost control with a woman like her, no matter how momentarily.

When he kissed her, in that instant she felt safe, as if she belonged, as if she didn't have to be lost. But now she felt even lonelier than ever.

Another knock sounded at the door and it was very clear Mary wasn't going to answer it. Emma quickly smoothed her skirt and tucked her hair back into its confining combs. She had no idea who would come calling on her, as no one had yet made their way to her cottage sanctuary. She only knew she had to get rid of them, whoever they were. And then she had to get rid of David, so she could be alone and think, and remind herself sternly why she was done with romance.

Any hint of the blighted thing was obviously very bad for her.

She pulled open the door, a polite smile pasted on her lips—and froze.

It was Philip Carrington. Henry's cousin and best friend, his partner in carousing. And the only one who had stood as *her* friend during her misbegotten marriage.

Philip stood on her doorstep in a stylishly cut greatcoat and impeccably fitted doeskin breeches, tallcrowned hat in his hand. The breeze tossed around his honey-coloured curls and he grinned at her in a show of dazzling delight.

For an instant, all Emma could do was gape at him. Surely he was some sort of illusion? It had been months since she refused his offer of help and left him in that dingy lodging house. She'd thought she would never see him again, yet here he was. Right on her doorstep.

Emma shook her head, mingled disbelief and delight sweeping through her. Philip had been her one friend during life with Henry, even though he had often been in trouble himself.

'Philip,' she gasped. 'Whatever are you doing here?'

'I came because I couldn't bear not to see you again, Emma. The Continent is a complete wasteland without you.' His smile widened and Emma remembered how all the ladies would flutter their fans at him. Would practically chase him down through the casinos and shopping stalls.

Yes, he was just as handsome as ever. As handsome as Henry had once been. But what was he doing there? They hadn't parted on the best of terms. And she wasn't one of his swooning admirers.

Even though she could see why those ladies were enthralled. His smile *was* disorientingly sensational.

But not half as disorienting as David's rare flashes of humour.

Oh, good heavens. *David.* David was just down the corridor in her sitting room. This was not good at all.

'Philip, I—I am quite astonished,' she managed to say. 'You should have written.'

His confident grin faltered a bit. 'No time to write, Emma my dear. I could travel faster than a letter and I was most eager to see you. I can see now I should have travelled faster. You are looking lovelier than ever.'

'Philip…' Emma said, her desperation growing.

'Blast it, Emma, I missed you so much,' he said. Before she saw what he was about, his gloved hand slid out and grabbed her wrist to pull her towards him. 'You are more gloriously pretty than I remembered!'

His arms closed hard around her waist and he lifted her completely off her feet. As she curled her fists into the fine fabric of his coat, trying her hardest to push him away, he twirled her around and around.

'Didn't you miss me, too, Emma? Just a bit?' he shouted. 'Say you did or I vow you'll break my heart!'

'Philip…' she cried.

'I can see I'm quite interrupting. I'll just take my leave, Mrs Carrington, and be out of your way,' David suddenly said.

Over Philip's shoulder, she saw David standing in the corridor just beyond the open door, his hair and clothes impeccable again. As if nothing at all had happened.

What was worse—far worse—was that he watched

her seemingly cavorting with Philip with no sign of emotion on his face at all. No frown, no anger, only that calm, cool mask she had come to dread.

The man who kissed her so passionately had completely vanished.

Chapter Eleven

'Philip, put me down!' Emma cried, hating the thread of desperation in her voice. 'This instant.'

'It's been so long since I've seen you, though, Emma,' Philip protested. 'Haven't you missed me just a bit? I...' Then he looked beyond her and saw David standing in the doorway. His teasing grin slowly faded and he lowered her to the ground. 'I didn't realise you had company. I thought that horse there was yours.'

Emma staggered back, trying to pretend to at least a modicum of dignity. She really just wanted to scream, or run away, or rewind the clock to take her back an hour before this all happened. Or really, if she had such a magic cloak, she should turn it back to before she made the supreme mistake of marrying Henry Carrington.

But all of those things were quite impossible. She straightened her shoulders and said, 'Philip, this is my neighbour, Sir David Marton. Sir David, may I present my late husband's cousin, Mr Philip Carrington?'

'A neighbour, eh?' Philip said as he offered David a bow. 'You have settled back here quickly, Cousin.'

'Is that not what home is for, Mr Carrington?' David said quietly. 'A place to belong, no matter how long we have been gone from it?'

'I'm sure my late cousin would want his wife to be with family, no matter what,' Philip said.

'And yet his own family has taken so long to call on her?'

Emma felt as if a conversation in some foreign language was going on over her head as Philip glared at David. She didn't like that feeling at all. And she couldn't like the solemn, watchful way David studied Philip. It made her feel like she had done something horribly wrong, when for once she had not.

'Mr Carrington has quite taken me by surprise today,' she said. 'I thought he was travelling on the Continent.'

'You were the one who left in such a hurry,' Philip said, a thread of querulous irritation darkening his sunny demeanour.

'Then I will leave you to be reacquainted,' David said. 'Thank you for the tea, Mrs Carrington. I am sure either my uncle or I will contact you regarding the books very soon.'

He gave her another bow and hurried down her garden path toward the gate where his horse was tethered. He moved with such swift, elegant dignity, so quick to leave her.

As if their dance, their kiss, had never happened.

Emma longed to run after him to catch his arm and

tell him everything. To beg him to believe her when she said she was not expecting Philip. But she knew she couldn't do that. It would surely only make him think worse of her and he wouldn't believe her anyway. Why should he? She surely looked the veriest wanton now, just like his wife.

With David, she always felt like one baby step forwards—or one great kiss forwards—pushed her ten steps back. She wanted so much more from him, even though she knew that was foolish indeed.

'Good day, Sir David,' she called as his horse turned on to the drive that led away from Barton land.

He gave her a quick wave and urged his horse to a gallop. All too soon he disappeared from her view.

'I hope not all your neighbours are quite so dour, Emma,' Philip said.

Emma's hands curled into fists as she turned back to face him. 'Sir David is not dour. He merely has many responsibilities, which he takes seriously. Unlike the Carringtons.'

Philip held up his hands as if in surrender and gave her a rueful smile. 'Pax, Emma. I am sorry I was too impatient to see you to write first. But I *have* missed you.'

Emma sighed and rubbed her fingertips against the headache forming at her temples. It really was not Philip's fault that the timing of his arrival was so rotten. Once he had been very kind to her when she had so little kindness in her life.

It wasn't his fault that he was part of a past she wanted only to leave behind.

'Do come in, Philip,' she said. 'I can ring for some

tea and you must tell me what you have been doing since I saw you last.'

Philip's grin returned and he offered Emma his arm to lead her back into the house. 'Missing you, mostly. It really has been horribly dull without you and Henry.'

'I find it hard to believe you could find no amusement at all,' Emma said. She hastily kicked the empty bottle of wine behind a sofa and piled up the used teacups on the tray before she rang for Mary and set about straightening the chair cushions. Her emotions were still roiling inside her, confusing and bewildering, but she was suddenly glad she wasn't alone.

'You would be surprised,' Philip muttered. He examined her little room with his hands clasped behind his back, frowning a bit as he glimpsed Murray. The dog whined at him and sat up at attention. Murray had never much liked Philip, Emma remembered. 'I was astonished when the housekeeper at Barton told me you were living alone here in this old cottage. Never tell me your sister cast you out?'

'Oh, no, nothing like that. Jane is in London right now and I felt too lonely in the great house all alone.' Emma sat down and gestured Philip towards the chair next to hers, trying not to think of how David had just sat there. Of how close she had come to him—only to be pushed away again.

'It still seems a harsh place for the sister of a countess,' Philip said. He fiddled with the china ornaments on her side table, a curious look on his face.

'You know how Henry left me placed,' Emma said softly, embarrassed to even mention his cousin's bad behaviour. Philip had encouraged Henry in some of it, true, but it was not Philip's fault he could handle it and Henry could not. Philip had tried to be her friend and now he had come all this way to see her. She couldn't be unfair to him.

'Do I?' he muttered. Emma could hear that hint of some darkness again and it made her fidget in her chair. But then he smiled and it seemed as if a grey cloud scuttled away. 'Yes, I fear my cousin did not deal well with either of us in the end.'

Mary hurried in with a fresh tea tray. For a second, the maid's eyes widened in astonishment to see a different man there. But Philip turned his sunny smile on her and she giggled as she set down the tray with a clatter. Her cheeks were bright pink when she dashed away. Such was the effect of Philip's angelic looks on every female he encountered.

Emma remembered that it was last a darkly exotic Polish countess, which made her wonder again why he had come so far to dull old Barton.

'No, I suppose he did not,' Emma said. She poured out the tea, knowing she would never offer a guest wine again. It only caused trouble.

'He left you nothing at all?'

A strange intensity in the question made her glance at him sharply over the teapot. 'You know he did not. But I am finding ways to look after myself.'

'Your family, I'm sure. Or perhaps you are planning to marry your ever-so-serious neighbour?'

Emma gave a choked laugh. Marry Sir David? Surely

it would as easy for her to fly to the moon. 'I am not the sort of wife Sir David Marton would require.'

'The more fool him, then.' Philip gave her another smile as she handed him the cup, a different smile. One quieter, more intimate. 'You really are looking lovely, Emma. The countryside seems to agree with you.'

'I am quite content here,' she said. 'I wish that you could find the same. You really have been a good friend to me, Philip. You deserved better from Henry.'

'Oh, I think I am closer to finding contentment than ever before,' Philip said mysteriously. 'Now, tell me more about your new life here, Emma. I find myself quite intrigued...'

David urged his horse faster down the lane until they were galloping, the wind rushing past and the hedgerows turning to a green blur as they soared by. Zeus was glad to have his head and tossed his glossy black mane back in joy. But the wild run didn't set David free.

Usually a fast ride released the tension built inside of him, took him out of himself, but not today. Today the recklessness and burning anger he kept tied up inside threatened to consume him.

He sent Zeus soaring over a ditch, bent low against the horse's neck as they flew. He had no right to feel jealous of anything Emma Carrington did, yet he feared that was exactly what fuelled his fury now. When he saw that man holding her in his arms, David just wanted to grab the blighter by his dandyish coat and plant a facer on him.

And then he wanted to grab Emma in his own arms

and kiss her until she never wanted to look at another man but *him*. Until she cried out his name only.

The fierceness of his primitive instincts appalled him. He didn't recognise himself—or at least not the man he had long strictly schooled himself to be. Responsible, reliable, never thoughtlessly angry. And he had now long lived by the dictates of control and decorum.

Until Emma. She brought out a recklessness he had thought conquered. Not even Maude, who he had once desired, ever made him feel that way. Her scandalous desertion had only made him more determined to exert control over every aspect of his life, to protect his daughter and his family name.

But Emma—she brought out the old wildness in him. Every time he looked at her, every time she smiled or laughed and he saw her green eyes brighten like a warm, lazy summer's day, he only wanted to be closer to her. To be a part of her light, fun spirit and see the world as she surely did.

Her husband had disappointed her, just as Maude had with him. But Emma didn't seem defeated by it. How did she do that? He wanted that for himself—he wanted *her*. Wanted her as he had never wanted anything else—wildly, passionately.

And he had to beat that down, just as he did every desire, every attempt of his darker side to defeat him. Passion had no place in his life. It only led to destruction and ruin. He needed order in his life and Emma Carrington was the very definition of chaos.

Why, then, did he keep remembering the way she felt

in his arms? The way she tasted, the smell of her perfume all around him, the sound of her sighs? When he danced with her, kissed her, he never wanted to stop. Never wanted her to go away.

And then that man—Philip Carrington—appeared. When David saw Emma in his arms, the two of them laughing as he spun her around, anger as strong as his desire threatened to overwhelm him. But he should have been grateful for Mr Carrington's timely arrival. It was a vital reminder to David that he always had to remember who he was and what his life was about. And who Emma was.

It was obvious Emma and Philip Carrington had once been close. The familiar way he touched her, the looks they exchanged, spoke of a friendship. Who knew what had gone on in Emma's life with a disappointing husband on the Continent? Perhaps Philip Carrington had been a comfort to her.

Even as a new wave of anger rushed through David at the thought of such 'comfort', his rational side knew he could hardly blame her. Henry Carrington had let her down in some way and she was alone in strange cities, far from her family. She had made mistakes, misjudged people, as everyone did. He himself had misjudged Maude and it almost ruined him and Beatrice.

He couldn't afford to misjudge again, no matter how beautiful or spirited Emma was. No matter how much her kiss awakened fires in him he thought long extinguished. He had to be very careful.

David turned Zeus down the lane towards home, drawing the horse in a bit. Zeus snorted and tossed his head, obviously not happy with being reined in and re-minded he had to be civilised.

'Believe me, old boy, I understand,' David said with a rueful laugh. Once wilder impulses were released, it was almost impossible to lock them away again. But it had to be done. He just felt that way because he had been too long without a lady's intimate company.

Yes, that was all it was. He had his natural urges and had suppressed them.

The gates of Rose Hill were just ahead and David glimpsed something most unwelcome there. His sister sat in her open carriage, waiting for the footman to open the gates. And beside her, the two of them giggling to-gether, was Miss Harding.

'Blast it all,' David cursed. This was the very last moment he wanted to see his sister and her friend, and play the genteel host.

But all his years of self-control were not for nothing. He slowed Zeus to a walk and felt a sense of icy calm and remoteness come over him as he moved closer to home.

'Louisa,' he said as he drew Zeus in beside his sis-ter's carriage. 'I didn't know you were planning to call today. And Miss Harding, a pleasure to see you again.'

'Miss Harding and I were just visiting Mr Crawford at the vicarage and I thought she might like to see Rose Hill since we were so close,' Louisa said with a giggle. 'Really, David, what have you been doing? You look quite wild! Not at all like you.'

David was sure he couldn't look half as wild as he felt. But he loathed the idea that it showed to other people. 'I have just been for a ride. Poor Zeus has been quite restless lately. If I had known you were coming—'

'Oh, Sir David, you mustn't be cross with your sister,' Miss Harding cried. 'It was entirely my fault. I have heard so much about the beauties of Rose Hill and I begged her to let me catch a glimpse for myself. Do forgive us for intruding.'

David bowed his head to Miss Harding, who smiled prettily back. She was all pink cheeks and bouncing pale ringlets in her fashionable beribboned straw bonnet and blue redingote, the very image of demure young ladyhood. The niece of an admiral, friend of his sister—exactly the sort of proper young woman he ought to be seriously thinking about at such a time in his life.

The sort who would grace Rose Hill and the area, look after Beatrice and give him more children—and never arouse his darker side with passionate desire. Yes, exactly what he needed.

But as she gave him a shyly sweet smile, all he could see was Emma staring up at him with brilliant green eyes and kiss-red lips.

'Not at all,' he said carefully. 'My sister and her friends are welcome at Rose Hill at any time. Please, do come inside.'

'I knew you would be glad to see us, David,' Louisa said. 'Dear Rose Hill is in such need of a feminine presence, isn't it?'

David led his sister's carriage up the gravelled drive to the front doors, which were opened by Hughes, the old butler who had been at Rose Hill since David's parents' time. He left Zeus with the grooms and helped Louisa down from her carriage.

As he handed down Miss Harding, she leaned gracefully on his arm and peeked up at him shyly from beneath the brim of her bonnet.

'Thank you so very much, Sir David,' she said. 'You are always so gallant.'

'You are very welcome, Miss Harding,' he answered politely. 'I hope Rose Hill doesn't disappoint you after the good reports you have heard.'

Still holding on to his arm, she tilted back her head to study the house's façade of pale-grey stone, with its twin stone staircases leading to the front doors and soaring rose-pink marble columns. The windows sparkled in the sunlight.

'Not at all,' she said. 'It is most pretty indeed.'

'You do not see any improvements you would make?'

Miss Harding's smile turned mischievous. 'Not at present. But I should have to see the inside. That is where ladies really excel, you know, in curtains and cushions and such.'

'Indeed,' David murmured, remembering how Maude had filled the London house with bolts and piles of fabrics and wallpapers and pillows the instant they arrived. Everything in the very latest style.

And then he thought of Emma's cosy sitting room, all books and family portraits and dog beds.

'Hurry up, you two,' Louisa called out merrily, pulling him out of his thoughts. Out of his impossible desire to be back in Emma's cluttered cottage, beside her. 'Stop whispering now. I am quite longing for a cup of tea.'

'Of course, Louisa.' David led Miss Harding up the steps into the cool shadows of the hall, with its black-and-white stone floor and rows of classical statues brought back by his grandfather from the Grand Tour. They hadn't moved since.

'Yes, I do see what you mean,' Miss Harding whispered. 'No colour at all.'

Before David could answer, Mrs Jennings the housekeeper, like Hughes a remnant of his parents' time, came hurrying over.

'Louisa, Miss Harding—Mrs Jennings will take you into the drawing room and send for some tea,' he said. 'If you will excuse me for a moment.'

'Oh, David dear, no need to be so formal,' Louisa said with a laugh. 'Rose Hill is still my family home, too. I can play hostess—until a new Lady Marton comes along, of course.'

Miss Harding blushed prettily and gave him a flashing smile before she hurried after his sister into the drawing room.

David went up the stairs toward the family chambers, shaking his head. He was no fool when it came to matchmaking family and friends. Almost everyone he knew had immediately begun producing their pretty young daughters, sisters and cousins as soon as Maude died. He saw their kind intentions and always knew one day he would have to marry. But being in no way prepared for the emotional demands of a marriage, and having his stunned and sad little daughter to think of, had sent him back to the quiet haven of Rose Hill. Alone.

He had foolishly not counted on his sister's tenacity on the subject of his marriage. Louisa hadn't learned much from the mistake of her friendship with Maude, it seemed. And now Miss Harding was her object.

David paused on the landing to glance back down at the drawing-room door. Laughter floated out to him, a softly feminine echo that Rose Hill hadn't heard in a very long time. He couldn't be unfair to Miss Harding. She *did* seem to be exactly the sort of lady he required as a wife—young, respectable, biddable. That she could be friends with Louisa was surely a mark in her favour; she would get along with his family.

But doubts lingered, a toxic mix of bad memories and a strong desire never to make a mess of his life again. He couldn't afford to make another wrong, scandalous marriage. Miss Harding bore some watching.

And yet—yet he couldn't get the memory of Emma out of his mind. Emma in his arms, Emma's lips under his. Emma driving him to bedlam with his need for her.

David pounded his fists on the carved railing and silently cursed, trying to drive the thought of her away. Emma was most decidedly *not* the sort of wife he needed. She was too impulsive. And he was not the man for her, not if she sought adventure as she had with her first husband. They were deeply wrong for each other.

If only his mind could convince his body.

He heard a rustling noise, a sigh, and he glanced up to see Beatrice on the landing above. She sat between two gilded posts, her legs dangling down and a doll clutched in her arms as she stared down at him with large, solemn eyes.

'Is that Aunt Louisa, Papa?' she said.

'Yes, it is. And where is Nanny? You should be in the nursery,' David said. He strode up the rest of the stairs to scoop his daughter up in his arms.

'She fell asleep by the fire. I was reading, but then I heard voices and wanted to know who was here.' She peered down at the hall far below. 'I was rather hoping it was Mrs Carrington.'

Beatrice was hoping to see Emma Carrington? David studied her closely and saw an interested light in her eyes that hadn't been there for a long time. He had thought he should not let Emma tutor Beatrice, not when he needed to learn to control himself around her, but if she could make Beatrice show an interest in something at last...

It was rather a conundrum.

'It is your Aunt Louisa and her friend Miss Harding,' he said as he turned toward the nursery wing.

Beatrice wrinkled her little nose. 'Miss Harding? Why is *she* here? She doesn't talk about anything interesting. At least she did not that time I met her at Aunt Louisa's.'

'She is here because she's friends with your aunt and you need to be polite to her.'

Beatrice looked doubtful. 'I'll be polite, of course. If I must see her.'

David tried not to laugh. He had to teach Beatrice to learn to be a proper lady, after all. 'You must, as they are visitors in our home. You said you see her at Aunt Louisa's house.'

'I must be nice because one day you might marry her?'

David stopped suddenly in his tracks, startled by her quiet question. 'Where did you hear that I am to marry Miss Harding?'

Beatrice stared back at him, wide-eyed. 'From Aunt Louisa, of course, when I went to play with my cousins yesterday. She was talking to Mr Crawford's fiancée, and she said she hoped that soon Mr Crawford would have another ceremony to perform—for you.'

'Well, it was wrong of your aunt to speculate like that,' David said, appalled to realise that surely now the whole village paired him with Miss Harding. He would have to have a word with his sister about little pitchers and big ears. 'I can't say what might happen in the future, but Miss Harding and I are not betrothed. If we were, *you* would be the first one I would tell.'

'Really?'

'Really. We are a family, you and I, and we must always be able to tell each other what we really feel.' David hugged his daughter close, an unbearable feeling of tenderness threatening to overwhelm him. She was his child and he would protect her in any way he could. And the first way he would do that was in being very careful about what new stepmother he brought into her life.

'Then Miss Harding is not to be my stepmama?'

'No one is going to be your stepmama at present. We do well enough by ourselves, don't we?'

Beatrice nodded and even gave a smile. 'For the present we do. But I must tell you honestly, Papa, that you don't smell very good right now. You should not be entertaining guests to tea.'

David laughed, relieved that her worries seemed to have passed. But if there was one thing he knew about Bea, it was that she was too good at hiding the depths of her feelings. Though she was quite right; the wine and the fast gallop outdoors probably did not make for an appealing perfume. 'What have we said about manners, Bea?'

'But you just said we should tell each other what we think.'

'I have just been riding and was just coming upstairs to clean up and make myself presentable.' David nudged open the door to the nursery sitting room. Nanny was indeed snoring by the fire and Beatrice's dolls were set up around their tiny table for a tea party. Open books lay scattered around everywhere and he remembered her need for lessons.

And her happiness at the mention of Emma's name.

Yes, it was definitely time for Beatrice's education to advance. She was becoming far too clever for the nursery. The realisation that his darling daughter was growing up, becoming a most independent spirit, gave him a pang.

He put her down on her small chair and picked up some of the scattered books to tidy them into a pile. Against his better judgement, he knew what he had to do.

'I do have some news you might like, though, Lady Impudent,' he said.

Beatrice frowned doubtfully. 'What is that, Papa?'

'I am going to look out for a governess for you, a lady who can help teach you all the things you want to know. In the meantime, so that you will be ready when she comes, you will go to the bookstore to have a few lessons with Mrs Carrington.'

'Mrs Carrington? Truly?' A smile suddenly burst across Beatrice's face, brighter and happier than any David had seen in a long while. And it was Emma who had put it there.

Emma who somehow made the world brighter and lighter just by existing. Emma—with her doubtful past and unpredictable spirit.

'Oh, thank you, Papa,' Beatrice cried. She jumped off her chair and came running to hug him around his waist, holding on tight. 'I will study so very hard with Mrs Carrington, you'll see. You are the best papa in the world.'

'Just promise me you will do your work and be very careful,' David murmured, holding Beatrice close. He hoped he was not making another terrible mistake.

Yes. This place would do very well.

Melanie studied the drawing room as she sipped at her tea and listened to Mrs Smythe chatter on. The colours were not at all stylish, of course, much too dark and heavy, but the elaborate white plasterwork of the ceiling was very pretty and the space quite large. It could accommodate some grand parties.

She thought of the rooms in Bath where she and her mother had lived for so long, the tiny little bare space they could barely even afford to heat. How very different Rose Hill was from all that! A whole different world, really. It would be so very splendid if she could bring her mother here and show it to her as their new house. If she could finally take care of her mother and not be a disappointment to her...

Melanie closed her eyes and imagined the look on her mother's face when they drew up to the portico of Rose Hill in a fine carriage. The delight, the joy—the relief that they would never have to struggle again. How wonderful that would be! To have a secure place. To be Lady Marton of Rose Hill.

And all she would have to do was marry Sir David Marton to get it.

Melanie's eyes opened and she felt as if cold water had just been flooded over her delightful dream. Marriage was surely a small price to pay for such a prize? She had been completely ready to marry Captain Whitney. And Sir David was far from unattractive. He was very handsome, indeed, and came with that lovely security.

But—but why did she feel nothing when she looked at him? When she danced with him? When Captain Whitney led her on to the dance floor at the Bath assembly rooms, it felt as if a wonderful fizz, like champagne, sang through her veins. That giddiness made her long to risk everything just to feel it again. And when it was gone—blackest despair.

She'd felt the tiniest fizz again when that gloriously

gorgeous Philip Carrington lifted her up on to his horse. He was so dashing, like a Galahad rescuing a fair damsel! It was like a dream.

But she couldn't afford dreams now. Dreams were what got her packed off to this dull village in the first place. Dreams were why they were so poor, because her mother fell in love with a poor curate who then died young. No, Melanie couldn't have dreams of great romance right now. She needed this house. Maybe some day, when she was established, she could find someone…

She just had to find a way to get all that.

The drawing-room door opened, interrupting Mrs Smythe's flow of chatter, and Melanie looked up to see Sir David come into the room. He had changed into a fresh coat and his dark hair was damp and combed back neatly from his face.

Something inside her perked to a new attention. Yes, he *was* good looking. Surely once they were married she could do something to make him more fun? More impulsive, more laughing. More like…

More like Philip Carrington.

No, Melanie told herself sternly. She wouldn't think again about Mr Carrington, no matter how beautiful or exciting he was.

'Sir David,' she said brightly. 'Your home is so lovely, I am quite, quite overwhelmed by it all.'

Then she saw the little girl who held his hand and she froze. She had met Miss Beatrice Marton before, of course, at Mrs Smythe's house. She was a pretty child, but so quiet and so strangely old for her age. It was a bit—spooky.

And Melanie had quite forgotten that Sir David and his lovely house came with a strange little fairy-child who seemed to see right through Melanie with her weird grey eyes.

'Say good day to your aunt and Miss Harding, Beatrice,' Sir David said.

Melanie made herself smile and rose to her feet to hurry toward them. 'Such a charming little girl, Sir David!' she cried. 'You must be so very proud.'

If this was to be her life—and she was grimly determined that it would be—she knew she might as well start now.

From the diary of Arabella Bancroft

I hardly know how to write this, but it seems my darling Sir William is not all that he appears. The king does invite him to court for his handsome looks and charming conversation, but his family has long been penniless. He is here to seek an heiress to marry, or failing that...

He must return to highway robbery as he did during the wars. My poor William. How desperate his life must have been, must still be.

And I am no heiress.

Chapter Twelve

'And this is *galgan*,' Emma said as she pulled the spiky little plant from the damp ground. 'It's very useful for fevers, but it looks a bit like *venich*, which has no good use and shouldn't be eaten.'

Beatrice carefully studied the plant and compared it to the drawing in the book she held. 'I don't think I can ever remember so much, Mrs Carrington.'

Emma laughed and added the new specimen to their basket. 'That's what I'm here for, Miss Marton, to help you learn.'

'May I try to find one on my own?' Beatrice asked.

'Of course. Just don't go too far.'

As Beatrice scampered away, her botany guide in hand, Emma straightened and stretched her back. She laughed as Beatrice happily dug in the dirt, the sun shining on her red-gold hair. They had only been out for an hour, and already the girl was glowing with the brisk, bright air of the outdoors.

Not bad for a first lesson, Emma thought happily.

Surely David Marton would be content that she was the proper person to teach his daughter.

Not that she cared about what David thought about her, of course. Not at all.

To distract herself, she snatched up the basket of plants she had gathered with Beatrice and turned to follow the girl. It really was a lovely day, the spring sun bright and warm in a cloudless sky, the rich smell of green growing things on the breeze. Back in nature, which she had once loved so much and had lost for so long, she could almost feel like she had come back to herself again. Her true self.

It was too bad her true self still insisted on thinking about David Marton and the way it felt when he touched her.

'Mrs Carrington! Look at this,' Beatrice called.

Emma started to follow her, when suddenly she heard the rumble of wheels coming along the lane over the hill. She turned and saw it was Sir David himself, driving his curricle. He looked as if he had been visiting tenants, for he was casually dressed in a dark-blue coat and fine doeskin breeches that clung to his strong legs. A wide-brimmed hat shadowed his face.

'How goes the lesson, Mrs Carrington?' he asked as he drew in the horse.

Emma walked slowly toward him, still caught between her daydreams of him and the reality of his sudden appearance before her. She was unsure how to react to him.

'Very well, I think,' she said. 'Botany seems a good subject to begin with.' Emma felt a blush touch her cheeks when she remembered how disapproving his sister once was of her muddied hems. 'Although I haven't had the chance to study it in a long time, I fear.'

'Papa!' Beatrice cried. 'Look at what I found.'

His smile widened, transforming his already-handsome face to something truly wondrous. He climbed down from his curricle and quickly tied up the horse before he strode towards his daughter. Emma hurried after him, holding on to her straw hat as the wind tried to snatch it away.

Beatrice's little face and pink muslin dress were streaked with dirt as she held up a clump of mud-trailing plants, and her own hat fell from her head. Emma remembered how beautifully turned-out the child always was and felt a jolt of alarm that David would upbraid her for letting Beatrice get into such a state.

But he knelt beside Beatrice and carefully examined the leaves she held out to him. He swept his hat off and let it dangle in his hand, and the wind caught at his dark hair and tousled it over his brow.

'Very nice, Bea,' he said. 'What is it?'

'It's a—a...' A frown flickered over Beatrice's little face. 'What was it called, Mrs Carrington?'

'*Galgan,*' Emma said.

'It's good for a fever,' Beatrice said earnestly.

'Fascinating,' David said. 'What else have you learned today?'

Emma couldn't help but smile as she watched them there together, the tall, strong, handsome man and the adorable child. The sunlight shimmered on their hair, dark and bright. It was such a tiny, perfect moment, so unlike anything she could ever have imagined in her life before. If she could only freeze time and keep it for ever, she thought wistfully.

'Mrs Carrington?' Beatrice said, and the moment jolted into full light-filled motion again.

Emma smiled and went to kneel down next to them. She told Beatrice more about the plants, concentrating on the little girl even as she felt David's gaze on her, studying her. She felt a flutter deep down in her stomach, a nervous self-consciousness she didn't know what to do with.

Eventually Beatrice scampered off to examine something on the slope of the hill, her hat bouncing by its ribbons on her shoulders. David held out his hand to help Emma to her feet and she smiled up at him.

'Miss Beatrice is very curious about the world,' she said as they strolled along the road behind Beatrice, side by side.

David laughed. Like his daughter, he seemed lighter outdoors, more natural. He made Emma feel more comfortable too. 'Too curious sometimes, I fear. It's kind of you to share your knowledge of botany with her.'

'I've forgotten so much of what I once learned. I've enjoyed rediscovering it today,' Emma said. 'I think—

Her words were once again interrupted by the clatter of wheels on the dusty road. Emma glanced back over her shoulder to see an extraordinary scene, a fine open carriage painted a bright, glossy red, driven by a coachman clad in red-and-gold livery. It looked like no other equipage in the area.

As she watched, astonished, the carriage lurched to a

halt and a lady's face peeked over its gilded edge. Like her vehicle, she was—different. Bright blonde hair sparkled under a copiously feathered hat and her beautiful heart-shaped face was set off by a marabou-trimmed pink spencer.

'By Jove,' she cried, her voice caught by the breeze like the toll of a silver bell. 'It *is* David Marton. My, but it's been an age, hasn't it?'

Next to Emma, David stiffened. She studied him out of the corner of her eye and saw that his earlier easygoing, smiling demeanour, the casual warmth that had drawn her closer, was quite vanished. A small frown curled his mouth downwards and his eyes were narrowed as he looked at the beautiful woman in the carriage.

'Mrs Dunstable,' he said, his quite deep voice giving nothing away. 'It has been a long time.'

She laughed again. 'It's Betsy, remember? You used to call me that, anyway.'

'You are a very long way from London,' David said. Emma felt as if she watched a theatre scene she had come to late and couldn't follow.

'I was just giving a ride to a friend who needed to come to your quaint little village,' Mrs Dunstable— Betsy—said. 'I quite forgot you had come to live in this funny little place. After your marriage, wasn't it?'

'Yes,' David said shortly, still so quiet.

'Yes,' Betsy echoed, her sparkle dimming just a bit. 'It really has been too long. It's good to see you again.'

'And you, Mrs Dunstable. You look very well, as always.'

The fine carriage went on its way and David led Emma back towards where Beatrice was digging in the dirt again. 'An old acquaintance,' he said briefly.

'Of course,' Emma murmured. Yet inside she was afire with curiosity, and a tinge of what felt ridiculously like—jealousy…

'How are you settling back at Barton, ma'am?' Mary the housemaid said as she brought the tea tray into Emma's little cottage sitting room.

'Very well, I think,' Emma answered, pulling herself away from wondering who Betsy might be. 'It's a bit strange coming back to the places I knew as a girl and trying to reacquaint myself with everyone.'

'You'll make new friends, surely, ma'am,' Mary said. The china clattered as she laid it out.

Emma thought about that one sunny moment as she watched David and Beatrice, of how perfect it all seemed. How quickly it vanished. 'I hope so. I shall have to go into the village more often, I suspect.'

'Or call on more neighbours, ma'am?'

Emma laughed. 'I don't think we have many of those, Mary.'

'There is Rose Hill, ma'am. My sister worked in the kitchen there, 'til she went off to Bath.'

'Did she?' Emma asked in interest. Servants so often knew everything that went on in a house. 'I just saw Sir David Marton and his daughter today.'

'My sister said it was a lovely place to work and Sir David is very generous to all the servants,' Mary said approvingly. 'When he was there. He used to live in London, you know, when Lady Marton was alive.'

'I had heard that. It does seem strange, considering how much he seems to care about his estate.'

'So he does, ma'am, everyone says so. But...' Mary paused and bit her lip.

Emma was intrigued. 'But?'

'Well, Mrs Carrington, I did hear that once, a long time ago, when Sir David was young, he got into some trouble in London.'

'Trouble?'

'I'm not sure what exactly. Drink, maybe, or an unsuitable woman,' Mary whispered. 'But then his father almost let the estate go to ruin while he was gone and he came back. That's all I know. Just a bit of gossip, ma'am.'

'Yes,' Emma murmured. It was clear the maid would know no more. 'Thank you, Mary.'

As the maid hurried away, Emma sipped at her tea and turned those intriguing titbits of gossip over in her mind. So, once upon a time, the responsible Sir David had had a wild streak. Perhaps that was when he knew Betsy. But Rose Hill had brought him back, just as Barton Park had for her.

Most intriguing....

Chapter Thirteen

'So, is young Miss Marton to join us today?' Mr Lorne said.

Emma glanced up from her book, blinking and startled to find herself in the dusty, quiet bookshop and not in the colour and chaos of Restoration England. She had been immersed in Arabella's diary for what felt like hours now. It was a welcome distraction from thoughts of David and all that had happened between them. Of the gossip she had heard from Mary.

She smiled at Mr Lorne and said, 'I believe so. That is what Sir David's letter said.'

She'd been most surprised to get his message after their day outdoors. And, she was ashamed to think of it now, excited too, when she had seen it came from Rose Hill. She hadn't seen him since that day, and she was sure he regretted that he asked her to help Miss Beatrice. She avoided the village, afraid she might see him there and become quite tongue-tied and ridiculous when forced to make polite greetings to him and pretend nothing had happened.

But that didn't mean she ceased to think about him. Unfortunately, that was not the case at all. At night, she laid wide awake in her bed, remembering his kisses. The wondrous, soaring delight, and how she never wanted them to end.

And the way David looked when he saw her in Philip's arms. So cold, so remote—as if they hadn't just been so very close. And when Mary told her the tale of Sir David's youth, it was as if she didn't know him at all.

Emma wanted to cry when she thought about it all. Everything was so tangled up and upside down. She was mooning over David Marton like a silly schoolgirl and she hated it. Like the silly schoolgirl she herself had once been, in fact, fancying herself in love with the handsome dance master, Mr Milne. She'd been a fool then and she felt a fool now.

David was no Mr Milne, preying on a girl's fancies, she knew that very well. He was no Henry Carrington, either, living only for the moment and the desires of that one instant. David was a respectable man, as well as a devilishly attractive one. But that made him not for her and her dreams of his kisses were a hopeless waste of time.

But then again—he *had* asked if he could send Beatrice to her today. Surely that meant something? Feeling silly, Emma carefully laid aside the old diary.

'Sir David says he intends to hire a proper governess for his daughter and wishes for her to have some lessons to catch up first,' she said. 'I agreed to help if I can, but I fear Miss Marton may be too smart for me.'

Mr Lorne chuckled. 'She is a clever one, that child.

The quietest ones often are. Sir David is quite right to keep her mind occupied so she won't get into mischief. But I wouldn't worry, Mrs Carrington, you are quite equipped to teach any child. Did you not go to school yourself?'

Emma shook her head, thinking of her school. There had been little education there, among the worldly, gossipy daughters of fashionable families. And the too-handsome, deceitful dancing teachers. 'A finishing school for stylish young ladies with dancing and a little music and French. And Jane and I never had a proper governess. I learned haphazardly from my father's library. At least he never cared what we read, we had free rein among his books.'

'Books contain every answer, if we know where to look for them,' Mr Lorne said as he shelved a new shipment of poetry volumes from London. 'I understand you visited my friend Mr Sansom?'

'I did. He was most charming. He gave me these old diaries from Barton Park. I'm finding myself quite fascinated by them.'

'Did you have any luck in getting him to sell us his collection?'

Emma smiled at his use of the word 'us'. It made her feel as if maybe she was finding her place at last, even if it was behind the counter of a bookshop. 'Not yet. But I am sure he will let us have at least some of them soon. In the meantime, I feel as if I have made a new friend here.'

'Friends are a good thing to have.' Mr Lorne gave

her a sly smile over a stack of volumes. 'I hear that another one of yours has recently arrived in the village.'

Puzzled and disconcerted by his words, Emma said,
'I don't know what you mean, Mr Lorne.'

'I heard that a relation of your late husband was lodging at the Rose and Crown.'

Emma almost groaned aloud. If even Mr Lorne knew
of Philip's presence, surely that meant everyone did.
And she had come home to Barton hoping to escape
gossip! Philip had sent her notes asking for another
meeting since that day of his sudden arrival, but she
wasn't yet prepared to talk to him and find out his true
reason for coming.

She realised then she should have settled things with
him that very moment. If only her head had not been
whirling from David's kiss!

'Mr Carrington is my late husband's cousin, yes,'
she said quietly. 'He is passing through on his way to
a business appointment, I believe, and stopped to pay
his respects.'

'Mrs Smythe and her friend Miss Harding were in
to buy some of the new Minerva Press titles yesterday,'
Mr Lorne said. 'They were all a-flutter about how handsome this Mr Carrington is, and how he promised to
attend the next assembly. I'm sure they would be most
sorry to see him leave again too quickly.'

'Yes,' Emma murmured. Philip was indeed handsome. But nothing at all compared to David.

She thought of Miss Harding dancing with David,
the two of them looking so right together. And Mrs

Smythe's hopes for her brother's new match. Miss Harding would be a fool indeed to let Philip turn her head.

But no more a fool than Emma herself was for letting David turn *her* head.

She laughed at herself and turned back to the brittle pages of the old diary in front of her. Better to lose herself in the hopeless romances of people long gone than worrying any more about her own.

The bell over the door jangled and Emma looked up to see Beatrice entering the shop with her nanny. The little girl looked just as tidy and pretty as ever, like a little candy box in a pink pelisse and net bonnet, her hair tied at the nape of her neck with pink ribbon, unlike her messiness when they looked for botanic specimens. But her usual quiet, watchful air, so much like her father's, had vanished in a new smile. She hurried eagerly to the counter on her little pink kid boots.

'What are we going to learn today, Mrs Carrington?' she asked, her eyes shining.

'No, Miss Beatrice,' her nanny chided. 'Remember your manners.'

'Of course,' Beatrice said, bobbing a curtsy. 'Good day to you, Mrs Carrington. Mr Lorne. So delighted to see you again.'

Emma laughed. 'Good day, Miss Marton. I'm very happy you're so eager to continue your lessons.'

'Oh, yes, I am,' Beatrice said.

Her nanny took her leave, saying either she or Sir David would return for the child before teatime, and Emma helped Beatrice change her pastel pelisse for an apron. Mr Lorne lifted Beatrice up on to the stool next to Emma's, behind the pile of books Emma had chosen for her.

'These look marvellous,' Beatrice said. Emma wondered where the pale, quiet little girl had gone. Beatrice fairly shone with excitement.

'I wasn't sure where you wanted to start,' Emma said. 'I found some children's books on English history and some pamphlets on botany...'

Beatrice examined a copy of Aristotle that was nearby. 'When can I learn Greek, so I can read this?'

Emma laughed again, delighted at her eagerness. The little girl quite chased away her earlier silly broodiness. 'I'm afraid that Greek is quite beyond me. I can teach you French, and a little Italian and German, which I learned on my own travels. You'll need a special tutor for Greek, when you are older. In the meantime, we can start learning about another young lady who was eager to learn...' Emma pulled a biography from the bottom of the stack. 'Queen Elizabeth. I think she would be an excellent example for you and I found this lovely biography written for girls just your age.'

'Oh, yes,' Beatrice said as she opened the book to examine the engraved portrait on the endpapers. 'I saw a book from my father's library about the Spanish Armada once. I didn't realise she was once a child like me.'

The time happily passed with Beatrice reading about the young Queen Elizabeth and asking Emma questions about Tudor England as she went along. Emma continued in between with deciphering the old diary, making notes of things she found interesting.

'What are *you* reading, Mrs Carrington?' Beatrice asked.

'A very old diary your father's uncle gave me,' Emma said, showing her the faded ink writing on the crackling pages. 'It was written in the 1660s by a girl who once lived at Barton Park.'

'Did she know Queen Elizabeth, then?'

'No, the queen had been dead many years by then. But she does write about Charles the Second, who once visited Barton after he gave it to one of his friends. She mentions the family at Rose Hill, too, though I fear it's the old castle and not the one you live in now.'

Beatrice's eyes brightened and she leaned closer to examine the pages. 'Really? What else does she say? What was her name?'

Emma gave her an abbreviated account of the life of Arabella Bancroft, a poor cousin of the Bancroft who was given Barton Park by the king. Arabella witnessed parties at the new house and heard rumours of Court politics, all of which she shared in colourful detail. Arabella also had a budding romance with a handsome Cavalier, which Emma feared would not end well.

But Beatrice didn't need to know that part. Emma told her what houses like Barton and Rose Hill were like two hundred years ago and about the treasures of lost Royalist gold Arabella wrote about.

'A lost treasure?' Beatrice said. 'It sounds like a storybook.'

'It is, in a way. I've heard tales of the legend of Barton treasure since I was your age.'

'But is it true?'

'I don't know for sure. My father always thought it was true, but he could never find out where it was hidden.' And it drove him crazy in the end. Emma could never forget that.

'But he didn't have Arabella's diary, did he?'

'He gave it to Mr Sansom a long time ago.'

'Then maybe there is a clue in it your father didn't see,' Beatrice said thoughtfully.

Emma was somewhat alarmed to see the same spark for adventure and romance in Beatrice's eyes that had once been in her own father's. And her own, she feared. 'It is just a local legend. Queen Elizabeth is a much more important subject.'

Beatrice reluctantly went back to her book, until the bell over the door rang again. Emma looked up, expecting a customer—only to find it was Philip. There could be no more avoiding him now.

'Who would have guessed the loveliest ladies in all the village could be found in the bookshop?' he said cheerfully. 'And I have been searching for them for days in vain.'

'Good afternoon, Philip,' Emma said. 'As you can see, I have been working.'

'Working too hard even to see your cousin, eh?' Philip said, but he didn't seem put out by her avoidance. He smiled and strolled over to lean his elbows on the counter. 'And who is this fair maiden?'

'This is Miss Beatrice Marton,' Emma said. She felt strangely unsettled, but she couldn't quite decipher why. 'Miss Marton, this is Mr Carrington, who was cousin to my husband.'

Beatrice gave him a doubtful look. 'How do you do, Mr Carrington?' She slowly held out her hand to him.

Philip gallantly bowed over it. 'How do you do, Miss Marton? You must be the daughter of that chap I met a few days ago, Sir David Marton.'

'Yes, I am,' Beatrice agreed.

'I'm amazed he is so fortunate to have such a beautiful daughter,' Philip said teasingly. 'I hope he is very protective of you and carefully guards such a jewel.'

To Emma's surprise, Beatrice laughed. 'You sound like a character in a book.'

'The book you are reading right now?' Philip said, peeking at Beatrice's volume upside down across the counter. 'A life of Good Queen Bess, eh? Sounds quite weighty for such a petite girl.'

'I like it,' Beatrice said. 'Maybe you could have been someone at her Court, Mr Carrington. They liked to give compliments too.'

'Very wise of you, Miss Marton, to know so much about the Elizabethan age already,' Emma said, quite enjoying watching their light banter. Beatrice was actually smiling. 'Never believe flatterers, no matter what era they live in.'

Philip laid his hand over his heart and affected a wounded air that made both Emma and Beatrice laugh. 'I vow I speak only the truth! But Mrs Carrington is quite right, Miss Marton. You must read all you can and learn all about the world and the people in it. Tell me more about Queen Elizabeth.'

Beatrice showed him some of the illustrations in her book, explaining the various chambers of old palaces, the food and gowns and servants. Emma was amazed she had already absorbed so much information.

'And this is a great banquet for a foreign ambassador,' Beatrice said. 'I wish I could have seen the dances then. Were they much like the ones we have now at assemblies, Mrs Carrington?'

Before Emma could answer, Philip held out his hand to Beatrice and said, 'If you would do me the honour of partnering me, Miss Marton, I would be delighted to demonstrate a Spanish gavotte. Which my mother once made me learn to show off at a fancy dress party when I was about your age.'

Emma frowned. 'I am not sure…'

'Oh, please, Mrs Carrington!' Beatrice said eagerly. 'I do so want to try it.'

'I, too, would like to see a gavotte,' Mr Lorne said, leaning on the crate he had been unpacking.

'Oh, very well.' Emma gave in with a laugh. 'We are meant to be learning lessons, after all. Dancing should be included.'

Philip helped Beatrice off her stool and led her to a cleared space in front of the shelves. He bowed low and she gave a giggling curtsy.

'First we step like this,' Philip said. 'Then to the left. Hop. Hop, clap and spin.'

Soon they were whirling and twirling between the piles of books, Philip humming horribly out of tune as Emma and Mr Lorne clapped in time.

'Look, Mrs Carrington!' Beatrice called merrily. 'I am dancing.'

Emma laughed to see the delight on her pretty little

face. 'So you are—and very well, too. Philip, you have hidden talents!'

'If my fortunes wane, I can find work as a dancing master,' he answered.

'May I have this dance, Mrs Carrington?' Mr Lorne said with a wobbly bow.

'I would be honoured,' Emma said, and soon the four of them were twirling and spinning amid laughter and cries.

'These are the best lessons ever!' Beatrice called out, just as the door opened amid a jangle of bells.

David stepped over the threshold—and went very still at the sight of their hilarity. His solemn gaze swept over them, casting a chill over their impromptu ball.

Emma staggered to a stop and Beatrice suddenly toppled over, her hair bow askew. Philip lifted her up, until he too saw David watching them in silence.

'Papa,' Beatrice cried, 'I'm learning Elizabethan dances.'

'So you are,' David said quietly. 'It's not quite what I envisioned when I said you should have lessons…'

'Sir David…' Emma gasped, suddenly cold and dizzy after the giddiness of the dance. David was the last person she ever wanted to look foolish in front of, yet she always seemed to end up doing it anyway. 'We were reading a book about Queen Elizabeth, and Mr Carrington came in…'

'I do see,' David said, still very still and serious looking. He strode over to Beatrice and quickly retied her hair bow, drawing her away from Philip. 'It's getting rather late, I fear. We should be going home, Beatrice.'

'But, Papa…' she began.

'Now, if you please. Nanny will have your tea ready.'

Emma saw something she had never before glimpsed on Beatrice's face—the beginning of a pout. She leaned over to grab the child's hat and pelisse, and helped her put them on. She felt flustered and unsure and she didn't like that feeling at all.

'You must take the books with you, Miss Beatrice, and tell me what you've read in them next time I see you,' Emma said.

'Oh, I will, Mrs Carrington. I promise, I will read them all,' Beatrice said. 'Can I come back here very soon?'

'I'm sure Mrs Carrington must be very busy, Beatrice,' David said. He took his daughter's hand and led her toward the door. 'We cannot monopolise all her time.'

'Oh, but—' Beatrice cried.

'Say good day, Beatrice,' David said firmly.

The pout became fully formed, but Beatrice obediently made her curtsy. 'Good day, Mrs Carrington, and thank you very much.'

Then, to Emma's surprise, Beatrice ran over to hug her around the waist. Emma longed to hug her back, to hold her close, but Beatrice left as quickly as she had come. She hurried back to take her father's hand, her eyes downcast, all her giggling gone.

'Good day, Mrs Carrington. Mr Carrington, Mr Lorne,' David said. He led his daughter away and the door shut behind them, leaving stunned silence behind them.

'Well,' Philip said jokingly, 'he isn't much fun, is he?'

Emma had the strongest urge to rush to David's defence. After all, surely she herself was in the wrong for letting Beatrice's lessons get out of control? And yet—yet she was angry with David, too. They had been doing nothing wrong. She ran out the door just in time to see David helping Beatrice up into his curricle.

'Sir David,' Emma called.

He turned back to look at her, his handsome face blandly polite. She had come to hate the way that expression concealed so much from her. 'Mrs Carrington?'

'I—I hope you aren't angry at the…er…exuberance of today's lesson,' she said, a bit out of breath after her dash from the shop and desperately eager that he should not be angry with her. 'It won't be that way again. Mr Carrington came in most unexpectedly and—'

'Mrs Carrington, please don't worry,' he said politely and yet somehow impatiently. 'It is none of my business who your relations are, of course. I must only be concerned with my daughter.'

And being with her would not be good for Beatrice? 'Of course you must be. I only—'

'David, dear! What are you doing here at this time of day?' Mrs Smythe and her friend Miss Harding suddenly emerged from the draper's across the lane, waving to David and turning his attention from Emma.

Emma turned away, most unwilling to let the ladies see how flustered she was. The last thing she needed was more gossip in the village. She rushed back into the bookshop and slammed the door behind her. As she turned to pull the shades down on the window, she glimpsed Miss Harding linking her arm through David's and smiling up at him.

Emma spun around and marched back to the counter where she blindly shuffled books around. Mr Lorne had vanished behind the shelves.

Behind her, Philip peered past the edge of the shade, an expression of amusement on his face.

'If that's the level of amusing company in this place, Emma, I'm amazed you stay here,' he said. 'Especially after Italy and Germany. There's nothing like that life here, is there?'

Emma remembered all those spa towns, the casinos and ballrooms, the drunken men. 'No, and that is why I came back here. That is why I am trying to make a new life here, to fit in.' And she was obviously doing a very poor job of it.

'With such dry sticks as that Sir David Marton? He even looks bored right now, talking to that charming Miss Harding.'

Emma slammed a book down on the counter in a sudden fit of anger. She'd once thought David a 'dry stick' herself, when she was young and stupid, before life with Henry taught her what 'amusement' could do. Now she saw how very foolish she was then.

Now that it was all too late.

'Sir David is a very respectable and amiable man,' she said. 'Why are you here, Philip? I know this place cannot amuse you.'

He looked back at her over his shoulder, a grin still on his lips. 'I came here to see you, of course, Emma. We parted much too abruptly after Henry died.'

'I had to come home. There wasn't much choice.'

'But there was. I offered you my assistance, Emma. Indeed, I was most eager to give it.'

Emma closed her eyes against the spasm of pain the memory of that terrible time gave her. She had felt so alone, so lost. She'd only wanted home, peace, a place to belong.

For a few precious moments, when David kissed her, she had felt just that.

'You were very kind, Philip,' she said.

His face darkened and he let the shade drop into place. 'I wanted to be more to you, Emma, and you would not let me.'

Disconcerted, Emma glanced toward the shelves where Mr Lorne was hidden.

'Let me walk you home,' Philip said. 'I can see we have much to talk about.'

Emma didn't want to walk home with him. She didn't want to be reminded of the past any longer, to be in the company of one man when all she wanted was to be with another. Another who didn't seem to want her. But she knew she had to hear Philip out, for once he had been her only friend.

She quickly gathered her hat and the diaries, and bid Mr Lorne goodbye. When they left the shop, David's carriage was gone and Mrs Smythe and Miss Harding were nowhere to be seen. But Lady Wheelington was walking past and she stopped to greet Emma with an airy kiss on her cheek.

'Mrs Carrington, my dear, how lovely to see you!' Lady Wheelington cried. 'I must hurry on my way, for I am meeting Mrs Smythe, Miss Harding, and my future daughter-in-law at the church to plan Sunday's flowers. I think we may expect an interesting announcement there soon.'

Emma was still distracted by everything that had happened so quickly, but she did not want to be rude to Lady Wheelington at all. 'Indeed?'

'Oh, yes,' Lady Wheelington said with a laugh. 'Mrs Smythe is quite sure her brother is on the very verge of a match with Miss Harding, which would be quite the *on dit* in our little community, don't you think? A new Lady Marton for Rose Hill…'

He was so near to getting engaged? To Miss Harding? Emma swallowed hard and hoped she didn't look as stunned as she felt. 'Quite the *on dit,*' she managed to agree.

'But then, one can never quite rely on Mrs Smythe's information,' Lady Wheelington said as she headed on her way. 'I just hope my son will have plenty to occupy him in his place as vicar now. Come to tea soon, my dear, and we will have a long chat!'

In a daze, Emma turned toward the road to Barton, Philip walking silently beside her until they had left the village behind.

'So your respectable Sir David is to marry that pretty Miss Harding,' he said. 'Amazing.'

Emma glanced up to see a flash of something like anger in his eyes. He quickly covered it in a smile. 'You know Miss Harding, Philip?'

'I met her when I first arrived. She and Sir David

seem quite different from each other. But then, we all must do what we must.'

'Is that why you are here?'

'I came because I wanted to be sure you are well.'

'You could have written to me for that, rather than taking such a long journey. I know how much you enjoy life on the Continent.'

Philip was silent for a long moment, the only sound the crunch of the dirt and gravel under their feet, the chatter of the birds in the hedgerows.

'I did wish to see you again, Emma,' he said, his tone darker, angrier than she had ever heard from him. 'But also I wanted to show you this. I have had it on my conscience for some time.'

'Conscience?' Emma said, puzzled. 'Whatever do you mean?'

Philip took a much-folded, faded piece of paper from inside his coat. As they stopped near the gates to Barton, he handed it to her.

Emma quickly scanned it and found it was a promissory note signed by Henry and dated nearly a year ago, right before his death. It appeared Henry had lost a game of cards to Herr Gottfried, a man Emma remembered all too well. Herr Gottfried had then signed it over to Philip.

It was for a great deal of money.

Emma did not know what to make of it all. 'Henry still owed you this money when he died? But he assured me he had paid off all his debts before…' Before he intended to run off with his married lover. Before he was killed in that duel.

Philip leaned his fist against the stone wall that guarded Barton. 'I didn't want to burden you with it, Emma. Not when I had hopes we could be—closer.'

'Philip…'

'No, don't say anything else. I see now that my hopes were impossible, that you want a different sort of life than we could have together. I was going to forget this note, but…'

'But what, Philip? Surely we can be honest with each other now.'

Philip nodded, his face still shadowed. Distant. 'So we can. The truth, Emma, is that I had to use much of my legacy from my mother to buy this note. Herr Gottfried was not a nice man and Henry would have been in a great deal of trouble if this debt had stood. Henry vowed to pay me back, but as you see he died soon after. And I have found myself in rather dire straits since then.'

'You came here to ask me to pay back Henry's debts?' Emma said, a terrible certainty dawning over her. Her troubles with Henry were far from over.

'I came to see if you could possibly be interested in me, care for me, as I do you, Emma,' Philip said. 'But as I see now that is impossible, I must ask for something else. I need the repayment.'

Emma stared down at the creased note in her hand. It was a great deal of money, much more than she possessed, even with her legacy from her own mother, which was to go to the bookshop. She had tried so hard to pay off Henry's debts to tradesmen, forcing her to depend on Jane to get home to Barton. Philip had said nothing of it to her before, but she had no reason to doubt him. Philip *had* helped Henry out of trouble. Why bring it to her now, though?

She looked up at him over the paper and it was as if she was watching a stranger. Philip stared back at her, his face as hard as granite. Every vestige of Henry's laughing, carousing cousin, a man she herself had counted on as a lighthearted friend, was vanished.

'I am very sorry for it, indeed,' she said slowly. 'Henry was a careless man to us both. I wish you had told me of this before.'

'Perhaps I should have. But as I said—I had hopes.'

And now that he realised she couldn't love him, he thrust *this* at her? Emma's head was spinning at how quickly matters had changed between them. She didn't know what to do.

'I am afraid I can be of little help, Philip,' she said. 'You see how I am set up here. I live on the kindness of my sister right now.'

'Surely she would help you settle a debt of honour for your husband? She is married to an earl, after all.'

Yes, perhaps Jane and Hayden could help. Yet Emma could imagine the looks on their faces as she told them of another of her failures. As she asked them for help again, after she had vowed to herself she would look after her own needs from now on. They had enough to think about now with the twins and the new baby. Baby Emma. Whatever would her namesake think of her wayward aunt?

Emma just had to find a way to fix this herself.

Surely Philip's pride could not be so hurt that he had entirely forgotten their friendship?

'I cannot ask Jane,' she said.

'Really? I thought families were supposed to always be loyal to one another. That is what Henry always said. That is why I tried to help him, even when it was to my own detriment.'

Emma nodded. She remembered that very well. The nights Philip brought Henry home drunk and babbling, his money gone. The day Philip tried to stop Henry from duelling. Yet she also remembered that Philip was very often the one who led Henry into trouble in the first place. Philip, who was so much cleverer about *finding* trouble than Henry could ever have been.

'Jane has already helped me so much,' she said.

'Then perhaps they might come to know more about Herr Gottfried and his friends,' Philip said in a granite-hard voice. 'And the circumstances under which this was obtained. Surely you remember them, Emma?'

Emma shook her head, appalled to think of the night she had gone to the casino at Baden with Henry, hoping her presence there would make him behave a little better. Far from it, of course. Herr Gottfried and his loathsome friends had made her horrible propositions in German she could barely understand—until one of them grabbed her and pulled her on to his lap.

Henry had only laughed, already filled with brandy, and asked the Germans if they cared to make *her* part of the wager. She'd been forced to slap the horrible grabber in the face and kick him in his fat leg with her heeled shoe before she ran away, their coarse laugh following her.

Philip saw her home that night and every vestige of her affection for Henry vanished for ever.

She would be so ashamed if Jane knew that sordid tale, knew the sort of life Emma really lived as Henry's wife. The people who had been around her. She'd hidden the incident with Mr Milne, the school dancing master, from Jane for so long. She meant to hide as much as she could. What Jane already knew was bad enough.

And now Philip of all people was trying to *blackmail* her? She longed to slap him as she had that German bounder! To kick him and scream at him. But impulsiveness was what had got her into this mess in the first place. She had to be calm now and work out the best thing to do.

She slowly folded the nasty note. 'I will find your money. Jane doesn't need to know about this.'

Philip gave her a stiff nod. 'I am sorry it has come to this, Emma. I had sincerely hoped...'

Emma held the paper out to him. She was careful not to touch him when he took it back. 'Just leave now, Philip. Please. I will send you word when I have decided what to do.'

'Very well. Just don't take too long. I don't wish to stay at the Rose and Crown any longer than necessary.' He turned and strode away down the road, back towards the village.

Emma watched until she was sure he was gone, then she spun around and ran through the gates of Barton.

She didn't stop running until she had gained the safety of her own cottage and locked the door behind her.

She tore off her bonnet and tossed it to the floor. The books under her arm followed and she sat down heavily on the wooden planks to bury her face in her hands. Why was everything in such a mess?

She heard the click of Murray's paws on the floor and he nudged her with his cold nose and a whine.

Emma wrapped her arms around his furry neck and hugged him tightly. 'I'm such a fool, Murray,' she whispered. He answered with a lick to her cheek that made her laugh. 'But we can't sit here for ever. We have to figure out what to do now.'

Murray barked as if in agreement. Emma gathered up the books, the old diaries Mr Sansom gave her. As she dusted off the faded leather covers, she suddenly remembered the old tale she was reading in the bookshop, the one her father had loved so much.

The stolen treasure of Barton.

From the diary of Arabella Bancroft

The treasure is real! I must scribble these words in pencil as I am running away forthwith. My William has found where it must be at—among the ruins of the old medieval castle of Rose Hill. We are going there to search it out before anyone can discover us.

Please God let it be there. It would be the answer to all our troubles and we could be together at last.

Chapter Fourteen

'Papa! Papa, where are you going?'

David turned from Zeus to see Beatrice standing at the top of the stone steps, looking down at him on the drive. She wore an old brocade curtain around her shoulders for a cloak and he was sure she was pretending to be Queen Elizabeth again. She had done that a great deal since her day with Emma at the bookshop.

The day he found them dancing so freely with Philip Carrington—in a way he himself could never have been free.

'On an errand into the village,' he answered. 'Where is Nanny?'

'Asleep, of course. I was reading in the window seat and saw you down here.'

David made a mental note that it was time to talk to nanny about retiring. It was clear Beatrice was becoming far too lively for her.

And for him. Every time he turned around now, his quiet, watchful daughter was into some mischief. He suspected it was Emma's influence.

She hurried down the steps, her cloak flowing behind her. 'You aren't going to see that Miss Harding, are you?'

'I am going to see the lawyer,' he said, making another note not to let Louisa talk too freely around Beatrice about her matchmaking attempts. 'Why would you think I was going to see Miss Harding?'

'Aunt Louisa brought her here that day and told me to be nice to her. Aunt Louisa likes her. But I don't, not very much.'

David knew very well he should not encourage Beatrice's new outspokenness, but he still wanted to laugh. He'd been so worried about her since Maude died, afraid her spirit had gone into hiding for ever. Now it was back, stronger than ever.

And he had the feeling it was Emma to thank—or blame—for that. Emma, with her own imaginative delight in life. Beatrice had spoken of nothing but her since that day in the bookshop.

But he wasn't sure that was a good idea at all. She brought things out in him he had thought long suppressed.

'That isn't very kind, Beatrice,' he chided. 'Miss Harding was most polite to you.'

'I don't think she means it. I think she is only saying what she thinks she ought.'

'Sometimes that is what being polite means, I'm afraid. But why would you think that?'

'The way her eyes crinkle when she talks to me,' Beatrice said.

'Miss Harding is a most respectable young lady. She might be in the village for some time.'

'I don't mind if she stays in the village. I just don't want to try to talk to her very much. She knows nothing about anything interesting. I doubt she even knows who Queen Elizabeth was.'

David struggled not to laugh. 'Well, you don't have to talk to Miss Harding today. Go and read your Queen Elizabeth book and try to keep out of trouble until I get back.'

'I will.' Beatrice slid the toe of her slipper along the gravel of the drive. 'Papa, when can I go to the bookshop again for another lesson? I must tell Mrs Carrington I need new books to read.'

Mrs Carrington—he wanted to see her too, far too much. And he didn't think that was a good sign. She was becoming too much a bright spot in their lives. 'I'm sure Mrs Carrington is very busy. But we'll see. We can talk about it when I get back.'

He bent down for Beatrice to kiss his cheek and then swung up into Zeus's saddle. At the turn of the driveway, he glanced back and waved. Beatrice waved back from the top of the steps. With her reddish-gold curls and brocade drapery, she looked like a young queen. He realised with a pang that his daughter was indeed becoming a young lady and very soon he would have to make decisions about her future and his own.

He had to do something he never liked to do—examine his feelings.

Outside the gates of Rose Hill, he started to turn towards the road into the village. Suddenly he changed his mind. He tugged on Zeus's reins and sent the horse galloping toward Barton Park instead.

It was time for Emma Carrington and him to cease dancing cautiously around each other, to fully acknowledge the lightning of attraction and caution and need crackling between them.

It was time for him to be honest with himself and her. It was time to find a way to end things, once and for all. Before it all went too far and his passion got the better of him.

The old castle at Rose Hill. Surely that was where it had to be.

Emma looked up from the open diaries spread on the table in front of her, surprised to see the light at the window was a pale pinkish-grey sunset. She had given Mary the day off and settled down hours ago to read Arabella's diaries and finish deciphering them. Now the day was almost gone and the pot of tea she made herself long gone cold.

But surely she had the answer now, unless Arabella somehow carried the treasure off later, after her lover died. Yet the diary ended abruptly and Emma had no way of knowing what happened to Arabella Bancroft without more research. Arabella could not have gone too far, not if her diaries stayed all this time in the village. And the couple's last refuge was in the old castle.

Emma stood and stretched out her aching back, sore after so long bent over the old books. Her eyes itched from deciphering the faded ink and she was hungry, yet she also felt strangely energised. The hunt for the

Barton treasure was a futile idea, surely. It had been a legend for so long and no one had ever found it.

And yet—if she *could* find it, she could pay back Philip with no one ever hearing the whole shameful story of her life with Henry. She could refurnish the bookstore, too, make a real life here again. And surely then Philip would know for good that she could never, ever live with him.

If nothing else, Arabella's story had taken her out of herself for a while. Given her something to think about, dream about, besides David Marton.

Emma sighed at the thought of him. She hadn't seen him since he took Beatrice out of the bookshop so suddenly. Surely he would never let his daughter see her again after the chaos of her 'lessons' and Philip's presence there. Surely he had seen she was no good example for a little girl like Beatrice.

Possibly he was even engaged to the pretty Miss Harding now, as Lady Wheelington said.

Emma hurried over to kneel down by the fire and stir the embers to life. Murray roused himself from his bed to watch her and whined as if to remind her what time it was.

'I know, you haven't yet had your tea, poor old Murray,' she said, reaching out to pat his head. 'Perhaps you and I should do a bit of exploring tomorrow? We could go take a look at the old castle at Rose Hill, see what we can find.'

And if David didn't catch them there. The last thing she wanted was to look silly in front of him yet again! To be caught trespassing would be too embarrassing.

As she rubbed at the dog's soft ears, Emma thought about the treasure. If it *was* at the old castle, it wasn't terribly surprising her father had never found it. Her parents were never great friends with David's, despite how near their estates were. The Martons were too respectable and conventional for the eccentric Bancrofts. They wouldn't have let him on to their land, so he mostly dug about on Barton Park.

Murray whined again and Emma smiled down at him. 'I know. I'm just as hopeless as my father. But I must do something to make Philip go away.' Or she would lose everything here she had so carefully begun to rebuild.

Suddenly, a knock sounded at the door. Murray barked, and Emma jumped to her feet, startled.

'Don't let it be Philip,' she whispered, a cold sweep of panic touching her. He had said he would give her time. Surely it hadn't been long enough.

She heard another knock, and she knew she couldn't just hide. Hiding never solved anything. She quickly smoothed her hair and her simple muslin day dress and hurried out of the sitting room, Murray at her heels.

She pulled the door open and to her shock saw it was *not* Philip on her doorstep. It was David.

The dying sunlight cast his dark hair in a golden halo and he looked more handsome than ever. She thought her heart even skipped a beat at the sight of him, just as the silliest poets always said.

'I am sorry for calling unexpectedly, Mrs Carrington,' he said.

'Not at all,' Emma gasped, still in the grip of surprise. 'Please, do come in. I was just about to make some tea.'

'Thank you, I won't trespass on your time very long,' he answered, patting Murray's head as the dog eagerly clambered to greet him.

'I'm glad of the company,' she said, half-truthful. She *was* happy to see him. But she also worried about what he had come to say. She couldn't help but feel ridiculously hopeful.

Murray glimpsed a squirrel in the garden and dashed to chase it as Emma shut the door behind David and led him to the sitting room. She was very conscious of him close behind her with every step, and she couldn't believe he was really there, in her home. Almost as if her daydreams had conjured him.

'Please do sit down,' she said as she hastily rearranged the chairs. 'Mary has the day off, but I have learned how to warm my own tea at least.'

David slowly lowered himself into the chair where he sat the last time he was there and Emma couldn't help but remember the champagne. The dance. The kiss. Oh, good heavens, the *kiss*. Emma hastily turned toward the fire and reached for the kettle.

'Don't go to any trouble, Emma,' he said.

At least he was calling her 'Emma' again. Surely that was a good sign.

Maybe it would be a good time to ask him about the treasure and the castle. But she had to curb her impulses and be courteous.

'I was just doing a little reading,' she said. 'I have been wondering how Miss Marton was faring.'

'She is well,' he said. 'That is what I wanted to talk to you about.'

'I am sorry about the way you found us in the bookshop,' Emma said quickly. 'Philip quite surprised us, you see, and when he saw Miss Beatrice was reading about Queen Elizabeth—well, I fear he can be a bit… er…spontaneous.'

'Like his cousin, your husband?'

Yes, too much like Henry. She could feel herself turning warm at the thought that David knew that much about her erstwhile family. 'Something of the sort. But you must believe me, Sir David, I would never endanger Miss Beatrice in any way. She is a lovely, clever girl and I am very fond of her.'

She glanced back at David in time to see the austere, solemn lines of his face soften a bit. 'She is, indeed, and I know she much enjoyed her time with you. She keeps telling me facts about the Elizabethan age every time I see her. But she has no mother now and I must be very cautious for her.'

Emma swallowed hard. 'Of course you must.'

David leaned back in his chair, his fingertips tapping at the wooden armrest. 'I am sure you must have heard something of how I lost my wife.'

Maude Marton's infamous elopement. 'I have and I am very sorry.'

'Bea doesn't know the truth, of course, but I will never allow her to be hurt like that again. I won't allow scandal to touch her.'

'I do see,' Emma said slowly. She wanted to wrap her

arms around herself, to hold away the hurt she feared was coming. 'You are saying you fear I would embroil her in scandal if she spent time with me?'

A frown flickered over his face and then his jaw hardened again. Emma turned away to tend to the kettle, afraid to look at him any longer.

'Beatrice likes you very much,' he said, so careful, so controlled. Emma wished with all her might she could shake up that awful control. 'Indeed, you are the first person she has shown enthusiasm for since her mother died. I would like to find a way for you to spend time with her, if you are agreeable. But we must be—careful.'

Emma spun around to face him. She bumped into her sofa and impatiently pushed at the piece of furniture. 'Because your fiancée might see things the wrong way?'

The frown became full-fledged. 'My fiancée?'

'Miss Harding,' Emma said, feeling disappointed that the rumours could be true.

'Miss Harding? I am not engaged to Miss Harding, or anyone else. Where did you hear that?' he said, a puzzled look replacing the frown.

'Well, I…' Emma stammered, suddenly confused.

'I assure you, I am not engaged to Miss Harding. My only concern, Emma, is my daughter. I hope you do not misunderstand me.'

'I—no, of course not. I…' Emma was utterly baffled. David always had her in a whirl. Her feelings for him, the puzzle of him. 'You surely must marry *someone*. Everyone says so.'

David suddenly rose to his feet, anger and amusement warring in his expression. 'Will *you* marry again? Because everyone says you should?'

'I have had quite enough of marriage,' Emma scoffed.

'And so have I. You shouldn't listen to gossip, Emma. Surely you and I both know how very wrong it can be.'

Emma shook her head and pressed her hands over her eyes. She wished she was merely watching this scene on a stage, that she could make the actors go back and erase lines, start again in a way she could understand. 'My life has been ruled by gossip, for as long as I can remember. There is no escape. I thought if I came home, I could escape it and begin again. But all I found is that it's even worse here. At least on the Continent, no one knew me, not really, but here, with people I care about so much…'

Emma spun around, unable to face him a moment longer. She had almost given herself away. The atmosphere in her little sitting room suddenly seemed to crackle, like on a stormy night when lightning flashed against the windows.

'People you care about?' he said softly.

She felt him move closer to her in the strained silence of the room, felt the warmth of his lean body. The clean, heady scent of him. How could he not know? Surely he saw how she had foolishly come to care for him. All the reasons she had disliked him when she was a silly girl—his quiet dignity, his care for the people around him, his subtle good humour—drew her to him now. He was all she was not and she craved that so very much.

She craved *him* and the way he made her feel when he was near. The way he made her want to be better, to be worthy of a life with him. But she had no idea how to even begin to do that.

'I would never want my actions to hurt Beatrice,' she said roughly. 'I know you think I am not the sort of woman she should be around. You gave me a chance and I just ruined it—'

'You have no idea what I think, Emma,' he suddenly burst out. She felt his hand close hard on her arm, spinning her around to face him. Her eyes flew open and she stared up at him to find his face dark and hard, his eyes glowing fiercely. 'You have no idea what I feel.'

'Because you will not let me see!' she cried, afraid she would start sobbing at the taut, hot emotions of the moment. At his nearness. 'You won't let anyone see.'

'I can't let anyone see,' he said. His other hand closed around her other arm, holding her with him. She could feel the tension in his whole strong body, as taut as a drawn bowstring. 'I can never lose control, too much depends on me. But I *do* feel, Emma. By Jove, but I feel so much, especially when you are near. I've never known anyone like you. I think about you far too much. I can't be like...'

Emma's tears fell in earnest now, she couldn't hold them back. She'd held them in far too long, held back her emotions that had been growing and growing for David until she feared they would drown her.

But now he was holding her close, words exploding from him in a torrent she would never have imagined could come from him. She wanted more and more of it, wanted to know everything about him.

'Be like what?' she sobbed.

Instead of answering with words, he pulled her closer.

Chapter Fifteen

Davin silenced her tearful words with the simple expedient of his mouth over hers in a hard, desperate kiss.

How she had longed for this! Dreamed of it in her lonely bed at night. How *right* it felt, her emotions swinging wildly from anger to hot desire.

And David seemed to feel the same. His tongue thrust into her mouth, as if he was hungry for the taste of her, and she met him with an equally fiery need. She felt as if she had jumped into a volcano, consumed by flames. She didn't want to escape, though. Ever.

Her hand slid from his shoulder down his hard, warm chest. Her fist curled into his slippery silk waistcoat and she drew him even closer. She could feel the alluring heat of his body through her muslin gown and she knew it still wasn't close enough. Feeling suddenly bold, she tugged open the buttons of that silk waistcoat and slid her fingers between the folds of his shirt to at last touch bare, smooth, warm skin. The lean, hard strength of him.

She felt him groan against her hand. He deepened

the kiss and she went up on tiptoe to meet him eagerly. She was determined to remember this glorious moment, every taste and touch, every glorious pleasure. His mouth slanted over hers and their kiss tumbled down into frantic need.

There was no turning back, not for her. Not for him either, as his hands closed hard on her waist and held her up against him. His warm lips traced the curve of her throat as her head fell back, and he kissed the soft skin of her shoulder through the thin muslin of her gown.

She remembered rumours that once upon a time David had not been quite so proper as he was now and it seemed sometimes that old naughtiness still came out. She was wildly glad to see it.

'David, please,' she whispered, burying her fingers in his hair. It slid like silk against her skin and she suddenly felt ecstatically happy.

'Oh, Emma,' he groaned. His hand closed over the gathered edge of her sleeve and he slid it down a mere inch. 'Let me see you, please.'

'Yes,' was all she could say. She was overcome by the raw, heady pleasure of his touch.

They tumbled back to the sofa and David drew her loose bodice down to reveal her lace-trimmed chemise. His dark head dipped and his lips closed over her aching nipple through the soft cotton. His other hand grasped the hem of her gown and chemise and he dragged them up over her leg until the fabric was wrapped around her waist. She wore no stockings, and she felt the heat from the fire on her bare skin, the fine wool of his breeches a delicious friction that made her moan.

And she felt his erection, hot and hard, straining against the confines of the fabric.

He laid her back against the cushions of the sofa behind them, his body heavy over hers, his mouth warm on her breast. She wrapped her legs around his hips and held on to him.

She was spread beneath him, vulnerable, open to all his desires—and her own. She closed her eyes and let herself fall down into the whirling, sparkling darkness of need.

'Emma,' he whispered. The top of his tongue circled her nipple as his hand slid over her bare thigh, drawing her higher and harder against him. He traced an enticing pattern on her skin, and then to her delighted shock she felt his fingertip press to the seam of her damp womanhood. She cried out at the rush of sensation from that one light touch.

'Do you want me, Emma?' he whispered roughly. 'As I want you?'

Did she want him? She had never felt anything like this desperate, primitive need.

'Yes,' she moaned. 'Yes, more than anything.'

He rose up over her and his mouth covered hers with a sizzling kiss. She felt his hand reach between them to unfasten his breeches, freeing his manhood at last from its confines.

'Emma, I'm sorry, but I can't wait,' he said hoarsely. 'I need you now.'

'Yes,' was all she could say.

With a twist of his hips, he slid deep into her and they were joined at last.

Emma arched up into him, crying out at the wondrous pleasure. She pushed his shirt away from his strong shoulders and held him close. She could hear his breath, the pounding of his heartbeat in rhythm with hers.

They moved together, apart and together again, deeper and deeper, faster, as the passion overcame them.

'Hold on to me,' he said as his lips slid along her neck and his arms came around her to draw her body tight against his.

She wrapped her legs close around his hips, holding on to him as she let herself move higher against him. She felt him thrust even deeper and she cried out at the sensations.

She called out his name incoherently, pushing her hands under his loosened shirt to trace the shift and flex of his muscles as he moved even faster. Even then she did not feel quite close enough. She wanted to be part of him and make him part of her. She hadn't realised until that instant that he was exactly what she longed for, for so long. And he was here with her, as close as two people could be.

How could she ever let him go after this?

He moved faster, less controlled, more frantic. It was never like this with Henry and his hurried, drunken fumblings. She'd never felt such pleasure before.

Deep down inside, she felt a hot pressure growing, expanding, covering her whole body. Sparks seemed to dance over her skin, consuming her. Every coherent thought fled, and all she could do was feel.

'David,' she gasped. 'What…?'

'Let it happen,' he said hoarsely. 'I'm here. I'll catch you.'

He buried his face against her shoulder and his body stiffened as he groaned at his own climax. He shouted out her name and suddenly drew out as delight exploded within.

He fell back beside her on the sofa, their arms and legs entangled. Emma closed her eyes and let herself float for a moment. She could feel David's weight pressed against her side, their heat of their damp skin pressed together, the night gathering around them to enclose them in its dark privacy.

'You are so very beautiful, Emma,' he whispered hoarsely.

Emma felt her cheeks turn warm and she turned her face away from him. It seemed ridiculous to feel so shy over a compliment after what they had just done, how intimately they lay together now, but the deep sincerity in his simple words made her want to cry.

'David,' she murmured.

He ran a gentle caress over her hair. 'Surely you've head that many times and far more poetically than I could ever say it.'

Emma turned on to her side and curled up against him as he covered them with his coat. She had never felt warmer, safer, than she did in that moment with his arms around her. It made her feel content, as she never had before in her life. She wished she could smash the clock over the mantel and make that moment stay for ever.

But she knew she couldn't. She could just revel in it now and hold him close.

She twined her fingers with his where his hand rested on her waist. She knew she had to give him honesty now.

'I've been given compliments before, yes,' she said. 'And when I was young and wilful, I let my head be turned by them. I hope I have learned better now, that I have learned to tell a sincere truth from a manipulative lie.'

David gently turned her in his arms so she looked up at him. His hair was rumpled, his eyes bright as he looked frankly into hers. He traced his fingertip lightly over her lips and the curve of her jaw, looking at her as if he studied her, memorised her. As if he really *saw* her. Not the scandal, but the real her.

'Well, you can believe me when I say that you are beautiful,' he said, his voice deep and rough. 'The most beautiful woman I have ever seen.'

He pressed a gentle kiss to her brow and Emma closed her eyes against the wave of emotion that swept over her. She turned again in his arms and listened to the crackle of the fire, the sound of his breath.

'Will you tell me what happened to you, Emma?' he said. 'What hurt you so much you can't believe anyone would think you are beautiful?'

Emma shook her head, thinking of Philip and how he insisted he had to hurt her because he cared about her so much. 'The past should be gone. I *want* it to be gone. But it won't let me send it away.'

'I know what you mean,' he answered slowly. 'There are people, things, that can never be changed or erased.'

Emma remembered what she had heard of his marriage, and she wondered if that was what he spoke of. If his wife still made him so cautious. 'Your wife?'

David went very still and she feared perhaps she'd said too much. Pried too far. 'Yes. She is one of those things that can't be changed or forgotten.'

Emboldened by the quiet, steady seriousness of his voice, Emma said, 'Did you love her very, very much?'

'I am sure you must have known what happened with Maude in the end,' he said starkly.

'I know she ran away and then died. But that doesn't mean that perhaps you didn't love her at first. I thought I loved Henry, until I discovered who he truly was. And then I mourned for my dream of him when he was gone.'

'Yes. I suppose I was much like that with Maude, though I never thought of it that way.'

'Do you try not to think of her at all?'

David gave a rueful laugh. 'I fear my sister and her love of a gossipy tale would never let me do that. She is still quite convinced there was just some misunderstanding between Maude and me that would have mended if she hadn't died when she did. Louisa thinks if she could just find me another woman like Maude…'

A woman like the pretty, vivacious Miss Harding? A better Lady Marton, a more faithful one, but just as sociable and perfect as Maude Cole once seemed. Emma shivered. 'But you don't?'

'Maude and I were mismatched from the beginning, though I was far too busy and too selfish to see it,' he answered. 'It was time for me to marry and she seemed very suitable. We got along well enough. I thought once she settled into being Lady Marton she would be happy. But I could never have made her happy. She wanted things I simply don't have to give.'

'I can't imagine that could be true,' Emma said. David was handsome, kind, perceptive, intelligent— and a wonderful lover, too. What else could the silly woman have wanted? He was all Emma could desire— if she hadn't been a foolish girl and ruined her future in one impulsive act. Now all she could have with him was this night.

'She wanted adventure. I have Rose Hill and my family and tenants to think of,' David said. 'She put all I care about most at risk. But she did give me Beatrice, so I can never hate her. My daughter was a great gift.'

'Yes,' Emma said quietly. 'Beatrice is a lovely child indeed.' And it was obvious David loved her with all his heart. She was another thing he would fiercely protect.

'Did you love your husband, Emma?' he asked.

Emma swallowed hard past the knot of emotion in her throat. 'I—I once thought I did. I thought I loved him so much that such a love would be worth defying even my sister's advice, that if we were only together all would be right in the end.'

'It didn't end up that way?'

'No,' Emma said. And then she told him something she had never admitted to anyone, not even herself. 'I was only a challenge to Henry. Once he had me, he wasn't quite sure what to do with me. And I was no great heiress who could support his lifestyle.'

She took a deep breath and went on. 'Before Henry, when I was at school, there was a dance teacher named Mr Milne. He flirted with me a bit and I must admit I was flattered. I was lonely at school, you see, away from family for the first time, and I wanted him to like me. I fear he took it for encouragement and tried to kiss me one night in a dark classroom.'

'Emma….' David said, his tone very dark. His arms went still around her.

She laughed. 'When I slapped him, he said I had lured him on with my beauty. That I could not blame a man for being so tempted when I wouldn't behave like a lady. That is why it is hard for me to believe it when someone says I am beautiful, that they don't want anything from me in return.'

In silence, David turned her again in his arms and softly kissed her lips. Looking into her eyes, he said, 'Emma Bancroft. You are truly beautiful.'

Emma was sure she would start crying at the stark simplicity of his words. With David, she believed them.

'Just sleep now,' he said, drawing his coat closer around her. 'I'll make up the fire and let Murray in. Don't worry about anything.'

Suddenly very weary, Emma nodded and closed her eyes. She let herself sink deeper into his arms and let the warm darkness of sleep close around her. It blocked out everything she worried about—Philip, money, the future, the past. All she knew was David next to her, holding her.

She knew it wouldn't always be this way. But she would hold on to it as long as she dared.

* * *

From the diary of Arabella Bancroft

We are discovered.

My cousin found out we had run here, and he cannot bear for anyone else to have the Barton treasure he is sure must be his. We hid in the old cellar, holding on to each other, but William was snatched from my arms. Now I am locked in my chamber and I fear my William is gone for ever.

Chapter Sixteen

David lay very still next to Emma, watching her as she slept. The flickering red-coral firelight gleamed on the tumbled spill of her golden hair and the smooth perfection of her skin. Her lips curved in a small smile, as if she was lost in a pleasant dream.

He would give anything to have been the one to make her smile like that. To give her that sort of happiness. But he feared he could never be that person.

David gently slid away from the enticing warmth of Emma's body and quickly righted his clothes before letting her dog in from the garden. Murray gave him a suspicious glance, but quietly settled into his bed by the fire. David found a blanket tossed over one of the chairs and tucked it around Emma so she wouldn't be chilled.

She sighed and stirred in her sleep, but she didn't wake. David sat down in the chair beside her and stared into the dancing flames.

He'd come to Emma's house, after pacing in front of her gates for a long time trying to decide what best to say, to tell her they should try to be as distant as possible. That it couldn't be good for them to try to be friends—not when he longed to kiss her every time he saw her. Not with that tugging rope of attraction always between them.

He remembered what she said about how their world was ruled by gossip. It was all too true. He had always tried to shield his family, his daughter, from it as much as possible. Especially since Maude's recklessness almost destroyed them. Beatrice didn't need to know such sordid things about her mother.

Emma couldn't help but attract gossip, with her beauty, her spirit, the impulsive affection of her nature. She was precisely the sort of person he had vowed to stay away from in his life.

And yet it was exactly those qualities—her glowing, vibrant, joyful life—that drew him close to her over and over. That made him crave to be in her presence.

Emma had an unquenchable glow within her that refused to be extinguished, and it warmed the coldness that had always seemed lodged like a paralysing shard of ice in his heart. Her passion for life, for sensation and fun and learning, made him want them too.

Ever since he saw her dancing in the old orchard, her arms outflung, her hair glowing in the sun, he had wanted her and all she was more than he had ever wanted anything. He fought against it, fought to stay frozen in his old, safe ways, but he couldn't stay away.

Emma murmured in her sleep and David reached over to gently tuck the blanket closer around her. He smoothed a gentle caress over her hair, letting the warm, soft length of it trail over his arm as a bolt of sheer, burning longing washed over him.

She was so fragile, so soft under his touch. The thought that anyone could dare hurt her, as her villain of a husband had, made him utterly furious. If the man wasn't already dead, David would find him and strangle him right then.

Emma's trusting, impulsive nature had led her into so much trouble. Once he had been sure she was something like his wife, willing to cause scandal for her own selfish ends. Emma was so very different from her quieter sister. But he saw now that Emma had none of Maude's cold heart. Emma would never willingly hurt a child as Maude had Beatrice. The fact that Bea, who was usually so very cautious, had clung to Emma so fast, and that Emma returned her affection and even understood what Bea needed in a way he couldn't, showed him that.

Emma's own stark pain over her past, the hope for the future in spite of it all, her love for her sister and willingness to work hard at the bookshop, showed him so clearly that he had been wrong about her.

And yet, the past was still there and always would be. Emma's impulsive nature was still there. And so were his own cautious ways. He couldn't afford to abandon them, not even if he had come to care too much for Emma. To want her, crave her.

Yes, he wanted to watch over her, to make sure she was never hurt again. He wanted that more than he had ever wanted anything. And that realisation scared him.

David pushed himself up from the chair, suddenly

restless to take action. He had to know the truth, the *whole* truth. Then he would know what to do.

He quickly put on his coat and bent down to kiss Emma's cheek one last time. Her skin was soft and warm under his lips, and desire surged through him. He wanted to crawl under the blanket with her, to claim her mouth with his and feel her body move against his again. But he steeled himself against the burning lust. He had work to do now and no time to lose.

Her eyes fluttered open, and she gave a sweet, sleepy smile. 'Is it morning? I thought maybe it was all a dream…'

A dream indeed. One David was reluctant to wake from, but he knew he had to. 'Not a dream, I promise. It's not morning yet, but I need to leave before it is.'

She blinked and the sleepy sweetness vanished. She looked worried before she turned on to her side, her face half-hidden from him. 'David…'

'I won't apologise, Emma, I promise,' he said fiercely. He couldn't bear to hurt her, as so many people had, to make her feel ashamed. But neither could he yet make her fully his. Not until he could be sure. And maybe that would never be possible. 'I will see you again very soon.'

'Of course,' she said, 'soon.'

David kissed her one more time, then hurried out of the cottage before he could give in to the strong temptation to stay. He had work to do now and he couldn't afford to let his heart lead the way. Not with so much at stake.

But he still couldn't help but pluck a small blossom from the first of the rosebushes over her door and tuck it into his pocket to remind him of Emma. Half-hidden beneath the bush, he glimpsed a folded letter, no doubt lost in the mail delivery. He slid it back under her door and turned for home, with his keepsake rose safe with him.

If only he could hold Emma just as safe.

Chapter Seventeen

'David! You cannot let Beatrice visit that woman again.'

'Good day to you, too, Louisa,' David said as he looked up from the estate ledgers open on his library desk just in time to see his sister sweeping into the book-lined room. The tall plumes on her bonnet waved madly, along with her lace-gloved hands. She was obviously in a state over something, as usual, but he was damned if he knew what it could be.

He could barely even see the numbers in front of him. All he could think about was Emma. Emma, as he had last seen her, sleepy and sweet, her skin bare to him.

'What seems to be amiss?' he said, pushing away those lascivious memories as his sister continued to flutter around the room.

Louisa plumped herself down in the armchair across from the desk. 'Is it true that you let Beatrice see Mrs Carrington? At the bookshop?'

Ah, so *that* was what this unannounced visit was about. He didn't like the pinched, disapproving look on Louisa's face when she said Emma's name. He sat back in his chair and studied her calmly over his steepled fingers.

'Indeed she did,' he said. 'Bea has proved to be quite fond of learning, and has been reading with Mrs Carrington while I look for a suitable governess. Is there some sort of problem, Louisa?'

Louisa threw up her hands. 'Brother, what can you be thinking! You are usually so very sensible; we all rely on you. But you must see that Mrs Carrington is not suitable to be a companion to a young girl like Beatrice. Children can be so impressionable. One can never be too careful.'

David almost laughed at his sister's temerity in lecturing him about parenthood, when everyone in the village saw how wild her sons were. But he could not laugh at her disparagement of Emma. Certainly not after what happened last night.

'Mrs Carrington is from a family whose estate has long neighboured our own,' he said carefully. 'Her sister is a countess and she herself is known to be a most intelligent lady. Bea likes her.'

'And I see that you do, too!' Louisa cried. 'Oh, David, how could you? And Miss Harding so very fond of you. I was so hoping you would escort her to the assembly rooms next week for the concert. I know she hoped so as well.'

David could see he needed to nip all this in the bud right at that moment. 'I never encouraged Miss Harding in any way, Louisa, you know that very well. And just because I allow Beatrice to spend time with Mrs Carrington does not mean I am contemplating anything improper with her.'

No, he was not contemplating it—he had already done it. And he wanted more than anything to do it again. The question now was, where did he and Emma go next? Would she have him? Or would they only be making a terrible mistake together, re-enacting the mistakes of the past?

Either way, it was not the business of Louisa or anyone else. He wouldn't let Emma be exposed to any more gossip.

'I think we have said enough on this topic, Louisa,' he said firmly. 'When I have made matrimonial decisions in the future I shall inform you of them. But no more matchmaking, I beg you.'

'Well,' Louisa huffed. 'I only ever try to help, Brother. And I am quite shocked at your lack of judgement when it comes to Mrs Carrington. Why, only just this morning I heard Lady Firth say that her butler, who had gone to run an errand a few towns over, saw her going into the shop of Mr Levinson the jeweller. And you know what *that* means.'

David froze. 'It probably means she was buying a gift for her sister's new baby.'

'Certainly not!' Louisa cried. 'Everyone knows Mrs Carrington is in no position to give expensive gifts to anyone, not after her shockingly bad marriage. Everyone also knows that Mr Levinson gives a very good price for jewels when ladies find themselves in shocking debt.'

David frowned as he tapped his fingertips on the

ledger page. He had always had the suspicion that he didn't know everything about Emma, not even after their night together. What had she been doing at Mr Levinson's shop this very day? It was true what Louisa said. Everyone knew that often ladies who found themselves in embarrassed circumstances went there to sell jewels. But Emma shouldn't be in such trouble now that she was home, now that she had Lord and Lady Ramsay to protect her.

But the Ramsays weren't home and Emma was alone. David had the sense that Philip Carrington must have something to do with it all, something Emma was hiding. Especially if he was like his rakish cousin.

The man's appearance in the area, his hanging around everywhere like the bookshop, was annoying to say the least. Louisa giggled about how handsome he was, how charming, but David didn't like the possessive way the man looked at Emma. He had to find out who the blighter really was, what he had in his past. That could require a trip to London, but now David did not want to leave Emma unprotected.

Whatever trouble Emma had got herself into, he had to find out what it was. Now.

David pushed himself back from the desk and strode to the library door. 'I'm sorry, Louisa, but I must go out on an urgent errand.'

'Right now?' his sister said. She scurried after him into the hall just in time to hear him send the footman for his horse. 'David, what is the meaning of this?'

'I will explain later, Louisa,' he answered, though his thoughts were far away, with Emma.

'You must come home with me at once,' Louisa said.
'I am meeting Miss Harding this afternoon and I am
sure all can be mended with her now you know the truth
about that unfortunate Mrs Carrington.'

The truth about Emma? David feared he had only
just begun to discover the many enticing, surprising
layers that made up Emma Bancroft Carrington. And
now he was afraid for her.

If she was in trouble…

David hurried out the front door and grasped Zeus's
reins to swing himself up into the saddle. He had to find
out what was happening to Emma. Now.

Beatrice stared down past the gilded railings to the
hall below, watching as her aunt burst into tears. Past
the open front doors she could see her father galloping
down the drive, not even wearing a hat. The footmen,
usually so perfectly postured and expressionless, gave
each other bewildered glances.

It felt as if Rose Hill had been turned upside down
and shaken hard. She hardly knew what to think.

Even in London, when her mother would breeze in
and out of the house so unpredictably and there were
often parties of odd people laughing in the drawing
and dining rooms, her papa was a quiet, calm constant.
Today there were tears and angry words, and her aunt
having hysterics.

Beatrice almost stamped her foot in consternation
that she hadn't been able to hear the whole conversation between her father and aunt. All she knew was that
Aunt Louisa said they should have nothing to do with

Mrs Carrington any more and that Papa should marry that silly Miss Harding.

Well, Beatrice was having none of that. Mrs Carrington was wonderful and Bea would *not* give her up. Ever.

If she was still a baby, she would have laid down on the floor and wailed out her woes. But grown-up ladies could do no such thing. Grown-up ladies had to find other ways to get what they wanted. Reading about Queen Elizabeth had taught her that. When Elizabeth was a young, powerless princess, she had to be very clever and very sneaky to stay out of trouble and achieve her ends.

Only when she was queen could she pitch fits.

Beatrice would just have to find a way to show her papa what was really good for them: Mrs Carrington. But how?

Aunt Louisa swung around to storm back toward the library. Beatrice ducked down so her aunt wouldn't see her. Only once the library door slammed shut did she tiptoe back up to the nursery.

Nanny was snoring by the fire, as usual. The Queen Elizabeth book lay open on the window seat and Beatrice went to fetch it. Yet she couldn't quite lose herself in its pages as she usually could. She stared out the window at the sunny day, trying to figure out what she should do.

Then she glimpsed the tumbling stones of the old castle in the distance and remembered Mrs Carrington's tale of the lost treasure and the parties they used to have at Barton Park and Rose Hill, when Charles the Second was king.

It was a nice day. Maybe she needed a bit of exercise. That was what nanny always told her—to run along and play, and not be bothersome. Usually Beatrice just wanted to sit and read her books, but today a bit of exploration sounded fun.

And just maybe she could slip over to Barton for a bit, too...

'I heard he has even been letting his daughter visit her. He must like her a great deal, though I must say I am surprised at Sir David.'

'Quite. A careful, respectable man like him—and Mrs Carrington? Most unaccountable.'

'But she is a countess's sister, so she would be a fair match for him, I suppose. If only...'

Melanie Harding had not stayed any longer in the doorway of the draper's shop to listen to old Lady Firth and her equally elderly friend gossip. She'd heard all she needed to hear.

He was never going to marry her. Rose Hill was never going to be hers. She hadn't imagined the look of polite indifference on his face when she called with Mrs Smythe. He preferred an old widow like that Mrs Carrington. The fool.

Melanie hurried down the street, not seeing anyone she passed or any of the enticing window displays. All she could think of was what she had lost, before it was even really hers.

Suddenly she caught a glimpse of Philip Carrington

striding toward the Rose and Crown, and some spark of reckless hope took flame inside of her. The sunlight gleamed on his poetically tumbled golden curls, and his shoulders looked so broad and strong in his dashing greatcoat. Surely he was far more handsome, far more interesting than David Marton could ever be.

And Melanie was quite, quite desperate. She did not want to go back to her uncle's dismal house.

'Mr Carrington!' she called as she hurried across the street toward him. 'What a delightful coincidence to see you here today. Do you perchance have time for tea?'

Chapter Eighteen

Emma paced the length of the forest clearing and back again. The coins in her reticule felt heavy, the fruits of selling her wedding ring and her mother's pearl pendant to a jeweller in a town several miles away. It hadn't been as much as she hoped, but maybe it would be enough for now. She desperately hoped it would be enough.

If she ever hoped to be good enough for David, she had to make Philip go away. His presence in the village was always a reminder of her past. She had to be done with all that now.

She turned and paced back again. The only sound she could hear was the harshness of her own breath, the brush of her boots through the leaves, the whistle of the wind in the leaves. Pale, watery sunlight filtered through the trees on to patches on the ground. She had never felt quite so alone.

Surely Philip would come? That was what his note said, to meet him here at this hour. Even despite his blackmail, she had to believe he would keep his word.

He couldn't be all bad. Her old friend must still be in there somewhere.

At last she heard the pounding of horse's hooves along the pathway and she spun around to see Philip come into the clearing. His hat hid his face and she couldn't see his expression.

'I thought perhaps you weren't coming,' Emma said.

A whisper of Philip's old grin flashed over his face, only to be quickly gone. 'I asked you to meet me, did I not? A bargain is a bargain, Emma. You have something for me, then?'

Emma held out the purse and he came down from the horse to walk towards her. Her chest felt tight and she wondered if this had perhaps not been the wisest place to meet him. They were alone, so far from everyone else.

Yet that was why it seemed like a good place. She couldn't let anyone see her with Philip. And she felt the weight of the small dagger tucked into her sash under her spencer.

He took the purse and opened it to peer inside. 'This isn't the amount we agreed,' he said angrily.

Emma took a deep breath, forcing herself to stay calm. 'I know. I will find the rest later. This is all I have now, but it is more than enough for you to leave here and establish yourself somewhere else.'

'It's not good enough, Emma,' he said.

'I know, but I want to help you, Philip. I do,' Emma said desperately. 'We were both ill treated by Henry and we deserve a new start. Don't we? I am willing to help you make yours, if you will help me make mine.'

Philip was silent for a long, heavy moment. He stared down into the purse. 'It's because of that David Marton, isn't it? He is the reason you are so very eager to be rid of me.'

'Why do you say that?' Emma said, trying to sound casual, to not give anything away.

Philip snapped the purse shut. 'I've seen the way you look at him. He's the reason you're so anxious to forget about your old life, your old friends.'

'Sir David has nothing to do with this,' Emma said, suddenly angry. 'My family…'

'Your family has nothing to do with this!' Philip shouted, frightening her. 'He isn't worthy of you, Emma. He is too dull, too…'

'No,' Emma cried, shaking her head fiercely. 'I won't hear you speak against him. He is the best of men. If anything, I am not worthy of him, or you would have nothing with which to blackmail me now.'

'Blackmail? Such an ugly word to use, Emma.'

'What else could it be?'

'I wanted to have you as my own,' Philip said roughly. 'When you wouldn't listen to reason, what else could I do?'

'So you claim to love me, yet seek to hurt me?' Emma shook her head, bewildered. But she saw one thing so clearly now, thanks to David. 'Once I mistook pain and drama for love, too. But no more. Love is not cruel, Philip. Love is—is…'

Philip suddenly lunged forwards and grabbed her in his arms. Panic and fear rushed over her, blinding, just like with Mr Milne and Herr Gottfried. She struggled to twist away, but he held her too tightly and she couldn't breathe. His lips came down on hers, suffocating her.

Philip was a skilled lover and he put all his expertise into that kiss, Emma could feel it through her fear. Yet his kiss was nothing like David's and she longed only to be free of it.

She managed to slip her fingers into her sash and grasp the hilt of the dagger. It was a ridiculous thing, an antique that once hung on the wall in her father's library along with his other curiosities, but now she was desperately glad she brought it with her. She yanked it free and pressed the tip to Philip's side.

He froze and his lips finally slid away from hers. 'Emma…' he said hoarsely.

'Just let me go,' she whispered. 'Let me go and leave this place. I can't love you, Philip. And you never really loved me.'

He slowly backed away from her and Emma held up the knife until she was several feet away. Even as he reached for his horse's reins, she held it firmly in her fist.

'Very well, Emma, I am going,' he said. 'But this strange spell Sir David Marton has you under will fade. You have too much life for him, too much spirit. I will be waiting for you.'

'Don't do that, please,' was all Emma could say. 'This is where I want to be, where I have always wanted to be.'

Philip pulled himself up on to his horse and wheeled away. To her deepest relief, he spurred the horse into motion. 'This isn't over, Emma,' he shouted. 'I promise.'

Only once the hoofbeats had faded did Emma let

herself drop the dagger. She collapsed to her knees on the ground and struggled not to cry. Not to give in to despair.

'Let him be gone,' she whispered. Let a new life truly be possible. Even if David didn't want her, even if she had to find a way forwards alone, their night together had truly changed her and she knew she couldn't go back.

She slowly made her way to her feet. She left the clearing and found the path back to the road. Philip was gone and there was no one else to be seen. She had to go home now. Back to her cottage, to Murray and poor Arabella's diary, and try to find that way forwards.

Yet she found her steps taking her not toward Barton, but in the direction of Rose Hill. At the top of a rise in the road, she could see the crumbling stone ramparts of the old castle. Arabella's last refuge with her lover.

Somehow Emma found herself drawn there now and she left the road to climb over a low rock wall and head toward its romantic allure.

Chapter Nineteen

The old castle looked stark and empty against the pale-blue sky as Emma slowly made her way toward it. The blank windows set in the crumbling, ivy-coated walls seemed to stare down at her, watching her warily as she approached.

How much those walls must have seen over the centuries, she thought. Wars, elopements, broken hearts, deaths and births, and still it looked on in silence. Suddenly she was glad she came there so impulsively. The old walls felt like a refuge, a place she could hide for a while and where she would not be judged. Her sins were surely only small ones compared to all the walls had seen.

Emma made her way carefully around the edge of the outer wall, studying the faint lines in the overgrown grass where chambers once stood. She wondered where Arabella and her swain had sheltered from their pursuers, what they felt as they held on to each other against the rest of the world. Were they frightened, or exhilarated by their passion?

She almost wished *she* could run away, too. Could just run and run until she collapsed some place just like this, hidden and ancient, protected by the old lingering spirits. Yet even here she knew there was no hiding. The past was always there, waiting. And running never solved anything at all.

Emma sat down on a low wall and studied the column of what must have once been a chimney in front of her. Perhaps Arabella had even stashed the treasure in a fireplace just like that one, before they were caught? How could it have been for her, knowing in that moment that all she hoped for was gone? That love could be real, but could be lost so suddenly.

'Help!' someone cried, a tiny, far-off sound.

Emma jumped up from her seat, her heart pounding. Had her melancholy thoughts of Arabella conjured the girl's ghost? Was a spectre about to float into view?

'Don't be silly,' she told herself sternly. No matter what the novels said, there was no such thing as ghosts. It was only the wind, whistling past the old stones.

'Help,' someone cried again, and she heard it very clearly that time. A real voice, not a ghost.

'Where are you?' she called back, spinning around in a circle to scan the castle grounds. She couldn't see anything but a few sheep grazing nearby, a wisp of smoke from the chimneys of Rose Hill. 'Can you hear me?'

'Mrs Carrington! Is that you? Help me, please.'

Beatrice. Emma's heart pounded even harder as a rush of panic seized her. 'Bea! Where are you?'

'Down here. Oh, help me, please.'

Emma followed the sound of the child's frightened

voice, but she still saw nothing. 'Keep talking, Bea, so I can find you. I'm here, I won't leave you, I promise.'

Beatrice started singing, a wobbly little nursery song, and Emma followed the sound until she found an old caved-in section of what must once have been a cellar. Beatrice's voice echoed up from its dark depths.

'Beatrice, darling, what are you doing down there?' Emma called, forcing down her own fear so she could help the girl. 'I can't see you.'

'It's so dark,' Beatrice said and Emma could hear the panic in her voice.

'Just move toward my voice, dearest. Are you hurt?'

'I—I don't think so. I was just looking around the old castle, I didn't see the hole in the ground and I fell into it. I can't find my way out.'

'You were here by yourself?' Emma said. She could hear a rustling sound as Beatrice moved around. 'Where is your father? Your nurse?'

'Nanny fell asleep, of course, and Papa dashed off on some errand. Aunt Louisa was there and I didn't want to talk to her. So I came exploring.'

'But why here? It's very dangerous, Beatrice darling.'

'I loved the stories in the old diary you showed me. But I will never, ever go off alone again, I promise!'

Emma knelt down at the edge of the opening and at last she glimpsed a pale flash in the shadows. Beatrice's little face peered up at her. She blinked in the ray of light and her cheeks were streaked with dirt.

'Oh, Mrs Carrington,' she sobbed. 'I'm so sorry. I am not as brave as Queen Elizabeth.'

'It's quite all right, darling, I'm here now.' Emma

sighed. 'I know what it's like to be tempted by adventure. We must get you out of there, though.'

'There's a stone here, I think. Maybe there were steps once?'

'Can you stand on it and reach for my hand?'

Beatrice clambered up and reached out her small fingers. But Emma couldn't quite reach her. She quickly studied her surroundings and came up with a desperate plan.

'I will lower myself down there and help you up,' Emma said. 'Then I will pull myself up again. Can you move back a bit?'

Once Beatrice went back into the shadows, Emma grasped the edge of the pit and eased herself down carefully until her feet touched the rough, broken stone. Once she was down in the old cellar, Beatrice suddenly hugged her hard around the waist, her face buried in Emma's skirt.

Emma hugged her in return, deeply thankful to have a safe, healthy child in her arms.

'I'm so, so glad you're here, Mrs Carrington,' Beatrice sobbed.

'You are very, very lucky I happened by today, Bea,' Emma said as she kissed the top of Beatrice's rumpled head. 'You might have been lost for days. Your father will be frantic. So we must get back to Rose Hill right now.'

'I'll be so good from now on, Mrs Carrington, I promise.'

'I know you will be. Now, let me lift you up.' Emma hoisted Beatrice in her arms and balanced carefully on the stone. Using all her strength, she lifted Beatrice up and over, practically tossing her over the edge and into the light.

But as Beatrice launched herself away, Emma felt her foot slip out from under her in a rush of panic. She toppled to the hard-packed ground and her ankle twisted painfully beneath her.

'Mrs Carrington,' Beatrice cried. 'What happened? Are you hurt? Say something!'

Emma could hardly breathe with the pain, but she didn't want to frighten the child any more than she already was. 'I—think I have injured my foot,' she managed to say. The pain swept over her in drowning, nauseous waves. When she tried to stand, she feared she would faint.

Beatrice let out a wordless wail and Emma feared the child would go into hysterics.

'Beatrice,' she shouted sharply. 'None of that now. You must—you must run home at once and fetch your father, or someone else who can help. You must be very strong and brave now, just like Queen Elizabeth at Tilbury.'

'I will be back in only a moment, Mrs Carrington, I swear it.'

As Emma heard Beatrice's running footsteps fade, she let the dizziness and pain overwhelm her. Darkness closed over her just as she glimpsed some toppled old shelves in the corner by the dirt wall.

'Hurry, David,' she whispered. Then everything faded.

Chapter Twenty

'Papa, Papa!' David heard Beatrice's cries just as he handed Zeus's reins to the waiting groom. He'd never heard such panic in her voice before and he spun around in alarm to see her running towards him across the lawn.

His usually quiet, composed, ladylike daughter was streaked with dirt, her hair tangled and sleeve torn. David raced toward her, frantic to know what had happened.

'What is wrong, Bea?' he said. He knelt down as Beatrice threw herself into his arms. He felt her little wrists and ankles, and nothing seemed broken, but she was shaking like a leaf in the winter wind.

'You must come with me right now, Papa,' she gasped.

'No, we need to get you inside and send for the doctor,' David said. 'You can tell me what happened in the house.'

'Yes, yes, we will need the doctor, but not for me.'

Tears were pouring down Beatrice's cheeks, choking her.

'What do you mean, Bea? What on earth has happened?' he demanded. 'I go into town for a couple of hours and look what happens!'

Indeed, the weight of the package he had had just redeemed from Mr Levinson's shop was still heavy in his pocket. The pearl pendant he had seen Emma wear twice at the assembly rooms—and which she had for some reason sold to the jeweller. He had brooded over it, over her, all the way back to Rose Hill, but that was lost in Beatrice's panic.

'Tell me what happened,' he said firmly.

Beatrice gulped in a deep breath. 'It's Mrs Carrington who needs the doctor. She fell down into the cellar at the old castle and hurt her leg. Now she can't move and she can't get out.'

It was *Emma* who had got into trouble with Beatrice? Emma was hurt? David felt his confusion and anger freeze in fear and the need to move immediately to save her. 'The old castle? She took you there?'

'No, Papa!' Beatrice frantically shook her head. 'I went there on my own, to look around. It seemed better than talking to Aunt Louisa. I fell down into the cellar first and she found me. She hurt herself helping me.'

'Come along, Bea, quickly, and show me where,' David said. 'There is no time for the whole tale now, but you will tell me later.'

'Yes, Papa,' Beatrice whispered.

David hastily retrieved Zeus from the groom and sent the boy to fetch more servants to help at the old castle with ropes and blankets, and then into the village for the doctor. As David swung himself back into the saddle with Beatrice front of him, he forced his concern for Emma down. She needed him now; there was no time for his own fear.

And who knew what they would find at the old castle.

Emma felt as if she were sinking down into the dark warmth of an ocean, drifting down and down as something dragged at her limbs and wouldn't let go. She fought against its hold, the suffocating heat, even though part of her just wanted to fall back into it. She knew she had to wake up.

But when she forced her eyes open, she realised why she just wanted to drown. Stabbing pain shot up her leg and she cried out.

Then she remembered where she was, what had happened. She lay alone on a dirt floor, the only light a small yellow circle high above her head. She could smell the damp, green smell of the dirt and rotting wood, it pressed in all around her.

How long had she been unconscious? Would Beatrice return soon?

Please, please, Emma thought. Let Beatrice be back soon with help, before she became mad with panic.

Emma took a deep, steadying breath and forced herself to sit up. She ground her teeth against the pain and dizziness, and was able to slide back until she could lean against the wall. As she waited for the wave of nausea to pass, she examined her surroundings. They were not promising.

Surely, this had once been a cellar beneath the old kitchens, but most of it was caved in now. A few old rotten shelves, surrounded by broken shards of crockery, lay haphazardly on the floor. The stone she had stood on to lift Beatrice out was indeed an old, broken step.

Emma shivered in the cold damp and closed her eyes. She thought of Arabella and her lost lover, sheltering in just such a place. And she thought of David, holding her in his arms, keeping her so warm...

'Emma! Emma, are you there?' she heard someone shout, pulling her out of her half-dazed dream.

She sat straight up. 'Yes, I'm here!'

David's face appeared above her, peering down into her prison. He was surely the most beautiful thing she had ever seen.

'Are you hurt?' he asked.

'Yes, I twisted my ankle. I can barely move, I fear.'

'Don't worry, I'll have you out in only a moment.' He disappeared again and a rope fell down through the opening. As Emma watched in astonishment, David nimbly climbed down the rope until he dropped lightly to the dirt floor. He wore no coat and the white linen of his shirt gleamed in the darkness. He seemed like an angel of rescue to her.

He hurried over to kneel beside her and Emma bit back a sob as he took her gently into his arms. She clung to him, knowing she was safe at last.

'Where are you hurt?' he asked roughly.

'My—my ankle. That's all, I think,' Emma answered.

He carefully eased up the hem of her skirt and slid her boot from her swollen foot. Her stocking was torn and spotted with blood, and she gasped as his strong fingers slid over it carefully.

'Not broken, I think, but badly sprained. The doctor should be waiting at Rose Hill, he can examine you there.' David yanked his cravat from around his neck and wrapped it tightly around her ankle. 'Bea said you fell helping her out of here.'

'Yes,' Emma said. She wiggled her toes; the pain was eased a bit by the tight bandage. 'I'm glad I happened by. I promise I don't usually trespass on Rose Hill property. Something just told me to come here today, I think.'

David shook his head, his face drawn in stark, serious lines. 'Come, we have to get you out of here. I will try not to jostle you too much.'

Emma nodded and braced herself as he lifted her high in his arms. The pain washed over her again, but she knew she could bear it in his embrace. He pushed her up and out of the opening, much as she had with Beatrice, and footmen waited there to catch her. The sunlight blinded her for a moment after the dank darkness of the cellar, but she heard Beatrice cry out her name.

'Mrs Carrington, I am so, so sorry,' Beatrice sobbed and Emma felt her little arms slide tight around her neck. 'I will never be naughty again.'

'Adventures are quite all right sometimes, Beatrice,'

Emma said, laughing despite the pain. 'Just not alone, promise me.'

'Never again, Mrs Carrington. I will only go on adventures with you.'

'I think Mrs Carrington is done with your adventures, Bea,' David said. 'Come, we must go back to Rose Hill. The doctor will be waiting.'

David lifted her gently into his arms and helped her into a blanket litter the footmen had fashioned. She closed her eyes, safe but scared. Was he angry with her for what happened? What could ever happen next?

'You are very lucky, Mrs Carrington, to be in no worse shape after such a tumble.' The doctor snapped his bag shut and gave Emma a stern glance. 'Only a sprained ankle, I would say. Nothing broken. But you must be very careful for a few days. No dancing.'

Emma grimaced as she sat up against the cushions of the *chaise* in one of the guest chambers at Rose Hill. The mild sedative she had been given was starting to take hold of her senses, but the ankle still throbbed. 'I think I can safely promise you I won't be dancing, doctor. I will stay safely by my own fireside for a long time.'

'I am most glad to hear it.'

'How is Miss Beatrice?'

'Only scared and a bit muddied. Not hurt, thankfully. I will stop by Barton on my way back to the village and leave word for your servants there.'

Emma nodded, most relieved. As the doctor left, she could hear him talking with David in the corridor, quiet mutters she couldn't quite understand. She propped her freshly bandaged ankle on a pillow and studied the room around her, with its comfortable chintz draperies and overstuffed chairs scattered around the flowered carpet. It was a pretty, comfortable, inviting room, one where she wished she could stay for days and days, wrapped in the warmth of Rose Hill. But she feared she would be gone from there all too quickly.

She had to be gone. Obviously her impulsive ways hurt the people she cared about most and she wouldn't hurt them any more. She had to leave them for their own good.

'I owe you a great deal of thanks, Emma,' David said as he entered the chamber. He softly closed the door behind him.

Emma laughed, the warmth of the room and the medicine, and David's presence, wrapped around her. She would enjoy them while she could, for those fleeting moments were precious. 'You were the one who climbed down a rope to rescue me, David.'

'You injured yourself rescuing my daughter.' He sat down next to her on the *chaise* and gently put his arm around her.

Emma rested her head on his shoulder with a sigh and suddenly the pain and fear vanished into a sweet, soft weariness. She remembered how it felt after they made love and he held her against him in the firelight. How all the turmoil and worry of life quieted in his arms. If only it could always be like that.

She ran a gentle touch over his shoulder, tracing a streak of dirt on his coat and smoothing the silk lapel.

'I am just glad I happened to be there to find her. Poor Beatrice.'

'Yes,' he said quietly, his heartbeat steady under her hand. 'Why *were* you there, Emma?'

She froze, her hand in mid-stroke over his coat. Oh, yes—why she had been wandering around the bleak ruins all alone. She had almost forgotten, in the drama of her rescue and the doctor's sedative, and now it all came rushing back to her. Philip and his crude blackmail scheme, and her fear and loneliness.

'I cannot tell you,' she whispered. 'It is all too embarrassing. And anyway, it doesn't matter now.' Or she hoped it did not matter, that Philip had left and she had time to get her life organised again.

'Emma, have you learned nothing about me? Your secrets are safe with me, as I hope mine are with you. I am no gossip like my sister. If you are in trouble...'

Emma shook her head. 'No more than usual.'

David's arm tightened around her and she felt him press a kiss to the tip of her head. She squeezed her eyes shut, afraid she would start to cry at his tenderness. Tenderness she did not deserve.

'Who has hurt you, Emma?' he said quietly. 'Is it some trouble to do with your late husband? Is it that cousin of his?'

Somehow David's very quietness, his still, gentle strength, broke something in her. She buried her face in his shoulder and held on to him as all the fear and pain of the past poured out of her. She trembled with the force of her emotion and wished she could wail with it all, as Beatrice had in the old cellar.

'Shh,' David whispered. He softly caressed her hair, holding her against him. 'Don't be afraid, Emma. I'm here. I'm your friend.'

Her friend. Somehow that word was so precious, yet so insignificant compared to what she felt for him.

But his closeness, his touch, the pain and the medicine the doctor had given her, all conspired against her. She found herself holding on to him and telling him about Philip. She explained that Philip had threatened to tell details about her life with Henry, that she had tried to pay him because she couldn't hurt Jane any more.

She didn't tell him about Herr Gottfried, or any of the other horrid people Henry knew, but she was sure what she *had* said was quite enough for David to refuse to have anything more to do with her. Her heart felt as if it cracked in two and crumbled away with the knowledge that David and Beatrice would be gone from her.

Yet she knew, deep in her soul, that it was right for him to know. After all they had done, all he had meant to her, at last she could give him her honesty. David had changed her life, made her believe that real goodness, real loyalty, was actually possible once more. That it could touch her life, however briefly, and leave it transformed for the better.

He had given her that. And surely now that he knew how great her past mistakes were, he would leave her. Yet she would always remember how his arms felt around her right now.

'I am so sorry, David,' she whispered brokenly. 'So, so sorry. You have been kind to me and I have been…'

'Shh,' he said again. He gently urged her to lie back

on the *chaise* and carefully tucked a fur-trimmed throw around her. 'You honour me with your honesty, Emma. I will never betray it.'

'You deserve so much more from me,' Emma murmured. Her head felt cloudy, dizzy, and she closed her eyes against it.

'Trust me to know what I deserve. What we both deserve,' he said softly, in a neutral tone she couldn't read. She wished now more than ever she could read his thoughts, but they were carefully hidden from her. 'Just sleep now. I will send for the carriage and take you back to Barton when you have rested for a while.'

Emma nodded, the darkness of exhausted sleep closing around her. Yet it was so different from the hot, painful blackness of the cellar. 'I wish I didn't have to leave Rose Hill.'

'You don't yet. Just sleep.'

She felt his hand cover hers, warm and strong, like a lifeline holding her above the drowning waves. She held on to it and let herself sleep.

The bastard.

David braced his clenched fists on the desk, fighting down the urge to break the wood under his bare hands. It wasn't the innocent desk's fault that his temper was up. It was that blighter Philip Carrington's.

How dare he threaten Emma? How dare he even come near her?

The force of his fury surprised David, since it had been so long since he felt anything even near to it. He kept his emotions so carefully at bay all the time; it was the only way for him to always see to his duties, the only way he could survive. But Emma had changed all that and he suddenly realised how very much. His feelings for her had changed everything. Only when he was afraid he would lose her, lose the vibrant light of her irrepressible spirit, had he known how much he needed Emma.

David pushed himself back from his desk and snatched up his riding gloves. Carrington had to know Emma was not alone now. There would be no more taking advantage of her gentle heart, her generous spirit. No more threatening her over the past. Philip Carrington was going to leave and he was going to do it now, even if David had to bodily toss him into the street in front of the whole village.

Even if he had to cause a scandal. After Maude, he had vowed never to cause talk about his family again. But now, when he thought of Emma's tear-streaked face, he knew so clearly that some things were worth facing scandal.

Some things were worth any sacrifice at all.

He strode out of the library, calling for the butler. 'Hughes,' he shouted. 'Have Zeus brought around at once. I have an urgent errand in the village.'

Hughes looked shocked as he emerged from the drawing room. 'Right now, sir?'

'Yes,' David said firmly. If he was going to start being shocking, he might as well start at home. 'Right now.'

'But—but someone is here to see you, sir. I was just coming to announce him—'

'No need,' a brusque voice said and a man emerged from the drawing room behind the butler.

It was Lord Ramsay, Emma's brother-in-law.

'Ramsay,' David said slowly, pushing down his martial urges to face the one man Emma wouldn't want to find her here. 'I didn't realise you had returned from London.'

Lord Ramsay slowly slapped his leather gloves against his palm. 'Jane and I just arrived back at Barton to find a curious message you had sent to the housekeeper there. My sister-in-law is *here?* With you?'

'She is here, yes, but she is resting,' David said as he made his way toward the stone-faced man. He considered the Ramsays to be friends, but he knew he had to tread very carefully with them now. 'She had a very trying experience today.'

Ramsay's eyes narrowed. 'I think you had best explain, Sir David, and quickly. My wife was frantic for word of her sister and it was all I could do to persuade her to stay at home while I fetched Emma back to Barton. Jane is tired after the journey and should not be wearied further.'

David led him back into the drawing room and shut the door. He quickly told Ramsay the whole sorry tale, as briefly and simply as possible. About how Emma rescued Beatrice and was injured herself. He said nothing of how Emma had come to be wandering around the old castle in the first place, of the growing…whatever it was between them. He couldn't even find the words for it yet himself, though he knew that he was coming to rely on Emma's presence in his life far too much.

Ramsay was quiet for a long moment; the only sound in the tense air between them the slow, thoughtful slap of the gloves.

'You and Emma have become friends of late,' Ramsay said.

'I have tried to be a friend to her, yes,' David replied carefully. 'When she will let me.'

Ramsay laughed. 'Yes, she can be a stubborn one, no denying that. Jane worried about her all the time we were in London, but I told her Emma was better off at Barton right now. I hope I was not wrong. Is she much injured?'

'She needs rest.'

'I have brought the carriage to take her home. I see that you are on your way to some errand, so we shan't intrude on your hospitality any longer.'

His hospitality? Such a tepid word for what David was coming to fear he wanted to offer Emma. But for now Ramsay was right—Barton was the right place for Emma while he took care of business. She would be safe there. 'I hope I may call on Mrs Carrington at Barton very soon. And Lady Ramsay, of course.'

Ramsay stared at David for a long moment before he finally nodded and David knew there was a silent understanding between them.

He would do right by Emma, the strangest, kindest, most spirited woman he had ever known. He just didn't know yet what right might be. Every instinct told him to grab her in his arms and never let her go again, never let his life be the arid, lonely desert it was without her.

But he had to make sure she was safe first. That he could make her happy.

Because when David held her there in the dank darkness of the cellar and felt the warm, vivid life of her against him, he knew with a terrible certainty that making her happy was the only thing he wanted to do.

He was leaving her?

Emma leaned against the window frame and watched as David rode away down the drive. He never even looked back. And she had never felt more desolately alone. She had no idea why that should be: he had rescued her from the cellar; he owed her nothing, especially not explanations for why he would leave her. But the pain was still there.

She closed her eyes tightly against it. She should have expected nothing else. She and David were truly nothing to each other beyond a couple of wild moments desperately seeking comfort in each other's arms.

But he had given her more. He gave her hope. And now she felt foolishly, unaccountably bereft.

There was a knock at the chamber door and Emma hastily swiped at her damp eyes. She turned away from the window, from the sight of the empty lawn, and limped back to the *chaise*.

'Come in,' she called.

A maid peeked in with a quick curtsy. 'Begging your pardon, ma'am, but Lord Ramsay is here to fetch you. He's waiting in the drawing room and wishes to know if you require assistance.'

Emma gave a rueful laugh. So that was why David

left—he had handed responsibility for her troublesome self over to her brother-in-law.

Surely she would no longer see him next to the fire in her cottage. Whatever was between them seemed ended, as suddenly and strangely as it had begun. And she had never felt quite so lost before.

She remembered her earlier resolve, to leave David and Beatrice behind for their own good, before her propensity for trouble affected them too. She knew now that was the only right thing. She sat down at the small desk in the corner and reached for a sheaf of paper to do what she had to do.

From the diary of Arabella Bancroft

I would not have thought such grief was possible. Such pain. Surely I will fall into pieces if I must breathe for another moment. William is dead, the treasure is still lost, and I am being sent back to London.

I hope those stinking streets will soon hold my doom.

Chapter Twenty-One

David took the rickety wooden steps at the back of the Rose and Crown two at a time. The inn was quiet at that time of day, the tavern room empty and no new guests arriving. But the proprietor said that villain Carrington was in his rooms, that he had come in hours before and locked himself away. And that Carrington also owed him money for the stay.

It was the perfect time for David to confront the blighter and tell him in no uncertain terms that Emma was no longer unprotected. She no longer had to fend for herself against predators like the Carrington cousins. She was at home now, where they took care of their own.

He was there to take care of her. She had done an admirable job of it on her own for far too long, but he would see to it she didn't have to again.

As David stepped on to the second landing, he could hear Carrington moving behind his door. David pounded on the stout wood.

'Who it is?' Carrington called out, muffled, impatient.

'It is David Marton,' David answered, equally impatient.

There was silence, thick and heavy. 'What do you want?'

'Open the door and I will tell you.'

'I have nothing to say to you.'

'That's too bad, because I have a great deal to say to you. Open the door, Carrington, or I will be forced to break it down. And I don't think you would want such a scene. It would just add to the amount you owe the innkeeper.'

Once, a 'scene' would have been the last thing David wanted as well. His respectability, his name, his daughter—they were everything. But now taking care of Emma was equally as important. She deserved that—and so much more.

So, yes, he *would* break down the door if he had to.

Finally there was a creaking sound and the door swung open. Carrington stood there, his cravat hanging loose, his eyes bloodshot.

David pushed him back in to the room and stepped after him, slamming the door behind him. 'I should have you up before the magistrate for blackmail. It's a hanging offence, you know.'

A smile twisted Carrington's cracked lips. 'So she told you, did she? I am shocked. Emma was always one to bear her burdens alone.'

'So you thought she would be an easy mark for your villainy?' David said, his fury growing. 'She is not alone any longer, and if you value your skin at all you will return her money to her and crawl back to hell.'

'The white knight, are you?' Carrington sneered. 'I tried to be that for her once. But I wasn't good enough for her. No title, I suppose. The little whore.'

David's temper snapped at that vile word. He reached out and grabbed Carrington by his stained shirtfront, the fierce urge to bash the smirk off his unshaved face burning through him. His fist pulled back...

'You leave him alone!' a scream rang out.

David spun around, his fist still twisted in Carrington's linen shirt, to see Miss Harding standing in the doorway between the small sitting room and the bedroom. She wore only a chemise and her hair fell in a tangled skein over her shoulders.

A different kind of shock overtook David's anger. Had Carrington been victimising *all* the women in the area? 'Miss Harding...' he began. With another banshee-like scream, she launched herself at him and pounded at him with her little fists.

Not exactly a victim, then. David had to let go of Carrington and try to hold her back. She was shockingly strong.

'Well, well,' he said, once she backed away, panting. Carrington took her in his arms and quieted her. 'This is most unexpected. I think we might negotiate after all, Carrington...'

'Emma!' David called as he ran up the stairs at Rose Hill. He found himself ridiculously eager to share the tale of Carrington and Miss Harding with her, to see her reaction and maybe hear her laugh at the awful absurdity of it all.

It was the strangest sensation, wanting to share something after being alone for so long. But he wanted to tell Emma everything. Share everything with her.

He pushed open the bedchamber door, only to find the space completely empty. The blankets on the *chaise* where she had laid were neatly folded. In his excitement, he had forgotten that her family had already taken her away.

Then he saw the note, neatly folded atop the desk, labelled with his name. A cold finger of disquiet touched his earlier excitement and the house suddenly seemed so cold.

He slowly took it up and unfolded it to read the words looped across the paper. It was short and all he could see was her last message.

I've seen now how I can only be a misfortune in your life, David. I cannot stop my hoydenish ways and I have led you and Beatrice into danger. I have been careless too long and I can't do it any longer, not to people I care about as I do you. So I must go...

David crumpled the paper into his fist and tossed it away in a sudden rush of anger, and—and of fear. He hadn't realised until Emma was hurt how much he needed her in his life, and in Beatrice's too. He would even face scandal for her.

If she thought she could run away now, she was much mistaken.

Chapter Twenty-Two

'Are you sure you feel quite well, Emma dear?' Jane said as their carriage rolled closer to the village. 'I fear you still haven't quite recovered from your fall. If you want to return home...'

Emma turned from staring out at the gathering darkness beyond the carriage window and gave her sister a reassuring smile. 'Of course not. I've been looking forward to this concert and feel perfectly capable of sitting and listening to music for an hour or two. You need an outing, as well. You've seen almost no one since you returned to Barton.'

'I've seen my family and that's all that matters,' Jane said firmly. 'Though I fear the twins have not exactly been helpful in expediting your recovery.'

Emma laughed. She had insisted on staying in her cottage to recover, but Jane and the children were there every day anyway. Jane came bearing picnic baskets of healing jellies and soups, the nurse carrying the gurgling, pink-cheeked baby Emma behind her and the twins running ahead of her. It was quite true that they chased Murray and knocked over piles of books in their wild games.

But they were the only things that kept her from brooding over David, remembering every moment with him. When he held her in his arms, kissed her so tenderly, she had dared begun to hope…

But she knew she was right to have left him that note. Perhaps David *did* care for her, in some way. In fact, she was sure he did. He was no cad like the Carrington men, no consummate actor who could feign affection for a lady until he got what he wanted and then left. He deserved better in his life. And she knew it was best if they parted now, before she created some terrible scandal in his life. She had to be sensible, practical, and do what was best for David and Beatrice. Even if 'best' was not her.

Why, then, did being so sensible make her feel as if she was being cracked in two?

'I love their company,' Emma said. 'And yours. I can't tell you how happy I am you're home, Jane! But I think it will do us good to get out of the house for a while.'

Even though her first instinct when Hayden suggested they attend the concert at the assembly rooms had been to hide in her cottage and lock the door behind her for ever. What if she saw David there and had to be polite? What if she ran into Philip and he made his vile threats again? But even in her fears she knew Hayden was right and she should go. This place was her home now. The sooner she faced down her fears and got on with her life, the better.

Jane sighed and tapped her folded fan on the edge of the carriage seat. 'I confess, as much as I adore my children, I am happy to have an outing. I'm terribly behind on the local gossip and you are of no help there since you spent all your time buried in the bookshop while I was gone.'

Emma was saved from having to admit she had not spent *all* her time in the bookshop when the carriage lurched to a halt outside the assembly rooms. They were a bit late, so there was no line of vehicles waiting to disgorge their passengers. The windows glowed with flickering light and laughter spilled out of the open doors. Emma took up the cane Mr Sansom had sent her when he heard of her injuries and followed Jane into the building.

'My dears!' Lady Wheelington called out as soon as they stepped into the hall. They had barely handed their wraps to the attendant when she took their arms and led them toward the ladies' withdrawing room, the only place for a quick gossip. 'Have you heard the very latest news?'

Jane laughed. 'Of course not. I have only just returned from the wilds of town. But do tell. The design in coming here tonight was to hear everything.'

Emma nodded, though she was not quite so sure. What if the news was that David was to marry Miss Harding? Or had gone back to London? How could she maintain her façade of polite interest then?

'Well, my dears,' Lady Wheelington said, 'it seems that deliciously handsome Philip Carrington, who appeared in our midst only a few weeks ago, has already vanished again. His rooms at the Rose and Crown are utterly cleaned out. And you will never guess who vanished with him!'

Jane was wide-eyed with interest, but Emma feared where this tale might be going, even as relief swept through her that Philip was really gone. But she knew she couldn't trust whatever trouble he left behind.

'I can't even imagine,' Jane said with a sidelong glance at Emma. 'You must tell me at once.'

'The admiral's niece Miss Harding!' Lady Wheelington cried. 'We all thought Mr Carrington was here for you, Miss Emma. And that Miss Harding was all set to marry Sir David Marton. That's what Mrs Smythe was sure of, anyway. And now they have eloped together. People are ever surprising, are they not?'

Emma was actually rather shocked by the ending of this tale. And—and relieved. Miss Harding was not to marry Sir David? David was free?

But even if he was free, that could mean nothing to her.

'Is it quite sure they have gone together?' Jane said. Emma could feel her sister's gaze on her and she feared the truth of what Jane would read there. Her sister knew her all too well.

'The impertinent girl left a note for her uncle saying as much,' Lady Wheelington answered. 'The admiral actually managed to rouse himself enough to send searchers after them, but no trace can be found.'

'How shocking,' Jane murmured. Emma hoped her sister was not remembering Emma's own 'shocking' elopement. All of that seemed to have happened to an entirely different person, a foolish girl who let her heart rule her head, when it was obvious her heart had no idea what it was about.

Yet how different was she now, really? She had certainly let her heart rule when it came to David.

'That poor girl,' Emma said.

'Ah, well. Perhaps Mrs Smythe will be careful of her matchmaking in the future,' Lady Wheelington said. 'Shall we go in? The music should be most entertaining tonight...'

As they followed Lady Wheelington into the ballroom, Jane linked her arm with Emma's and whispered, 'I thought you said your husband's cousin did not stay long in the village?'

'He didn't, obviously,' Emma whispered back, still bemused by all they just heard. 'He just stopped to pay his regards. I had no idea he was involved in a secret romance.' With Miss Harding—who everyone expected David to marry.

'If you want to call it a romance,' Jane said. 'Lady Wheelington is right—people are ever surprising.'

Emma studied the crowd as they found seats at the side of the room, near the doors to the garden. She didn't see David there, or even his sister. Which was most surprising, since Mrs Smythe was never one to miss a social occasion.

Emma was relieved not to face him again quite yet, but also felt the pangs of sharp disappointment. She managed to smile and chat with the people who stopped to greet Jane, but all the time she wondered where he was. Where he had gone.

The musicians on their dais in front of the rows of chairs finished tuning their instruments and launched into their first selection, saving Emma from having to make further polite conversation. It was a lively, slightly out-of-control rendition of a local folk song and under its noise she could lose herself in her wistful thoughts.

Suddenly she felt a warm prickle at the back of her neck, as if someone had just trailed a caress over her skin. She rubbed at the spot with her gloved fingertips and glanced over her shoulder. Yet she was already quite sure of what she would find there. No one else's presence could ever give her that sudden lightning-shock of awareness.

David stood just inside the doorway, a lean, austere figure in black-and-white evening clothes, his hair swept neatly back from his face, his spectacles gleaming. He looked so different from the dusty, dishevelled man who had rescued her from the cellar. He looked like the Sir David she had once thought so cold and remote.

But now she knew the truth of what was hidden in him. She knew the real fire of his passion and it had warmed her for her whole life.

And despite all her resolve to let him go, to forget him, she realised that was the last thing she could ever do. David was emblazoned on her heart. She couldn't forget him.

She tried to turn away from him, to hide what she was feeling, but his gaze found hers across the room and she couldn't let go. An expression flickered across his face, a flash of pleasure that was so swiftly gone she feared she had imagined it.

He gave her a small nod, and as she watched he slipped out the door into the garden.

'Excuse me for a moment, Jane,' Emma whispered.

'Are you unwell?' Jane asked, a concerned look on her face. 'Shall I come with you?'

Emma shook her head. 'I won't be long.'

Once she was sure Jane's attention was on the music again, Emma quickly slipped out the door behind him. As the darkness of the evening closed around her, her heart pounded in her chest so hard she could barely breathe. Barely think.

She scanned the pathways, but she couldn't see him and for an instant she feared he had already left. Or worse, was hiding, appalled she had followed him.

Then a ray of stray moonlight fell on a dark silhouette, half-hidden at the far end of the garden. He waited under the tree where they once kissed, so still he could almost have been a stone Roman statue. Yet the warmth of his living body drew her to him.

'How have you been, Emma?' he asked quietly when she drew close to him, moving carefully with her walking stick.

'Very well,' she answered carefully. 'My sister has been an excellent nurse. How is Miss Beatrice?'

'She is quite well and asks after you daily. Her behaviour has been exemplary since her little—adventure. A new, younger nanny helps as well.'

Emma had to smile to think of Beatrice. 'I am glad.'

A silence fell between them, and in the moonlight she could feel David studying her quietly, carefully. 'I am very sorry I haven't written,' he said at last. 'There were a few matters I had to take care of before I could see you again and once I was sure you were safe with your sister and brother-in-law.'

'Matters?' Emma asked curiously. 'What can…?'

As she looked up at David in the moonlight, she glimpsed a flash of sudden laughter in his eyes, and a suspicion struck her. 'David, did you have something to do with this shocking news of Philip and Miss Harding?'

A muscle flexed in his jaw, almost as if he tried not to smile. 'I have no idea what you are speaking of, Emma. But I do assure you, Philip Carrington will not be causing you trouble in the future.'

'I must admit that I am not sorry to see the last of him,' Emma said slowly, still reeling from the knowledge that David had got rid of him somehow. 'But poor Miss Harding…'

'I believe you mean the poor new Mrs Carrington.'

'They married?' Emma cried, even more shocked than before.

'They did, for better or worse. You are done with him, Emma, I promise.'

'But what did you…?'

'Never mind that now,' David said. He reached inside his coat and took out two small items he held out to her. 'I believe these are yours.'

Emma stared down at his hand to see the pearl pendant she had sold to pay Philip, and the tiny bunch of silk forget-me-nots she lost from her sash the night of her first assembly back here.

Amazed, she murmured, 'Where did you…?'

'I obtained the necklace from Mr Levinson's shop, where it had sadly been misplaced,' David said. 'The flowers I confess I have been keeping far too long.'

He had kept her flowers? Emma swallowed hard at the knowledge that he had done such a thing. 'How did you know I went to Mr Levinson's? I was desperate and I heard Lady Wheelington say once that ladies sometimes went there.'

'It doesn't matter how I found out,' David said with a laugh. Emma stared up at him, astonished to see him laughing—and confused.

She had no idea what was happening. She'd been in despair, sure she could never see David again. Now here he was, smiling at her, giving her back her necklace—with the whole village merely feet away, where anyone could come across them.

'The only important thing is that I did find it,' he said. 'And that I can say this now—no one else will ever hurt you again, not while I'm here. And I won't let even you stand in our way, Emma. My dear, noble-hearted Emma.'

Emma shook her head, afraid to hope. She had hoped for so many things so many times before and been so cruelly disappointed. Did she dare endanger her heart one more time, for the thing she hoped for above all else?

'David, what do you mean?' she whispered. 'What are you saying?'

'I am saying I have never been happier in my whole life than when I am with you, Emma,' David said. 'I am saying that you have shown me the joy of what being alive can mean. I didn't realise before you that I was only living a half-life. Don't make me go back to that. When I read your note, I was so angry, so unhappy to think I would never see you again. I never want to feel like that.'

Emma was so confused. It seemed like the world had turned upside down. 'But—I haven't seen you since I came back to Barton. I thought you were angry with me for leading Beatrice into trouble. That you...' She choked on her words, unable to go on.

'I am so sorry, Emma dearest. I went to town for a few days because—well, because I didn't feel I could declare myself to you without this.' David reached into his coat again and withdrew a tiny box.

As Emma watched, her heart pounding, he opened it to reveal an emerald ring surrounded by smaller diamonds that sparkled in the moonlight.

'It was my mother's, and her mother's before her,' he said. 'It never seemed to belong to Maude; I could never bring myself to give it to her. But I think it is rightfully yours. It's the colour of your eyes. The colour of summer, which is how it feels whenever you're near.'

Emma was sure he must have deep feelings for her, if it made him so poetic. As she watched, David slowly knelt before her and held out the ring.

'It is yours, Emma, if you will have me with it and Beatrice, too. She adores you, as I do,' he said solemnly. 'I know I am not exciting or adventurous. Life at Rose Hill will have no casinos or court balls. But I promise to always love you, to always work as hard as I can to make you happy.'

Tears pouring down her cheeks, flowing freely as she let her emotions fly out at last, Emma knelt next to David and covered his hand with hers. 'You already make me happier than I ever thought possible. There at Rose Hill, with you and Beatrice—that's where I felt I at last belonged. I didn't think you wanted me.'

David laughed, a glorious, musical sound she had heard too rarely. But maybe now she would hear it every day for the rest of her life, if she dared hope for that. 'I want you more than anything. I don't think I realised quite how very much until you were hurt and I feared to lose you. Please, Emma, say you will marry me. Or do I have to run into that concert and declare that I have ruined you in front of everyone to make you say yes?'

Emma had to laugh at the image of David, her calm, cool David, making such a dramatic scene. 'Such scandal! Just like me, I fear.'

'I'm not afraid of any scandal, as long as we face it together. All of the things I have guarded against all my life—none of them matter next to you.'

And nothing in her life mattered next to him, either. He was truly the best man she had ever met. The only man she wanted. 'Then, yes. Yes, Sir David Marton, I will marry you.'

David took her hand and slipped the ring on to her finger. It *did* look like summer, she thought as she looked down at it. Like warmth and light, and the promise of a happy life where she belonged. The promise of a life with David, the man she truly loved.

She threw her arms around him as he drew her close

for a long, sweet, fiery kiss that said everything she ever needed to know.

As his lips trailed to her cheek, she smiled as happiness greater than any she could have ever imagined broke over her. 'Oh, David,' she whispered. 'I suppose you are not such a dull old stick after all…'

From the diary of Arabella Bancroft

It has been a year since I last wrote in this book, and I am sure this will be my last entry. I have not been able to find words, find light, for so long, but today the sun has come out again. Today is my wedding day.

I shall never forget the glorious love I found with my sweet William. But George Marton is a good man who I have come to care for. And with him I can leave London—and seek the treasure once more…

Epilogue

One year later

'Oh, Lady Marton, it looks lovely. Just perfect.'

Emma stepped back to survey the new window display of books freshly arrived from London. Mrs Anston, the young widow she had hired to manage the shop after Mr Lorne retired, clapped her hands as she looked at the array of volumes.

'Yes, Mrs Anston,' Emma agreed as she slid one book just a shade to the right. 'I think you are quite right. We should be ready for our re-opening party next week.'

Wiping her hands on her apron, she turned to scan the space. There were just as many books as ever, but now they were neatly shelved in categories, with displays laid out on tables from the attics at Rose Hill and Barton Park. A few comfortable chairs and sofas were also scattered about for easy perusing of volumes and pretty yellow curtains hung at the newly scrubbed windows.

It was a lovely sight indeed, her idea of the perfect bookshop. And it was all her own.

Emma had feared that once she was married, she would have to give up the shop and Mr Lorne would close it. But David had insisted she keep it, and even found Mrs Anston, the widow of a kinsman of his, to run it for her. Part of Mr Sansom's library had already found buyers, the beginning of Emma's antiquarian clients, and new book-buying ventures to London were all the 'adventures' she ever needed again.

Well—that and what happened in the grand, curtained bed at Rose Hill every night. *That* was proving to be quite adventurous indeed.

Emma felt herself blushing fiercely to think of it and she quickly turned away to readjust a display. Yes, life as Lady Marton was continually proving to be all she had ever dreamed. And more.

Beyond the window, she heard the church bell toll and she glanced up, startled. 'Is that the time already? I must go…'

'Don't worry, Lady Marton, I will unpack the last of the new books,' Mrs Anston said. 'You can't be late today.'

'No, indeed, or my sister would be furious.' Emma quickly changed her apron for a satin pelisse and tied on her bonnet. Her pearl pendant gleamed at her throat. She glanced in the mirror to see that her cheeks were still pink, but hopefully everyone would just think it was the spring day, the happiness of the occasion. Not that she had been daydreaming about what her husband did to her in their bedchamber.

She gently smoothed a caress over the still-small bump under her pelisse. It was still a secret to all but her sister, but in a few months Bea would have the new brother or sister she persisted in begging for.

Emma smiled to think of it. Her family. Her husband and children. Their home. All things she had once thought could never be hers.

With a quick goodbye to Mrs Anston, Emma hurried out of the shop and towards the church. Lady Wheelington's carriage was already there, outside the churchyard gates, and Mrs Smythe and her rambunctious brood were making their way up the path.

Jane and Hayden waited with the vicar at the church door, the twins helping little Emma toddle around on her leading strings. Beatrice tumbled around with them, laughing, until she saw Emma walking toward them.

'Mama!' she called, and dashed towards Emma to hug her. 'I got to hold the baby. He is very small, but I was so careful.'

'Of course you were,' Emma said with a laugh. Bea was always careful, always polite, always with a book in her hands. But she was learning to play too, which Emma was happy to see.

'And he's named Edward, just like Queen Elizabeth's brother,' Beatrice said. 'Come and see.'

'Yes, Emma, come and see your godson,' Jane said, holding up the lace-swathed baby in her arms. Hayden beamed down at them, every inch the proud papa. 'You were almost late for his christening.'

'I never would have missed this for anything,' Emma said. She took baby Edward carefully from her sister, marvelling at his tiny nose and silky lashes, the sweet scent of him. She couldn't believe that very soon she would have one of her own.

She felt a gentle touch on her shoulder and glanced up to find her husband smiling down at her. Even after a year of being married, just the sight of him made her heart swell and the day turn golden-bright.

He bent to kiss her and Emma knew that finally she was right where she belonged. For ever.

* * * * *

HISTORICAL

Where love is timeless

COMING IN JANUARY 2014

A Marriage of Notoriety

The scars she keeps hidden…

The mysterious *pianiste* is the Masquerade Club's newest attraction, captivating guests with her haunting music. What is the true identity of the lady concealed beneath the mask?

Only Xavier Campion, the club's new proprietor, recognizes Phillipa Westleigh, the lady with whom he once shared a dance. Concerned for her safety, Xavier escorts her home each night. But when their moonlit strolls are uncovered, the only protection Xavier can offer is marriage!

The Masquerade Club

Identities concealed, desires revealed…

Available wherever books and ebooks are sold.

REQUEST YOUR FREE BOOKS!

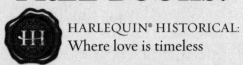

HARLEQUIN® HISTORICAL:
Where love is timeless

2 FREE NOVELS PLUS 2 FREE GIFTS!

YES! Please send me 2 FREE Harlequin® Historical novels and my 2 FREE gifts (gifts are worth about $10). After receiving them, if I don't wish to receive any more books, I can return the shipping statement marked "cancel." If I don't cancel, I will receive 6 brand-new novels every month and be billed just $5.44 per book in the U.S. or $5.74 per book in Canada. That's a savings of at least 16% off the cover price! It's quite a bargain! Shipping and handling is just 50¢ per book in the U.S. and 75¢ per book in Canada.* I understand that accepting the 2 free books and gifts places me under no obligation to buy anything. I can always return a shipment and cancel at any time. Even if I never buy another book, the two free books and gifts are mine to keep forever.

246/349 HDN F4ZY

Name	(PLEASE PRINT)
Address	Apt. #
City	State/Prov.	Zip/Postal Code

Signature (if under 18, a parent or guardian must sign)

Mail to the **Harlequin® Reader Service:**
IN U.S.A.: P.O. Box 1867, Buffalo, NY 14240-1867
IN CANADA: P.O. Box 609, Fort Erie, Ontario L2A 5X3

Want to try two free books from another line?
Call 1-800-873-8635 or visit www.ReaderService.com.

* Terms and prices subject to change without notice. Prices do not include applicable taxes. Sales tax applicable in N.Y. Canadian residents will be charged applicable taxes. Offer not valid in Quebec. This offer is limited to one order per household. Not valid for current subscribers to Harlequin Historical books. All orders subject to credit approval. Credit or debit balances in a customer's account(s) may be offset by any other outstanding balance owed by or to the customer. Please allow 4 to 6 weeks for delivery. Offer available while quantities last.

Your Privacy—The Harlequin® Reader Service is committed to protecting your privacy. Our Privacy Policy is available online at www.ReaderService.com or upon request from the Harlequin Reader Service.

We make a portion of our mailing list available to reputable third parties that offer products we believe may interest you. If you prefer that we not exchange your name with third parties, or if you wish to clarify or modify your communication preferences, please visit us at www.ReaderService.com/consumerschoice or write to us at Harlequin Reader Service Preference Service, P.O. Box 9062, Buffalo, NY 14269. Include your complete name and address.

HH13R

*From Bronwyn Scott comes the incredible new quartet
RAKES WHO MAKE HUSBANDS JEALOUS, featuring two
fantastic full-length Harlequin Historical novels and two
very sexy Harlequin Historical Undone! ebooks. Read on
for a sneak preview of our first hero, Nicholas D'Arcy…
the talk of the* ton *for all the wrong reasons!*

"I'm going swimming. How about you?"

Annorah drew her knees up and hugged them. She used to
love to swim, but that was before she grew up and swimming
was ruled as something ladies didn't do. A lady couldn't very
well swim in her clothes, which made the activity lewd *and*
public. "The water will make my skirts too heavy."

Nicholas grinned wickedly. "Then take them off."

He was going to have to debate with her about it.
Nicholas heard the regret in her voice, as if she was merely
making the appropriate answer. Well, he'd see what he
could do about that. He rose from the blanket and shrugged
out of his shirt. It was perhaps not as gracefully done as
it might have been. The shirt was wet and it stuck to him.
He threw it on a hanging branch and his hands went to the
waistband of his trousers.

"What are you doing?" Annorah's voice barely disguised
a gasp of excitement mixed with trepidation.

"I'm taking off my trousers. I don't mean to swim in
them," he called over his shoulder.

"What *do* you mean to swim in?"

"In my altogether. You could swim in your chemise if
you preferred," he suggested.

HHEXP1213R

"I couldn't." Annorah hesitated, biting her lip.

"Then take it off, too." He pushed his trousers past his hips and kicked them off, leaving only his smalls—a concession to her modesty. He turned around and Annorah blushed, her gaze looking everywhere but at him.

"Don't tell me you're embarrassed by my natural state." Nick spread his arms wide from his sides and sauntered toward her. He couldn't resist having a bit of fun. If he'd learned one thing about her this afternoon, it was that she could be teased—the wildness inside was very much alive once she let down her guard. He rather enjoyed getting past that guard, as he had in the river.

"It's not that."

"It isn't? Then is it perhaps that you're embarrassed about your natural state? I think your natural state would be quite lovely." He reached a hand down to her and tugged, letting the teasing fade from his voice. "Come on, Annorah. It's just the two of us. You've been eyeing that swimming hole since we got here. You know you want to." *You want to do more than swim, and if you'd look at me, you'd know I do, too.*

He had her on her feet and then he had her in his arms, kissing her—her throat, her neck, her lips. She tasted like wine, her body all compliance beneath his mouth. A soft moan escaped her. His hands worked the simple fastenings of her gown. He hesitated before pushing the dress down her shoulders, giving her one last chance to back out. If she resisted now, he'd let her. But she didn't. He smiled to himself. Sometimes all a person needed was a nudge.

Don't miss
SECRETS OF A GENTLEMAN ESCORT
available from Harlequin® Historical January 2014

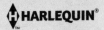

HISTORICAL

Where love is timeless

COMING IN JANUARY 2014

Rancher Wants A Wife

A marriage to save them both...

Among the responses Cassandra Hamilton receives to her
advertisement as a mail-order bride, one stands out—
Jack McColton's. Since she last saw him, tragedy has made
her a cautious woman.

Jack is mesmerized by his new bride—Cassandra might bear
the scars of recent events, but she's even more beautiful than he
remembers. They both have pasts that are hard to forget, but
can their passion banish the shadows forever?

Mail-Order Weddings

From blushing bride to rancher's wife!

Available wherever books and ebooks are sold.

H HARLEQUIN®

H ISTORICAL

Where love is timeless

COMING IN JANUARY 2014

From Ruin To Riches

A lord in want of a wife

Julia Prior is in desperate straits when she meets a gentleman with a shocking proposal. Close to death, William Hadfield, Lord Dereham, sees Julia as the perfect woman to care for his estate—if she will first become his wife....

Marriage is Julia's salvation—as Lady Dereham, she can escape her sins. Until three years later, when the husband she believes to be dead returns, as strong as ever and intent on claiming the wedding night they never had!

Available wherever books and ebooks are sold.